W9-CVY-107

MALL SNIPER

"Police Officers," the M.A.G. lieutenant shouted, the barrel of his service revolver pointed directly at the gang leader about to throw a garbage can into a mall boutique's front window. "Sit the fucking trashcan down or I'll plant you in it."

"Hey, pig. Plant this!" One of the skinheads grabbed his crotch.

"Eat some pavement, assholes!" Abel's partner, Sgt. Thorton appeared in front of the Malibu's headlights. A shotgun had replaced the regulation flashlight at the last moment. The headlights' beam silhouetted its gleaming, no-nonsense barrel. "Now!"

Slowly, the six skinhead gang bangers complied, dropping first to their knees, then completely prone across the cool blacktop. They were used to the routine.

Abel walked over to the leader with the big mouth. "You and your girl friends all look like curfew violations-in-the-making to me," he said, nudging him with his foot. "Even in your pussy Army surplus cammies."

"Hey, fuck off. We're all legal," the leader snickered. "Everyone's old enough to vote, or they don't ride on my wheels."

"Cut the shit and break out some ID. One hand on your head—"

Suddenly, two shots rang out from the roof above them. Abel and Thorton dropped into a squat immediately.

"The roof!" Abel shouted. "Get on the horn and request Air One down here. We gonna need some heavy back up!"

LITTLE SAIGON

ABEL'S WAR

NICHOLAS CAIN

LYNX BOOKS

New York

LITTLE SAIGON: ABEL'S WAR

ISBN:1-55802-089-6

First Printing/March 1989

This is a work of fiction. Names, characters, places, and incidents are either the product of the author's imagination or are used fictitiously. Any resemblance to actual events, locales, or persons, living or dead, is entirely coincidental.

Copyright © 1989 by the Jeffrey Weiss Group, Inc. and Nicholas Cain
All rights reserved. No part of this book may be reproduced or transmitted in any form or by any means electronic or mechanical, including by photocopying, by recording, or by any information storage and retrieval system, without the express written permission of the Publisher, except where permitted by law. For information, contact Lynx Communications, Inc.

This book is published by Lynx Books, a division of Lynx Communications, Inc., 41 Madison Avenue, New York, New York, 10010. The name "Lynx" and the logo consisting of a stylized head of a lynx are trademarks of Lynx Communications, Inc.

Printed in the United States of America

0 9 8 7 6 5 4 3 2 1

DEDICATION

For Joe Padilla, Jeff Reilly, John Pruett, Mike More-
house, Joe Bowland, and Glenn Miller—and all the
other *Seventies Cops*.

ACKNOWLEDGMENTS

Special thanks to the following Southern California
Law Enforcement officials for technical advice:

Officer Kurt Owens
Sgt. Dan Lyons

(Neither of whom had any control over the contents of
this work)

LITTLE SAIGON

ABEL'S WAR

≡ CHAPTER 1

THE IMAGE HAD remained with Victor all these years: burned and sizzling flesh, peeling back from the frail contours of Kim's face as flames consumed her entire body. He would never be able to exorcise the gruesome scene from his mind, or purge the pain and guilt from his soul. He could still hear Kim's inhuman, wailing cries as she knelt on the sidewalk, a crackling halo of fire rising from billowing silk pantaloons to consume her white *ao dai* gown. White for mourning. Kim was forever in mourning over South Vietnam's gloomy destiny. Her home, Saigon, had become the City of Sorrows.

It was a vision that haunted Victor both days and nights, but mostly in Southern California's mid-morning haze and humid breeze—heavy with an odd, memory-triggering combination of smog and incense—hurled him back to his tour of duty in Vietnam. Mere months, spent in a faraway land where one year could equal two lifetimes.

The flashbacks lingered as he limped along on his one remaining leg, down the side streets behind Little Saigon's main strip, scraping the asphalt with his crutches as he passed the maze of back alleys he had come to know like the scars crisscrossing his knuckles.

The vet appeared to be in his early forties. His hair

billowed out over his ears in scraggly puffs, and a gray stubble covered his cheeks and chin. A black patch concealed a hollow eye socket over his right cheekbone.

Victor stared at the stump where his right leg used to be, then shifted his eyes to the broken-down van sitting a short distance away—the black, '65 Dodge that had become home, refuge. In the light of the streetlamp, his eyes focused on the bumper sticker's white-on-black proclamation: LOST IT IN THE 'NAM. "Got that right," he muttered to himself and looked down the empty street.

Approaching midnight, he decided—based on the lack of pedestrian traffic. Not quite the witching hour yet, though: The fish market, fashion boutiques, and jewelry and souvenir shops were all locked up tight behind iron grilles and steel shutters, but cars remained parked outside the brightly lit ring of bars, restaurants, and nightclubs encircling New Saigon Mall.

The empty bottle of Vietnamese *ba-muoi-ba* beer fell from his pants pocket and bounced off the blacktop with a hollow clang. The glass did not shatter, and that disappointed him. He bent forward, but it rolled out of reach before he could grab it—so he could smash it against the brick wall of the nearby Golden Buffy Gift Shop. By then, it no longer seemed worth the effort. "Fuck it. Don' mean nothin' no how, no way." Lapsing into a tense silence, Victor seemed to reconsider. "I miss you, Kim," he whispered finally.

He glanced down at his brass belt buckle—it bore a raised skull and crossbones, the skull sporting a soldier's helmet, the banner below bragging: AGENT ORANGE HEALTH CLUB—LIFE MEMBER—then stared over at the van again. Through the open rear doors, coming to rest on the AR-15 carbine hanging from the cab wall. It was the legal, semiautomatic counterpart to the M-16 he had carried for so many years in-country.

Shaking his head in mild resignation, he scanned the parking lot again—dark and guarded by shifting shadows despite the long line of antique, French-style light poles leading down through the middle of the suburban shopping plaza and disappearing in the swirling blue mists. Only a few of the lights worked.

Dozens of posters were taped to huge billboards running along the storefront—all the same, all bearing the likeness of Mai Tran, latest in a never-ending string of popular "new wave" vocalists entertaining the new immigrants of Little Saigon. Her long hair pulled way back to reveal high cheekbones, and nothing more than a wisp of red satin draped over her creamy shoulders to conceal firm, upturned breasts, the beautiful singer's expression was one of contempt mixed with defiance.

Victor reached down into the old army rucksack propped against the gutter beside him and retrieved another bottle of lukewarm beer. "Fuck it." He popped the cap with the church key hanging on a chain around his neck with his tags.

A sudden flurry of sounds jerked the drunk vet from his flashbacks and self-pity. A sleek two-door sedan, painted a dull shade of silver with the headlights blacked out rushed down the narrow alley, crashing into a line of trash cans. As it turned onto the main strip, Victor noticed that the entire car—grille, hubcaps, fenders—was painted in the same color scheme as its bullet-riddled body.

Crouching back into the shadows, he watched three hands holding bricks emerge from the automobile's passenger side as it cruised slowly in front of the Pho-75 Restaurant. Bricks flew from angry fingers like *chi-com* stick grenades arcing out into the night: end over end, whispering death twirling through the fog.

Floor-to-ceiling plate-glass windows shattered and collapsed, onto the blacktop. As the plate-glass windows disintegrated, the crash of their long shards was drowned out by a squealing of tires as the big car roared off into the night, its occupants laughing hysterically.

No words. No warnings. None of the usual gang slogans. No drive-by shooting here tonight. Just laughter.

Victor could not tell if the gang was Asian or white. He wondered why he even cared. Punks were punks. And they were ruining Little Saigon.

As the car squealed through the parking lot in a defiant doughnut of burning rubber, he tried to jot down the license plate number, but the contents of too many bottles of *ba-muoi-ba* had found their way through the ulcers, into his head. Even if he could focus on the rapidly fading yellow-on-blue digits, he wasn't sure he was in enough of a give-a-shit mood to remember them.

After the car's driver ignored the concrete exit ramps and soared right off the parking lot's raised curbing—throwing a shower of sparks out from its undercarriage when it crashed back down onto the street pavement—he rose to an unsteady crouch and hopped over toward the van's rear doors where his crutches were propped against a short timer's calendar bearing the year 1975.

The swinging front doors of Pho-75 burst open as the dozen or so patrons who had still been boldly congregating inside now rushed toward the parking lot, bent over, eyes wide and wary—eight men and four women. There were no screams. Just the routine, orderly evacuation. The calm before the secondary blasts. It reminded him of Old Saigon, and the satchel charges Viet Cong terrorists would fling into open-air cafés on Tu Do and Le Loi and Pasteur streets.

Motors on three expensive BMWs, a Jaguar, and a beat-up, primer-gray Pinto rattled to life. The Jag shot out of the parking lot first, sliding sideways onto Bolsa Avenue and leaving dual clouds of burnt rubber swirling behind as it raced west toward the Pacific Ocean that lay six miles beyond the already closed McDonald's.

Victor watched the noodle shop's owner bolt the front door, place a Closed sign in the entryway, and begin pulling bamboo shades and curtains over the shattered windows.

The old, familiar rush of fight-or-flee adrenaline pumping through his veins, flooding his belly, Victor briefly considered departing for greener, more peaceful pastures himself, but already the night was alive with police sirens. Someone in Little Saigon had actually broken with tradition and phoned the authorities. It sounded like a half dozen black-and-whites were converging on

his little plot of sacred turf from four different directions
as electronic yelps, wails, and hi-los closed in on the
scene.

Static-laced radio transmissions drifted from the brown,
1974 Malibu coupé parked at the entrance to a dark alley
that ran off the Bolsa Strip, several blocks east of Pho-
75. The messages being exchanged over local airwaves
sounded formal, the jargon street cop and military.

Its motor running, a small cloud of steam lingered
behind the Malibu's dual exhausts. The two veteran detectives sitting in the front seat looked more like a couple
of L.A. Dodger fans staking out a favorite pitcher's estate
than cops in their jeans, black running shoes, and dark
blue baseball caps. Beneath their dark bomber-style jackets, however, both men carried automatics. As backup,
they also carried an arsenal of smaller, snub-barreled
revolvers in ankle holsters. Five-inch block letters across
the backs of their jackets read M.A.G., the acronym for
the Metro Asian Gang task force. The force's emblem—
a red dragon prowling a field of green bamboo—graced
the bright yellow patch sewn across the front of the caps.

"Don't touch that sucker!" Feigning surprise, the
stocky investigator leaning against the passenger-side
door leveled a rigid forefinger in mock reprimand as his
partner reached for the ignition key and started to turn
off the car's idling motor.

"When the little red dial falls below the big E on the
dashboard there, it means we're running on fumes,
chump."

"But you *know* the starter on this piece of shit has
been acting up all week. I don't know *why* we didn't take
one of the Plymouths. One of the eighty-*nine* models.
Something *new*. There's nothing like the smell of a new
car."

"You love this 'piece of shit,' and you know it. Hell,
it's perfect for this part of town: From a distance, the
Viets think it's just another Chicanomobile. After dark,
they probably figure us for a coupla fag *cholos* from Santa
Ana. And you *know* no other unmarked unit anywhere

in Metro has a souped-up four-forty under the hood. Shit,
this is a classic, man—one of the last of the police pursuit packages from the seventies, when punks didn't mess
with *real* cops 'cause—''

"Cause they were the meanest motherfuckers in the
valley." Thornton fiddled with the car's passenger-side
spotlight handle. "Yeah, save it for some maggot who
gives a flying fuck, Luke."

The detectives were in their forties—though both men
sported better physiques than many of the hot-dog rookies coming out of the police academy. Behind the steering wheel sat Lt. Luke Abel, the task force's Orange
County team leader. His partner, Sgt. Glenn Thornton,
rode shotgun tonight. Instead of a twelve-gauge, Thornton's hands were occupied with a giant, creme-filled
longjohn roll from Mah's Donut Shack.

Abel—the one pushing forty-four but with over twenty
years of combined law-enforcement experience under his
belt—reached down to lock the dash-mounted police scanner on the local P.D. frequency. Tilting the brim of his
cap back, he ran the fingers of his gun hand through
wavy brown hair, which was full and combed straight
back. "Celebrating anything important?" he glanced
over at his partner, who was attempting to keep the roll's
creme stuffings from dripping down onto his lap.

Thornton stared back at the M.A.G. lieutenant with a
blank face. "Well, I survived my wife's cooking again
this evening," he said, finally. "Korean *bullgogi* with a
side plate of *kimchi* strong enough to kill a water buffalo.
Actually, *this*,"—he held up the longjohn like a lead-
filled sap—"is to make up for the empty stomach I left
home with tonight."

"I thought you liked Korean food," Abel fired back.

"Twenty-one times a week is pushin' it a little." He
sighed. "When I first met her back in Chong Dong Nee,
all she ever wanted to do was steal an MP jeep and head
for the Pizza Hut in Taejon."

"That's what you get for—" Abel began, but his partner cut him off after filling his mouth with part of the
roll.

"I should have married a Viet instead," he mumbled, mouth full now. "Like you . . ."

Abel's grim frown grew deeper, and he glanced out the window.

"Sorry . . ." Thornton cursed himself silently.

"Forget it."

Thornton glanced at his watch. "She feeds me nothin' but that gook food out of revenge—she's pissed 'cause of these seven-P.M.-to-three-A.M. shifts we've been working. When we gonna rate white man's hours, Luke? Nobody works seven-to-three except street cops in the bag and emergency room nurses."

"We've been working the late cover shift for three years, Glenn," Abel reminded him in a sour tone.

"Yeah, well, I admit I *used* to like it—the action, the adventure, the endless supply of badge-sucking nymphs—but after five years, it's old."

"Three," Abel repeated.

"Hell, look at us," Thornton finished the longjohn and raised his hands in surrender. "Four years chasing gook gang bangers and we're still sittin' in dark alleys, comparing passing license plates with numbers on the hot sheet."

"Don't let your old lady hear you talking like that." Abel almost grinned.

"Shee-it." Thornton rolled his window down and tossed a small, wadded-up bag at a nearby trash can, missing by several feet. He reached down into his side pocket and produced a package of cupcakes.

"You keep eatin' that shit—" the lieutenant resumed studying passing license plates with his pair of folding mini-binoculars—"and it'll alter the chemical *im*balance of your brain. Ever hear of the Twinkie defense?"

"That's exactly why I eat this crap," Thornton maintained. "I'm gonna be ready for the deputy D.A. if I ever fuck up and waste one of these gang-banger pukes without righteous probable cause." He motioned toward a freshly waxed Nissan Maxima passing slowly by on the six-lane boulevard in front of them.

The sleek new four-door sedan was loaded down with

an obnoxious collection of young Vietnamese self-styled studs clad in various shades of black—their hair slick with gel and feathered to the sides or simply spiked straight up. All in their late teens or early twenties, they never seemed to notice the fifteen-year-old undercover Chevy parked in the shadows. They were directing their attention at a cherry red Celica, cruising slowly in the next lane of traffic alongside their own set of chromed wheels and polished plastic. The customized Toyota convertable was crammed to capacity with gang girls from a friendly faction of the area clan—their skimpy leather outfits of the punk-rock variety, their Tina Turner frizz with silver or purple streaks.

Abel chuckled lightly, but his face remained somber, unsmiling. Thornton couldn't remember having seen his partner grin once in the last several weeks, in fact. And that was unlike Luke.

They were waiting for a black Porsche Cabriolet 911, with partial personalized California license plates that read MERC. The type of plates that cost an extra five bucks at the Department of Motor Vehicles Registration counter and had been new in 1987 but discontinued now: off-white with gold letters and an orange, setting sun. Driver wanted for strong-armed robbery of little old Vietnamese ladies in the Bolsa and Brookhurst districts. Beat them up and snatched their purses. Wore a ski mask, so identification was proving to be difficult.

The computer hit on the license MERC-IT, a Porsche stolen out of a ritzy neighborhood in nearby Westminster only last week. His instincts told him that it was probably related to the Westminster paramilitary gang known as the Mercs, but Abel didn't want to make hasty conclusions or assume anything right now—ten years at L.A.P.D. and three more at Santa Ana, not to mention his first seven in Old Saigon, had taught him that much.

M.A.G. was an elite arm of the Department of Justice, which all peace officers referred to as simply D.O.J. Their numerical strength fluctuated depending on transfers, retirements, and the mortality rate, but thirty or so officers were usually assigned to the Los Angeles-Orange County branch of the task force, which concentrated largely on Asian-gang crime, and maintained three sub-stations in Southern California—on Hill Street, in L.A.'s Chinatown, on Atlantic Boulevard in Monterey Park, and on the Bolsa strip, an enclave of Vietnamese refugees in neighboring Orange County to the south, better known as Little Saigon.

Drawn from police and Sheriffs' departments throughout the L.A. metropolitan area, officers selected for M.A.G. duty by their patrol commanders, and approved by the Justice Department liaison, were automatically promoted to detective and given free rein to travel wherever their investigations led them. Traditional territorial boundaries between agencies—often held sacred by all street cops—were largely ignored by the men of M.A.G.

Street cops working marked cars from departments throughout Los Angeles and Orange County wanted to get into the elite Metro Asian Gang task force. But M.A.G. was a small, tight-knit group composed of low-profile law-enforcement veterans, and access to their ranks was difficult.

Currently, trouble between the Chinese and Vietnamese gangs was escalating, and the department's crime-control stats were reflecting an increase in criminal activity throughout Little Saigon—surpassing even the notorious extortion activities going down in Chinatown to the north. It was M.A.G.'s current orders to both stem the tide of residential robberies taking place on both sides of the Bolsa Strip, and prevent all-out warfare between the roving gangs of young hoodlums as the Tet Lunar New Year festivities approached.

Presently, only four sworn agents and two civilian Community Service Officers, or C.S.O.s, were assigned to the Bolsa office. The agents were teamed up into two pairs, both of which worked the action-packed cover shift.

The C.S.O.s—both former Vietnamese refugees who had gone on to earn naturalized U.S. citizenship status—

worked an odd assortment of hours as interpreters, juvenile project specialists, and even undercover operatives when the need arose. The remaining officers in M.A.G. were assigned to the Chinatown substation, due to an increase in organized rackets and Triad gang activity escalating in East Los Angeles and the San Gabriel Valley. The upcoming return of Hong Kong to communist Chinese control panicked underworld bosses in that part of the world and they were looking for a new base of operations.

"What're my chances of talking you into cruisin' on over to the Can Tho Cabaret and—" Thornton began.

Abel silenced him with a raised hand. "Did you hear that?"

"Breaking glass," Thornton affirmed, cleaning up his culinary mess in the blink of an eye—all business now, as he reached for the radio microphone. "A *lotta* breaking glass!"

Abel placed his fingers on the ignition key but did not immediately turn it. "Which direction?" he glanced up and down the boulevard—now suddenly empty of traffic.

"That way." Thornton pointed toward the glowing facades that were New Saigon Mall, five or six blocks to the west.

"I think you're right for a change." Abel was scanning storefronts in the opposite direction, however. They all appeared dark. Except for the bars and some restaurants, Little Saigon's business district usually died at seven or eight o'clock each night.

He finally turned the ignition key and, though the starter began grinding loudly, the engine itself refused to turn over.

"This damn piece of shit!" Thornton brought his fist down on the dashboard, and cracker crumbs flew from his side of the car.

"Mellow out." Abel raised his hand a second time, urging calm. "It's just a bad starter, that's all—needs to cool down a little bit more. We've been running this crate into the ground for the last two weeks. She needs a rest."

"That's what my old lady always says whenever the sarge here is in the mood for a little action." Thornton patted his crotch.

Less than a minute later the Garden Grove police channel of Emergency Communications Station 18 was broadcasting reports of a possible window smash, burglary-in-progress at Pho-75—phoned in by a passing Rapid Transit District bus driver. Shortly thereafter, their blue and red roof lights flashing sluggishly but sirens off, two marked units from Garden Grove P.D. zoomed past them.

≡ CHAPTER 2

"LET'S GET THIS fucking show on the road, Lucas!"
Thornton complained loudly as he punched out the dashboard again.

With the Malibu's battery sounding on the verge of
death, Abel closed his eyes tightly and turned the ignition key for the tenth time.

"Fan*tastic*!" Thornton erupted as the entire car
shuddered and the powerful V-8 under the hood finally
rumbled to life. "Now just promise me you won't turn
this mother off again until we clock out, bud!"

Abel nodded, slammed the gearshift into drive, and
sent the rear tires spinning. His eyes drifted from his
driving as he raced to the call for cover—though a cop
is taught to scope out the street blocks ahead of his unit
as it rolls along, and to eyeball the homes and busi-
nesses along his beat even at thirty or forty miles an
hour. His concentration shifted to the storefront signs,
still glowing.

In the morning, the streets would be bustling with activity—shoppers with Asian features everywhere. There
would be some Latins here and there, but few white folks
in sight—other than the usual quota of commuters locked
in their automobiles.

The stone-faced holdouts would be in evidence behind shop windows every few corners or so, watching the changes and the strangers and what they perceived to be the growing loss of business as more and more Caucasians moved away from the strip. But refusing to sell out. Feeling like foreigners in their own hometown . . . Refusing to give in to the newcomers who they wished would go back where they came from: Vietnam.

After South Vietnam fell to the communists in April of 1975, refugees flocked to California by the tens of thousands. Former embassy employees, ARVN soldiers, civilians who had worked for America's MACV or DIA or CIA. A million boat people would perish over the next ten years as they followed their relocated relatives, trying to survive the treacherous, shark-and-pirate-infested South China Sea in their quest for freedom. Eventually, nearly 100,000 ethnic Vietnamese would settle in the Orange County communities of Garden Grove, Westminster, and Santa Ana, thirty-five miles south of Los Angeles. It was your textbook melting pot of Asians, Latins, and Europeans. L.A.'s suburbs to the south. To the north, another 65,000 ethnic Chinese from Vietnam would end up in Alhambra and Monterey Park, San Gabriel and Rosemead—blending in with the 200,000 Asians from Hong Kong and Taiwan who already resided in the suburbs on the edge of East L.A.

The Viets quickly turned what some longtime residents considered to be the ghetto of Bolsa into a thriving commercial sector. Vacant, dilapidated buildings and long stretches of ramshackle warehouses were torn down after a few wealthy Vietnamese immigrants purchased two miles of land and began leasing it to the other refugee businessmen—those who had been lucky enough to smuggle their gold bullion out of Vietnam without having it stolen by Thai pirates or confiscated by U.S. Customs. New, modern buildings, many brightly decorated in the Oriental fashion, quickly went up: everything from food markets and jewelry stores to import-export shops and audio-video outlets using bright, proud neon to advertise their wares in colorful Oriental slashes.

Most of the storefront signs included a smaller English
translation beneath the business's name or service offered, but it was only the blatant and foreign Vietnamese
script most Orange County natives seemed to notice. And
were offended by.

None of the closed-in, crowded congestion common-
place in Chinatowns across the country was evident in
Little Saigon. The main strip, Bolsa Avenue, was a wide,
six-lane affair. Comprising the southern border of the
Vietnamese shopping district, it ran east and west through
the communities of Garden Grove, Westminster, and
Santa Ana, but only a two-mile stretch—from Magnolia,
east to Euclid Street—was considered Little Saigon. The
refugee enclave extended north another mile to Westminster Avenue.

The housing was spread out and orderly—not like Old
Saigon. There was a wide array of two-storied storefronts
and sprawling shopping plazas. Much of the architecture
remained American, with the exception of two giant
malls boasting dragon spires and arched roofs. In front
of the impressive Man Wah commercial complex, two
white marble lions "guarded" the access drives and
glass-plated main doors. Across the boulevard, and a few
blocks west, several larger-than-life statues of immortal
Buddhist deities greeted visitors to the New Saigon Mall,
a cavernous two-story structure with a train-depot flavor
about it. Even this late at night, gold floodlights made
the building's sloping, red-tile roof sparkle beneath a rising crescent moon.

As they approached the sea of flashing emergency
lights converging in the distance, Abel saw an old mama-
san standing in the bamboo doorway of one of Bolsa's
medical clinics. She was wearing a straw conical hat, a
purplish tunic, baggy black calico trousers and was holding a bowl to her face. He watched her maneuver the
chopsticks as she scooped the food into her mouth. And
his eyes were drawn to the flag flapping proudly thirty
feet above her: the golden flag with three horizontal red
stripes—symbol of pre-1975 Vietnam, the homeland they
would return to someday.

A half dozen black-and-whites blocked Pho-75's west access drive, and Abel immediately scoped out the situation even before he brought the Malibu to a stop: several plate-glass windows totaled, no suspect vehicles being detained, zero onlookers yet as far as crowd control went. There was no telltale odor of gunsmoke on the sticky, late night breeze. No fleeing felons bagged by the boys in blue.

Two vehicles remained at the scene other than the P.D. units, and he recognized both of them: the restaurant owner's long, late-model pickup truck, and a beat-up old van. The lieutenant knew instantly that Vic the Vet was not involved in this kind of vandalism. But the disabled ex-GI was certainly getting skeptical treatment from the beefy patrolman standing over him.

Abel and his partner dismounted from the Malibu and started toward the semicircle of uniforms and leather gear crowding in around the rear doors of Victor's black van.

"What's the story, guys?" Abel raised his voice as the patrolman in charge resumed waving his finger in warning at the tight-lipped, one-legged ex-soldier swinging casually from side to side inside a hammock suspended from the van's ceiling.

The officers who glanced back over their shoulders at the familiar voice did not seem particularly pleased to discover that two M.A.G. agents had monitored their call and decided to investigate. "Victor's drinking in public again," one of them said with bored indifference.

Thornton glanced over at the damaged picture windows along Pho-75's west wall, forty or fifty feet away. "Did Vic do *that*?" he asked.

"Fuck no I didn't do that!" the Vietnam vet's outburst came as a drunken slur.

"I keep warnin' him to quit drinkin' this ten-percent firewater in public," the first officer on-scene advised Able, "but he never pays me no heed. I keep warnin' him to take the juice *home* before he opens it up, but—"

"This *is* my home!" Victor proclaimed. "You tell

'em, Lieutenant Abel! Tell 'em to cut me some slack, man. . . ."

"I think it's time the scrote found a *new* home," one of the rookies present muttered. "County *jail*. Christ, lookit that fucking assault rifle he's got in there!" His hand rested on the black Pachmyre grips of a holstered pistol butt.

"It's legal," Abel replied without emotion. "If Victor planned on usin' it, there'd be a dozen P.D.-blue corpses gracin' those cruisers back there. Am I right, Victor?"

"Shit," the vet responded, still swinging. "Just memories, Lou. You know that. I got no fight with your boys. My war's over."

Shrugging, Abel walked over toward the black '65 Dodge van.

Victor still lay in his hammock, parked in the heart of Little Saigon, stump protruding for all to see, ignoring even the M.A.G. lieutenant, staring up at the gang graffiti that shadowed bright Oriental lettering atop the storefront walls identifying this shop or that restaurant—neon closing in on his turf, his private parking lot, his temporary stall in life.

Abel scratched at the stubble on his own chin as he studied Victor's stony features. He reflected on the man's past—as much as he knew about it—and tried to devise a way to get the uniformed cops back out on the street without taking him into Headquarters for an attitude adjustment. Hell, Victor had been hanging around the Bolsa Strip since before the snarling marble lions and giant Oriental arches went up in front of Man Wah Center years ago.

He was *part* of Little Saigon—he added to the tense atmosphere of the place. And he was no troublemaker. Tonight, it was pay back. Abel owed Victor—one vet to another.

When he was in that rare, good mood—and sober—he sometimes even surprised the M.A.G. agents by supplying them with little tidbits of information about Bolsa and its side-street denizens that no one else in Little Saigon seemed privy to.

Victor could read most of the crypticly twisted graffiti that closed in on him like the ghosts haunting his nightmares. He could distinguish between the ethnic Vietnamese hoodlums—Steel Dragon—and those with Cholon-Chinese in their blood—the Blue Bamboo Boys. He knew the gang-banger monikers and all their leaders: Willie Wu, Snake Eyes, Bullet Hole, Weasel Breath, Bone Chips, Louie-Louie. He'd watched them grow up.

From the far side of the parking lot, a woman's carefree laughter drifted out through the nearest nightclub's swinging front doors—a few words of her singsong voice carrying to him on the breeze as well before fading against the sudden din of traffic rushing past on the Bolsa Strip after a signal light changed down the block.

"I said, *Break-out some ID*, asshole!" The giant cop waiting between the van's open doors finally lost his patience. He drew his PR-24 nightstick and delivered a swinging crack to one of the rear-door handles for emphasis.

Abel gently grabbed the officer's bulging bicep and pulled him off. "So how's it hangin' tonight, Victor?" he motioned for the uniformed officers to give them some breathing room as he stared up at the black POW/MIA flag flapping lazily from the van's extended radio antenna: the silhouette of a prisoner's head behind barbed wire.

"Same old shit, Lieutenant . . ." Victor responded with the usual respect when he spoke to Abel—as if he were conversing with his old platoon commander back on the outskirts of Gia Dinh Providence. He slid down out of the hammock and balanced himself precariously on the van's rear bumper, good leg dangling over the edge. It reminded Abel of the gunships cruising low over Saigon, the grunts on board fresh in from the boonies and crowding the open hatch, M-16 rifles across their thighs and legs dangling out over the landing skids.

Victor locked eyes with Abel, and a silent bonding of

old warriors seemed to pass between them as he sized up the two anti-gang investigators.

Lt. Lucas Abel, though tall and healthy-looking was not stocky. The chest and upper arms of his jacket were tight across hard muscles. The man stood about five foot ten or eleven, and probably weighed one hundred eighty or ninety. His face seemed dark and weathered—but it was not beach-bum brown . . . more the golden, bronzed shade earned from spending many years working under some exotic, tropical sun. Rough and weathered.

His eyes gave him away, though. At times, they seemed those of a hundred-year-old man—on other occasions, those of a predator. His hair was dark brown, combed straight back, but dry and full.

Along his left cheek, just under the eye, a horizontal scar announced he'd paid his dues. The scar was an inch and a half long and an eighth of an inch wide, but blended with the dark texture of his skin rather than standing out. It made Victor think of the gang members in Chinatown who wore scars all across their bodies like combat medals. Luke Abel had been issued *this* medal back on the streets of Saigon, more than twenty years earlier, in 1968.

His partner, Detective Sgt. Glenn Thornton, was two or three years younger and as many inches shorter than Abel. His build was stockier and somewhat muscular, with wide shoulders. Always clean shaven, with prominant, almost intimidating brows, he wore his medium-length black hair parted along the left side.

"Tell us what you saw here tonight, Vic." Sgt. Thornton finally broke the weird trance.

"All I saw was a car speeding recklessly through the lot." Victor aimed his statement at Abel when he finally spoke. "A souped-up car full of punks."

"Can you describe the car?" Thornton asked. "Did you happen to get a license number?"

"Were they Vietnamese gang bangers?" Abel added.

"All I remember," Victor sighed loudly, "was that the car was silver. Totally silver, if you get my drift." When the two M.A.G. detectives responded with bewildered looks, Victor said, "Hubcaps, grille, even the radio antenna. Painted silver."

"Gang bangers." Thornton nodded sullenly, as if he'd just been told they'd have to work a double shift now.

"As far as the punks, I didn't see no faces. They didn't drop a hammer on ol' Vic, so ol' Vic didn't look too hard in their direction, you know?"

"Yeah, we understand," Thornton responded, but he didn't seem too happy with the arrangement. "Any gang slogans yelled?"

"Nope. Sorry, Sarge."

Abel frowned as well. The kids who tore a new wall into Pho-75 could be just about anybody. And the owner probably wasn't talking.

"I say we take this douchebag in for further questioning." The burly patrolman was standing a couple inches over Abel again.

"Maybe a couple hours in a holding cell will refresh his memory," the officer's rookie partner chimed in.

"Why don't you two cool it down on Vic here," Abel said. "He's paid his dues."

"And he's our pal." Thornton's remark came across as semi-comical, and a few officers turned away, hiding their grins.

"Look, *I* served in the Nam, too, ya jerk!" The big cop glared down at Victor. "Marines. Iron Triangle."

Victor's eyes surveyed the patrolman's stocky frame, head to toes. "Looks like you brought everything home, too, *amigo*. Including your balls. I'm happy for you."

Taken aback by the remark, and not quite sure if he'd just been insulted—Abel wasn't sure either, actually—the patrolman shot back: " 'Brought everything home'?" He cocked an incredulous eyebrow. "This sure as shit ain't my home, sleezeball. This is Little Saigon."

"Come on." Abel's chest expanded importantly. "None of this verbal bullshit is getting any of us anywhere." He turned to the uniformed officers and said, "I'll tell you what, guys—Sergeant Thornton here vol-

unteers to do the paperwork on the restaurant vandalism
over there . . ."

"I do?" Glenn's eyebrows came together as he glanced
up at his partner.

". . . if you'll just agree to turn this little incident
over to us. It's gang related, after all."

Heads turned as the officers surveyed the jagged shards
of glass protruding from Pho-75. There was definitely
enough damage there to qualify the call as a bona fide
felony 594—criminal mischief—but arrests seemed un-
likely. Massive amounts of paperwork didn't.

"It's all yours." Half of the police officers were already heading back to their cars.

"I shit you not, Lieutenant," Victor said, speaking to
Abel though his eyes had locked onto the giant patrolman's. "I don' want no trouble. I only want to be left
alone, man. . . ."

"Aw, fuck it." The uniformed weight lifter turned and
started over toward his unit. "It's all yours, Lou." As
soon as his back was to Victor, he winked at the lieutenant with a suppressed grin.

"We know you don't want no grief, Vic." Abel
reached out and patted the disabled vet on the shoulder.
He recalled their bar talk the last time he and Glenn had
taken Victor "into custody" and carried him, punching
and screaming, into Anh Adams's Can Tho Cabaret. That
was the night he told them about his lost love Kim.

"We're outta here, Lou. . . ." A black-and-white
rolled up silently beside him. Inside, Officer Gorilla and
his rookie stared up at the lieutenant.

"Thanks for the favor," Abel said.

"Just don't try and sweep this crime under the rug."
Gorilla's eyes narrowed with mock suspicion. "I *know*
how you M.A.G. boys are always hoggin' the glory, then
tryin' to get out of the paper work."

"That's the only thing I hate about this job." The
rookie spoke out of place, rambling off on some bizarre
tangent about his twelve-month probationary period as
his field-training officer's eyeballs rolled skyward.

"Yeah, well, all I know is rookies these days sure got

the balls to complain so early," Sergeant Thornton growled. "In the old days, when *I* was a rook, we didn't gripe and groan until we had that five-year star sewn onto our sleeve."

"Yeah, when was that? Nineteen-oh-niner?" Gorilla giggled.

"The seventies, fuckwad. When cops were really cops and not social workers. These days, you gotta worry about the ACLU and NAACP—even the Citizens Advisory Commission. Back in the seventies, when the Brotherhood of the Badge meant something, you didn't worry about the letter of the law—you just did what was *right*."

"Spare me the spiel, Sarge." With a loud sigh, Gorilla switched the car's headlights on. "I've heard it a hundred times before from your buddies exiled from M.A.G., back onto the Night Watch."

"Sayonara," Abel muttered, as the cruiser coasted out of the parking lot. "Don't shoot yourself in the prick, peckerhead."

The big patrolman responded by flipping him the bird out his window without looking back.

"Lovely personality," Thornton remarked.

Abel didn't seem disturbed. "He's good to have around in a bar fight."

They walked over to the Pho-75 and banged on the locked front door until the owner appeared. "I need you to sign an incident sheet," Abel told the restaurateur. "I don't think there's enough evidence here to rate a full-fledged crime report."

"Why you want me sign anything?" the man shook his flabby jowls and ran a set of stubby fingers back through his close-cropped, silver hair. "I don't know who do this. I don' *want* to know! Only misunders'anding— tha's all."

"You haven't received any extortion demands lately?" Thornton asked.

"Ex-*what*?" the owner tilted his head to one side.

"Ep lay," Abel translated into pidgin-Viet. *"Cuoag doat."*

"Oh! You speak Vietnamese?" the old man's eyes lit up.

"Not enough." Abel's expression told the owner he was in no mood for compliments or grammatical corrections.

"Well, no . . . no, I get no problems from nobody here. We pay some piaster to the gang—you know, Steel Dragon boys—but just to . . . to 'keep undesirables out of Pho-75. . . .' " It sounded as though the last few words were a recital, taught him by the gang bangers should he ever be approached by the police. An overhead lightbulb seemed to illuminate his features as he suddenly brightened up, recipient of a heaven-sent idea. "I think VC do this to me, Officer." He turned to face Sgt. Thornton, who stood clear of the conversation, arms folded across his chest as he counted falling stars. "Do you know what VC is, mister?"

"I got a gut feeling," Thornton said sarcastically, without looking down from the night sky.

"You ever been to Vietnam?" the old man pressed the M.A.G. sergeant for a face-to-face show of respect.

Abel knew his partner well enough to realize they'd all be standing there until morning before Glenn gave in. "Yeah, *I've* been there," he said. "But VC would have blown this place off the face of the earth, friend. VC woulda raped your daughters and lopped off your wife's head. Now do you want to level with us about what happened tonight, or not?"

The old man turned and surveyed the damage to his restaurant with a critical eye. "The insurance will take care of it," he decided quietly. "So sorry, Officers, but I think I have nothing more to say about this unfort'nate event. Bookoo thanks for your time. Police got here very quick."

"But not quick enough," Thornton muttered.

"Let's split." Abel sighed in resignation as the owner bowed slightly, then walked back into his store and closed the door.

"Jesus," Abel listened to the series of deadbolts slide into place. "Typical Vietnamese attitude: Hear no evil, see no evil, speak no evil. Don' even *think* no evil, or it will surely befall you with a vengeance.''

The M.A.G. lieutenant turned from the bright multi-colored fluorescent lamps lighting Pho-75's entryway, cursing under his breath at the temporary loss of night vision. He was in the mood to invite Victor over to the Can Tho Cabaret for a cup of coffee, but the Vietnam vet and his beat-up black van had silently vanished.

≡ CHAPTER 3

THE HAZE-CHOKED MORNING felt like daybreak in some steaming port in the tropics. There was a hint of impending rain in the air that gave the city that special smell, that bittersweet taste of danger lurking beyond the bend that real cops love so much. Day-watch troopers would even patrol with their windows rolled down, air conditioners off.

Blistering heat and the aroma of steaming rice cakes made the old, retired *canh-sat* or Old Saigon street cop think of his riot squad days in South Vietnam. As he stared at the two police Plymouths parked across the street, joss smoke—offerings from dozens of sidewalk shrines bristling with incense sticks—drifted by on the humid ocean breeze, reminding him of the Buddhist temples that once lined Cong Ly and Le Van Duyet streets in Old Saigon. The sun had climbed above the skyline now, and was burning away the fog. Sun dogs danced in the halo of water crystals high overhead.

His eyes focused on plumes of steam rising from the squad cars' rumbling exhaust pipes, then, searching once again for his son, scanned the groups of noisy Vietnamese youth leaving a hot-dog stand. The sight of their spiked hair and untraditional garb creased the former *canh-sat*'s grim features—their unruly and boisterous an-

tics in public mirrored his eldest child's own disrespectful behavior of recent weeks.

But the old man's eyes always returned to the two police cars and the contrasting Asian architecture rising up
behind them through the swirling mist. In the distance,
storm clouds loomed on the dark horizon, bringing back
monsoon memories of his own days patrolling the rain-
slick streets of Old Saigon.

Brightly decorated and intricately carved Oriental
arches rose at an impressive slant nearly three stories
above the two police cars. The spires, covered with
blood-red tiles, glistened beneath the arid, Southern California sun, and marked the entrance to one of the largest
shopping plazas catering to the refugee community. The
massive arches were adorned with good-luck symbols
and Vietnamese script. A set of seven-feet-tall snarling
lions, carved from white marble, guarded the entrance
to one of Little Saigon's many sprawling shopping and
arcade plazas.

The black-and-white police cars were parked side by
side with their drivers' windows open. Newly washed,
they shone on the side of the road, beacons of power and
protection, their undented metal bodies reflecting the
sluggish collage of the traffic passing by on the Bolsa
Strip. Without leaving their cruisers, the two officers sitting inside exchanged handfuls of interagency hot sheets
and a moment of shop talk as several Asian women in
gossamer-thin Vietnamese gowns strolled past, their dark,
sloe eyes carefully averted.

A dozen young schoolgirls from the nearby private
Catholic school appeared in front of one police unit.
"You!" a tiny seven-year-old with straight black hair
pointed at her own reflection in the patrolman's mirrored
sunglasses.

"Good morning, young lady," he responded with a
friendly and casual salute.

The schoolgirls erupted into unrestrained giggles. Half
returned the salute. The air was filled with pidgin-English
chatter as they skipped on down the busy, commuter-
clogged street.

The officers' police cars were parked on Bolsa Avenue at Bushard Street in the heart of Little Saigon. They were both street veterans in their early thirties, born and raised in Orange County. When they walked a foot beat through their districts, both officers towered above most of the area's transplanted residents. The new immigrants treated them with politeness and a tolerant respect—not the disdain and suspicion afforded the often-corrupt white-shirted *canh-sats* of Old Saigon.

Abel's brown Malibu pulled up into the long, vacant field on the south side of the street, across from the two marked units. Municipal work crews were clearing debris from the five-acre lot, which was to be used for the upcoming Lunar New Year celebrations—Little Saigon's annual Tet Festival. The three-day event would feature a carnival-like atmosphere of rides, games, and entertainment, with several new cars raffled off and a Miss Indochina beauty pageant to highlight the final night's activities.

Inside the Malibu, the two M.A.G. detectives turned toward a nervous Asian youth standing on the corner. The boy was clad entirely in black, and his wary eyes had been darting back and forth, scanning passing vehicles, yet apparently failing to spot the approaching Malibu until Abel and Thornton had pulled up right beside him. He appeared genuinely startled when the two-door sedan slid to a sudden stop.

The black jean outfit and spiked hair identified the youth as a possible gang member. Though gangs in Little Saigon wore no identifying *colors* as their criminal counterparts in other communities did, almost all members of the seven groups fighting for control of the Bolsa Strip sauntered about in public wearing various shades of black from shirt to shoes. The black jean *jacket* identified this youth as a runner for the Steel Dragon gang—the area's most vicious and heavily armed.

The two M.A.G. agents accepted a grudgingly surrendered piece of crumpled paper from the gang banger.

Slipping on a pair of wide black sunglasses, the youth

quickly departed, losing himself in the throngs of morning shoppers crowding the sidewalk along the Bolsa Strip.

The two-door Malibu coupe slid out onto Bolsa, rear tires spinning. With a cloud of burned rubber left behind, Abel sped west along the strip, in the direction of Magnolia Street.

Pham, the retired *canh-sat*, felt a nauseating pain swirl about in his gut. The boy across the street was his son. He wondered briefly what his son had told the two detectives to make them leave in such a hurry. His eyes shifted to resume their careful scrutiny of his son's suspicious activities, then he raced across Bolsa's six lanes of honking traffic unscathed, attempting to latch onto him.

As Abel's car vanished down the haze-cloaked street, the ex-Saigon policeman caught up with his son, grabbed him by the collar of his shirt from behind, and whirled him around.

It was beginning to be a daily routine. The boy wandered the streets instead of attending school. His father would find him down on the Bolsa Strip, and an argument would ensue. The ex-cop had little patience with proud teenagers. He ruled with the edged hand of a jujitsu master, but there was little respect for the wishes of elders in this new country.

The youth's father was punching the boy around now as he dragged him in the direction of a bus stop down the block. The old, retired *canh-sat* didn't want his boy running with the gangs. But he didn't want him working the street as a snitch, either. That would mean a death sentence.

The two patrolmen sitting in the marked cars did not miss a thing. They saw the old man slap the young kid on the head a couple of times, and they watched the brown Malibu squeal out of the parking lot and race off down Bolsa. But they didn't seem particularly concerned.

"Where you think them two M.A.G. hot dogs are going?" one of the officers asked.

"Probably to the shitter."

"What about the kid and the old man?"

"Hell, that's ex-Sergeant Pham. Was a Saigon cop for twenty or thirty years, the way Lieutenant Abel tells it. Retired from the Vietnamese National Police back around seventy-four or so. . . ."

"And South Vietnam fell to the commies a year later."

"And that's all she wrote."

The officer frowned and went back to his lapful of paperwork.

A few minutes later, the dispatch was sending a multi-toned *Attention*! scrambler over the radio set. *"All units!"* a female's tense voice barked. "At Bolsa and Magnolia, M.A.G.-Thirteen is requesting assistance. Gang fight at that location! Units to respond identify. . . ."

In the middle of the intersection of Bolsa and Magnolia, a calm-faced Luke Abel was using choke holds to restrain two members of the Steel Dragon gang—one in each arm.

Twenty-seven patrol cars from four different agencies quickly converged on the location—their sirens wailing and emergency lights flashing—once word had criss-crossed the radio waves that there was a gang fight in progress and one lonely M.A.G. unit on-scene.

"Who called in the cavalry?" Abel glared at his part-ner as the sea of black-and-whites skidded up all around them.

"Don't look at me!" Thornton was keeping three other gang members at bay with a PR-24 nightstick while of-ficers waded into the melee of two or three dozen com-batants and began separating the two enemy factions of Vietnamese. He raised both hands in a bewildered pose before reaching for a set of handcuffs. "I guess half the county monitored your call, though—and just happened to be passing through the sector or something!"

Thornton laughed as he directed his three prisoners to spread-eagle on the blacktop. Eyes taking in the stream of police cars speeding up to the scene, they complied without protest.

"What you got?" A tired-looking sergeant alighted from his unit carrying a riot baton and gas mask.

"Just a . . . *disagreement*!" one of the out-of-breath gang members—a tall and agile one—snarled as he struggled against Abel's thick forearm. "Nothing we couldn't handle . . . *privately*."

"Shut up, Lui," Abel directed. "Or I'll choke your young ass out!"

" 'Disagreements' are not handled *privately* in the middle of the street!" Thornton told the gang leader.

"Steel Dragon clan versus some boys from Blue Bamboo," Abel told the watch commander. "They must have just got out of a kung-fu movie or something," he added. "No weapons."

"Too bad," the patrol supervisor took the prisoner off Abel's hands as Thornton handcuffed one of the others.

"Want us to charge 'em with Assault on a Police Officer anyway?" a nearby officer, his hands full of flexicuffs, asked Abel.

"Just Disturbance."

"How 'bout Resisting Arrest?" The officer didn't seem to think misdemeanor arrests were worth the paper work.

"Disturbance will suffice," Abel repeated, making eye contact with the patrolman this time.

"Yes, sir." The other's tone was laced with such respect and awe that it brought a smile to Thornton's face.

"One of these days I'm gonna kick your white ass, Abel!" Lui thrust his chin forward after the sergeant handcuffed the gang leader behind the back and began leading him off to a patrol unit. But the lieutenant didn't seem flustered by the threat.

"You and whose army?" he responded dryly. "You're nothing but a half-cocked fruitcake."

"I don't need no army!" Lui hissed, narrowed eyes scanning the reactions of his friends. "You just better watch your back, Abel!" He kicked out at another officer as he guided him into the cage car's backseat, but missed. "My Dragons'll find out where you live, and we'll burn down your house and gang bang your wife, motherfucker!"

"Better watch his *back* is right!" Thornton sneered.
" 'Cause you're nothing but a cowardly *back*stabber,
asshole."

Le Van Lui was a twenty-year-old troublemaker who
had persisted in remaining a thorn in Luke Abel's side
for the last three years. He was tall for a Vietnamese—
about five foot eight—which may have accounted for his
popularity among the area's apprentice hoodlums: they
looked up to him.

Unlike most of the younger gang bangers who ran with
him, Lui did not spike his hair or wear it long. It was
always neatly trimmed and kept in place with a thin coat
of mousse. He was rarely seen in public without his
trademark sunglasses—dark lenses and thick black
frames. Spiders and the inscription "Widow Maker"
were tattooed at the edges of each wrist. Though slender,
his limbs and torso were covered with rippling muscles
that gave him a lean, predator look.

A holding-cell officer had tagged him with the nickname Louie-Louie two years back, when the Rascals song
was playing on the book-in room's radio. Among cops,
the nickname stuck, though any gang member brazen
enough to call Lui by it risked losing his tongue to a
rusty straight razor.

"Sometimes you're so full of shit." Abel just laughed.
To the watch commander, he added, "Go ahead and tag
Resisting onto his jacket this time, Sarge. I seem to have
split a shirt seam *subduing* the subject." He raised an
arm and examined the tear running from elbow to arm-
pit.

"It'll be my pleasure," the supervisor nodded.

Leaning against his car's open door, Abel stared at Lui
for a few moments. Now propped up in the backseat, the
gang leader's face was pressed up against the unit's rear
window. His nose and chin were flattened to the point
of appearing almost comical, but there was no masking
the hate in the Vietnamese youth's eyes. For the first time
in his career, Abel actually felt slightly unnerved by a
prisoner's threats.

Usually, they flew in one ear and out the other. It was

all just part of the job, and most arrestees forgot their promises to do bodily harm long before they reached the jail. But there was something different about Lui. Abel had made fun of him here today. Lui had lost face in front of his men. That could mean trouble.

Thornton motioned his partner away from the prisoners. "What'd that little runt kid tell you back there, Luke?" he asked. "First, you jackin' around in pidgin-Viet, next thing I know we're flyin' balls to the wind down here to this half-assed street rumble."

"At least I warned you to break out the nightstick, didn't I?" Abel produced the wadded-up piece of paper his informant—the *canh-sat*'s son—had handed him ten minutes earlier.

Thornton opened it up and sighed as he read the hand-scrawled tip.

BOLSA & MAGNOLIA—ELEVEN A.M. SHARP
FIGHT BETWEEN STEEL DRAGONS & BLUE BAMBOO
MAYBE

"You know that kid is a retired Saigon cop's son?" He gave Abel an accusing glance.

"Not so loud!" Abel snapped, even though Glenn's words had been a mere whisper.

"No 'maybe' about it. Both sides showed up." Thornton's eyes darted about, counting prisoners. "Just goes to show you how stupid these punks are: fightin' in broad daylight at a major intersection."

"Maybe they're tryin' to tell us something."

"Probably just preparin' for the martial arts contests at the Tet Festival." The M.A.G. sergeant was no longer smiling.

"You don't know how close you are to the facts," Abel said.

"What?"

"That *canh-sat*'s kid advised me there's a power struggle going down in Little Saigon. Between Steel Dragon and Blue Bamboo.

"How deep is the *canh-sat*'s kid in, Luke?"

"His name's Ricky Pham. He's a low-echelon runner—just got initiated last week. They made him knock over a jewelry store at the New Saigon Mall. I got word of it beforehand, and managed to set everything up nice and pretty so no one got hurt. I think Lui bought the act. But you never know."

"Louie-Louie's no dummy," Thornton said.

"I know. And if he finds out our kid's papa-san used to be a *canh-sat*, we might really be up against a brick wall."

"You never know." Thornton folded massive forearms across his chest and leaned back against the Malibu. "Bein' an ex-Saigon cop might be a *plus*, as far as Lui's boys are concerned—and from what I've read about the *canh-sats*. Regular mobsters, weren't they?"

Abel rubbed at his closed eyelids. "Let's just say I knew a lot of . . . colorful characters on the Vietnamese National Police Force," he said.

"Well, thanks multitudes for keepin' me in the dark about this kid," Thornton said in an injured tone. "I thought we was *partners*, boss: I tell you who *I'm* cultivatin' as a snitch, and you tell me who *you're* tryin' to mold—that way we don't get our wires crossed."

Abel dismissed Thornton's irritation with a shrug. "I didn't think it would really lead anywhere. I didn't go out tryin' to recruit the kid. He just keeps followin' me around. *He* came up with the role of informant. I figured it couldn't hurt to see what he produced in the way of gang intel'."

"Hey, Abel!" Lui was yelling from the backseat of the patrol car. "Can we get this show on the road? My old lady's waitin' at police headquarters to bail me out, so I can go straight to my lawyer and *sue* your racist ass!"

"Yeah, hold onto your *ying-yang*, Louie-Louie. We'll be right with you." Abel shook his head in resignation. Lately, M.A.G. duty just didn't produce the job satisfaction it used to.

"Well, duty calls," the sergeant grumbled without

sincerity. ''You guys comin' over to Book-in to question these scrotebags?''

''Yeah, we'll be over there later.'' Thornton nodded. ''Much later.''

''They stop servin' lunch at the jail at thirteen hundred hours sharp,'' the supervisor winked back at the two detectives.

''That's *disgusting*!'' Thornton's features wrinkled in rebuke.

''It keeps hair on my balls.'' The watch commander's wave brought the verbal exchange to a close.

≡ CHAPTER 4

A YOUNG BOY was setting up his shoeshine crate on the nearby corner. The fluid movements of his shoulders and hands displayed a confidence that made him nearly invisible in the swirling haze of Little Saigon—just another street urchin, as he dropped into a casual squat and began unfolding his box of rags and polish. The boy's actions told any potential hostiles prowling the rooftops that he was not a worthy target of opportunity. Abel's eyes looked elsewhere for the trouble.

Farther down the street, several teenage girls in black pantaloons and turquoise blouses were opening a storefront floral display and positioning their bright flowers amidst a row of leaning tamarinds. Abel checked his watch: 0845 hours. They were late.

Beyond the girls, shafts of sunlight burst forth through a wandering storm cloud not unlike a giant Chinese fan slowly opening. Dark sheets of rain poured down at a slight angle from the cloud, yet all around it the panorama remained a bright, fresh aquamarine.

Two young women wearing silk blouses, slacks, and leather boots all in black—obvious gang garb—seemed to glide through his peripheral vision before disappearing behind the swinging bamboo doors of a nearby nightclub—open, even at this hour. For an instant, they had

both locked eyes with him, and he felt a cold tingle run
down his spine. Their dark almond eyes were icy and
laced with hate. They reminded him of the "Hanoi
whores" of so long ago—who enticed drunk GIs up into
dark flophouses only to slice off their penises with a rusty
straight razor.

M.A.G. Lieutenant Lucas Abel stared at the Vietnamese script shouting back at him in hot pink neon above
the nightclub's tusk-white arches as they pulled up: IVORY
DRAGON LOUNGE. His partner rammed the gearshift into
Park as he smiled at a slender, sloe-eyed Vietnamese
woman passing by just a couple of feet beyond the driver's window. Unlike the gang bangers, she wore a more
traditional *ao-dai* gown. It clung to her figure from throat
to hips and, slit along the sides from the waist down,
billowed freely about the thighs with each breath of warm
breeze.

Abel gauged his partner's hungry grin: Glenn Thornton was ready to produce his infamous goo-goo-eyed
wink, but the woman was ignoring them. Silent and un-
approachable. Exotic and mysterious.

His eyes returned to the sign hanging above the lounge
a few shops down from the entrance to their second-floor
office. Suddenly, he felt himself get ready: ears perked
waiting for the locomotive-like roar. But there was no
scream of incoming rockets to tear open the heart of the
city . . . no flares floating along the charred and blackened rooftops . . . no VC snipers wearing tire-tread sandals or armed with AK-47s waiting for him in the night.
He waited until it passed.

Behind them, a bus roared by. His eyes focused on the
logo. Orange County Rapid Transit District. Orange
County, California. Hometown America.

His eyes drifted to a nearby newspaper rack. Again,
everything was in Vietnamese. The date on the lottery
sign read February 3, 1989. Viet Cong rockets had not
descended on Old Saigon in fourteen years.

Twenty-one years had passed since Charlie assaulted
the embassy during a surprise predawn Tet attack, departing in defeat and disgrace and leaving seven ounces

of Chi-com lead in various parts of MP Sgt. Luke Abel's torso. Twenty-four years since a communist satchel charge destroyed half the military police headquarters on Tran Hung Dao Street—the incident that shattered young Luke Abel's image of himself and the world, and led to a seventy-two-hour running gun battle that left over a dozen of his best friends dead and the back alleys and side streets of the city he had come to love laced with gunsmoke and blood trails.

Despite his loss of innocence . . . despite the drastic and permanent change in his own hometown, Orange County had always been safe . . . "protected." Luke's love for Vietnam aside, he had always sought to keep the war and its players separate from Garden Grove, California. Now there were more Viets than childhood friends living on the block where he grew up. Most of the white folks had moved away in the last ten years or so . . . to the more fashionable and exclusive suburbs nearer the beach: Laguna, Huntington, Newport.

Despite all the contrasts and changes, Little Saigon was the only place in the L.A.-Orange County metropolis where Abel's adrenaline surged without the stimulus of echoing sirens or gunshots in the night. The *ao-dai* clad women strolling along Bolsa and Brookhurst and Bushard did that to him. He stared at their long black hair and saw, instead, the Casablanca-style ceiling fan in his old third-floor Thanh Mau Street apartment in Saigon twirling overhead as he lay on blue satin sheets, the side of his face against Xinh's breast, her heart still thumping rapidly from their fourth session of lovemaking in half as many hours . . . both of them listening to the jets racing their engines two miles away, at Tan Son Nhut Airport . . . wondering if they would survive another night in the Paris of the East.

Abel glanced out Thornton's window. The street signs read BOLSA and BROOKHURST. The street signs were in English. Ninety percent of the shop signs were in Vietnamese, but the street signs remained English. This was California, not Vietnam, he reminded himself—Orange County's Bolsa Strip, not Tu Do Street. Abel rubbed at

his eyes and the dreamlike vision of Saigon's skyline in
flames slowly disintegrated, like withered fragments of
the past, peeling back in gold and orange shards, away
from his mind.

"Home sweet home," Thornton announced from outside the car as his door slammed shut. The detective
sergeant was staring up at the brass sign imbedded over
the red brick stairwell that led up to their second-floor
offices:

M.A.G. TASK FORCE—LITTLE SAIGON SUBSTATION
VAN PHONG CANH-SAT GARDEN GROVE

Someone had scrawled a large A over the O in FORCE.
"No-account little gang bangers," Glenn reached up and
rubbed some of the purple lipstick off with the palm of
his hand as he rushed up the steps.

The police substation was nestled in the middle of a
bustling shopping center and occupied the second floor
of a former sweatshop-turned-Chinese-market now. Several of the cubicles on the ground floor, behind the market, were reserved for the use of interagency teams, such
as Abel's, and the local detaining facility. A small, private parking lot for police personnel was located in the
expanded alley behind the crowded market and, though
the access drive opened out into a residential neighborhood behind Bolsa and away from the business district,
there was no escaping the somewhat exotic sights and
sounds of Little Saigon's Bolsa Strip.

Upon leaving their unit, Abel noticed that the oppres-
sive humidity was permeated with a more pleasant fra-
grance. Overpowering even the scent of nearby flower
stalls, the aroma of boiling noodles and spicy seafood
from the dozen or so restaurants surrounding the substation drifted up to tease Abel's nostrils.

"My stomach's starting to growl," he announced in a
semi-hopeful tone. "How long you going to be?"

Thornton glanced back down at him as they reached
the heavily bolted substation door and removed a single
key from the handcuff pouch under his jacket. "*Ti-ti,*

GI." He used the Viet slang for "little bit." "Just wanna
enter those Dragon wagons into the computer before
some poor fuck in a black-and-white stops one of 'em
for a burned-out taillight and gets his ass blown away."

"Yeah, I guess that would be felony stupid," Abel
sighed as the tumblers rolled free and Thornton pushed
the door inward.

"On *our* part," the M.A.G. agent added. The constant chatter from three police radio monitors within
reached their ears, but neither man bothered listening to
the individual transmissions.

Abel headed directly for the coffee machine sitting on
a table against the far wall of the cramped office, while
Thornton dropped a pile of red 10851/Auto Theft cards
atop a computer terminal and sat down at one of the three
desks that took up the east side of the small room. Along
the opposite wall, two weapons racks, behind bullet-
proof glass, and nearly a dozen metal file boxes, made
use of every last inch of free space.

A small corridor beside the coffee machine led to rest-
rooms in the back. There was no fire exit. The only
window was a large one beside the front door, but it was
also covered with bars and presently shuttered. Outside,
it was approaching nine A.M., but an odd sort of twilight
reigned in the M.A.G. offices. The only illumination was
from the two computer consoles. Glenn Thornton's face
glowed green as he sat down in front of one, stale doughnut in hand.

"Shouldn't Verdugo be manning the fort in here today?" Abel said as he lifted the half-empty coffeepot
from its holder and held it to his nose.

"Dispatch advised me he called in sick this morning." Thornton flinched when the computer responded
with a loud beep to the first entry code he attempted to
type in. ". . . When I was on the way over to pick you
up. Forgot to tell ya, Lou. . . ."

Abel frowned only slightly: Sgt. Verdugo ill? That was
the last surprise he expected to get today. Verdugo *never*
called in sick. The phone rang and broke into Abel's
thoughts.

"Are we here?" Thornton glanced up from his computer with little enthusiasm.

"You better answer it. I told Dispatch we'd be here before I coded out downstairs."

Without any visible emotion, his partner set down the half-eaten doughnut and picked up the black receiver. "M.A.G. SubStation, Sergeant Thornton."

Abel could hear the caller's gruff, booming voice from the other side of the room. Special Agent Frank Sanders.

"Yes, sir." Thornton was nodding respectfully, but his tone was one of mild annoyance. "Right, Commander . . . yes, sir . . ." He glanced back and crossed his eyes at Abel, who began grinding his teeth instead of laughing. "Uh, right . . . we'll be there ASAP, boss. . . ."

After Thornton replaced the receiver, Abel asked, "What did that asshole want?"

"Did you know anything about an interagency briefing this morning?"

"Christ!" The M.A.G. lieutenant slapped his forehead with the palm of his hand. "I completely deep-sixed it."

"Mental block to the max, eh, Luke?" Thornton snickered. "They say that's what starts to go first, you know. . . ."

"We better head over there." Abel shook his head from side to side. "Jesus, how am I supposed to make any arrests around here if all they have us doing is baby-sitting the guys in uniform?"

"You'll get over it." Thornton followed him back out the door, slamming it shut behind him. "You always do."

Franklin Sanders was the local Justice Department liaison. He ran the Metro Asian Gang Task Force on paper, reporting to the U.S. Attorney General and the governing councils of every city that contracted for M.A.G. services. In his fifties, with gray, close-cropped hair, the man sported a slightly protruding jaw and an eagle's beak of a nose. His eyes were dark and intense. They grew wary whenever Luke Abel was the focus of his attention.

Though he had never fought in any overseas war, "Seoul food" and armchair critiques of past military conflicts were his personal obsessions. He could always be found lurking in the many restaurants along Garden Grove Boulevard's Koreatown, refusing to venture southeast into Little Saigon unless it was absolutely necessary.

Despite his fondness for war gaming, current police matters—and task force missions in particular—seemed to bring out the worst in the man. The technical commander of the M.A.G. team, Sanders was also its strongest obstacle in the law-enforcement bureaucracy and went out of his way to badger Lieutenant Abel about tactics, strategy and deployment. The men referred to him as the colonel, and frequently joked about the aroma that was often on his breath: *kimchi*, a potent, foul-smelling spice composed primarily of rotten cabbage. Abel sometimes called him the Korean Fried Chicken.

This morning, he was in a mood to resume the Korean War.

"I don't need this," Thornton muttered, as they coasted up to the rear entrance to one of Garden Grove P.D.'s briefing rooms and spotted Sanders rocking back on his heels in a doorway, arms folded across his chest, chin up and lips pursed—as if he'd caught two schoolboys cutting class.

Before Abel could formulate a reply for his partner, Sanders had stormed over to the driver's window. "It's about time!" He glared, checking his watch for emphasis. "The briefing's about over. I'd like you two to update the uniformed troops in there about this upcoming Tet Festival the Viets are getting so excited about. Throw in the latest info about your alleged escalation of the gang problems down on Bolsa, and wrap it all up with your personal hypothesis as to what you think the P.D.'s in for. Keep it brief, too. Chief Daniels was kind enough to invite us over—"

"For coffee and rolls?" Thornton cut in.

Sander's sarcastic grin vanished. "Just get in there and

make M.A.G. look good—if that's possible. I've noticed some animosity between you boys and the line troops working the squad cars. I won't have an elitist attitude ruining the open-door image of cooperation we're trying to present over at—"

"We'll do our best, boss." Abel frowned as he opened his door and got out of the Malibu. "I'll give 'em the usual propaganda."

Sanders straightened up to match the lieutenant's height, flattened down the lapels of his sports coat, and smirked. "By the way, where're Sergeant Verdugo and Detective Zamora?" He glanced into the backseat to make sure none of the M.A.G. agents was pulling a fast one on him.

"Vinnie called in sick this morning," Abel responded. "Rachel's on the way."

"And Miss Vo—uh, that C.S.O. of yours?"

"Over at the Vietnamese Cultural Center, tryin' to keep some of the kids on *our* side of the law."

"Oh, I was hoping she'd be here." Sanders began massaging his temples. "It always looks good when Chief Daniels sees all of M.A.G.'s resources at work."

"I felt her talents were more needed at the center." Abel stood his ground. "Here, she'd just be warming a chair."

Sander's expression wrinkled into one of mild disapproval.

A late-model, dark blue, unmarked Plymouth pulled up beside their Malibu, and an attractive Latina in tight jeans and a form-hugging peasant blouse alighted from the driver's side—eyes wide and unsmiling. "Did I do something wrong?" She froze.

"Glad you could make it, Zamora." Sander's look of impatience deepened.

Thornton and Abel both nodded with mild affection. More than a fellow detective, this gal was a brother cop. "The boys in blue are waiting inside for your briefing on the trouble brewing in Little Saigon." Glenn grinned in anticipation of her reply.

A policewoman for five years now, Zamora had barely

passed the academy requirements because of her height:
five foot two. Weighing in at a petite hundred and ten,
she was constantly jogging and working out to make up
for her small size. She was Sgt. Vinnie Verdugo's partner. Today, she was working solo.

"Me?" She swept her long dark hair back over a
shoulder. "Not *me*, gents! *I* don't give briefings. I *attend*
them." She sounded adamant.

"Just fucking fibbing." Thornton wrapped an arm
around Rachel's shoulder as they went into the building.

"If I could have your attention, guys." Abel tapped the
podium lightly, hoping to attract the attention of the hundred or so uniformed patrolmen occupying ten rows of
folding metal chairs arranged in a casual semicircle below his speaker's platform. The briefing room was cavernous and held over three hundred seats—many with
tables lined up in front of them—but only a third were
occupied this morning. "I know I don't have to tell anyone here that the shit's about to hit the fan in Little Saigon."

"We've got it under control, Lou!" an anonymous
voice called from the back of the room. "We don't need
no undercover hot dogs comin' in an makin' waves with
the Viets."

Mild laughter and even some applause filled the briefing room. Abel was bright enough to realize what had
really just been said: The Viets rarely reported crimes,
which made for less paperwork. Why all the fanfare about
Bolsa? The Viets were always ripping each other off, and
they would continue to do so. So why the big public-
relations blitz to get them to trust the police more? It
was only going to make their job more complicated in
the long run.

He decided not to bring up the recent odd rash of
racially motivated incidents, but to stick with something
he had hard intelligence data on. "It's been brought to
our attention that discontent among the Viet gangs in
Little Saigon is on the rise. Especially Le Van Lui's Steel
Dragons . . ."

Another crescendo of laughter rose up to scoff at Abel. "Punks," somebody muttered. "Nothing but limp-dick scrotes tryin' to impress the slanted pussy they peddle on Bolsa . . ."

"The Steel Dragons," Abel continued, ignoring the jibes, "is the biggest and most powerful of the seven gangs fighting for turf along both sides of the strip. Up until now, they've pretty much kept to themselves. . . ."

"Being curteous enough to dump their bodies north of the county lines," another voice volunteered, "in the L.A. River."

"But as of late, the gang bangers have become more brazen—especially in the extortion rackets. Our P.R. campaign is paying off: More and more victims are coming forward. As you know, the Vietnamese Cultural Center is sponsoring their annual Tet Festival next week. It kicks off on February seventh. It's a big thing with these people." Abel detected a general murmur of discontent rising from the ranks. "It's like our New Year's, Christmas, and Fourth of July all rolled into one. Everyone will be there. Including the gangs.

"We've heard some rumors that the gangs plan to flex some muscle, disrupt the event—make some kind of political statement about their strength and influence, probably with the business end of a sawed-off shotgun. . . ."

"They don't have the balls," a shout rose from the unmoving sea of dark blue, but Abel noticed most of the grins were gone.

"Now I'm not here to tell you I think the Viet gangs are up to more than their usual dose of violence. But there may be some outside influence at work this year, trying to use the Tet Festival to make the eleven-o'clock news. All I'm asking is that you guys forward a copy of all field interrogation cards to M.A.G. until it's over." Abel motioned toward Rachel. He was glad she'd worn her tightest jeans today. "Detective Zamora here"— several wolf whistles erupted as she stood up and took a bow—"with the help of our C.S.O.s, will feed them, along with data from any police reports involving the

Viet community, into our stats computer to get a handle
on what to expect.''

Abel had to give Sanders credit: Bringing Zamora to
the briefing was good strategy. She was a knockout, and
half the department had tried, unsuccessfully, to get into
her pants at one time or another. Having her in charge
of stats would motivate more of the street cops to come
to M.A.G. with information and paper—if only for the
opportunity to share a paper cup of P.D.-issue brew with
the lovely detective.

"So feel free to drop by our substation whenever you
get some solid intel' about the gangs and any of their
activities that might relate to the upcoming Tet Festival,''
Abel nodded down to the men. "You all know where
we're located. M.A.G's here to serve the cops as well as
the Vietnamese, guys. I know you hate to waste doughnut time dealing with the gang bangers. Leave 'em to
us—that's why we're here . . . so you'll have more time
to deal with 'real' crime, away from the Bolsa Strip. Any
questions?''

Not a single hand in the assemblage of one hundred
badges rose into the drifting blue clouds of cigar and
cigarette smoke.

"That was easy,'' he told Thornton later.

"I just don't understand why these guys get so uptight
when we come around.'' His partner shook his head,
genuinely bewildered.

"They just don't like plainclothes supercops invading
their turf. They figure they've got everything on their
beat under control, so why all the big deal about some
Asian punks. To them, we're Feds, and you know how
city cops hate secret agent types. I can understand it. I
was the same way.''

Abel proceeded immediately to the nearest wall phone
hanging alongside an access corridor leading from the
briefing room to the outside parking lot reserved for police units. Community Services Officer Vo Thi Luyen
answered on the second ring.

"Abel here,'' the lieutenant said. "Just wanted you to

know Sanders is on the prowl. He cornered us over here at headquarters, and thought you'd be present—seemed pretty disappointed that you didn't show. He just might try sneaking over there to catch you guys goofing off.''

"Vo Thi Luyen does not goof off, Luke," came the confident reply. Abel smiled. He knew the petite, attractive C.S.O. was afraid of no man, let alone the Korean Fried Chicken. "Besides, I'm covered: I knew nothing about the briefing and was scheduled to be here at the center since last week and—"

"I know all that," Abel interrupted. "Forget it. I'll be by to drop off some intelligence reports the dicks here at the P.D. managed to put together. I need to pick up your paperwork from the last few days, too.''

"I'll be here."

≡ CHAPTER 5

"HERE'S ANOTHER BATCH, Luyen."

"Thanks." Luyen took the basketful of miniature Vietnamese flags from the schoolgirl and set them in a crate. "Almost done now."

"The Tet celebration is going to be great!" The girl's smile served to brighten up Luyen's morning—it was a catalyst she needed, after having worked half the night on publicity flyers about the upcoming event.

"Yes it is." Luyen's eyes scanned the cultural center's gymnasium, which had been transformed into a factory where high school students—primarily children of Vietnamese refugees—worked on decorations and banners for the festival. The center's sports activities had been temporarily moved outside—she could hear young boys bouncing a basketball beyond a dual set of open bay doors. Inside, the faces were mostly female.

It pleased her that there were still so many young people who refused to be intimidated or influenced by the gang activity sweeping Little Saigon. Instead, these youths put much of their energy into shaping pride over their background and cultural heritage, and finding ways to explain Tet to the Americans and help bolster community relations with the center's neighbors.

Luyen stared at the cluster of girls working diligently

nearby: all dressed conservatively, their hair still straight and jet black—not bleached, streaked, or permed like the gang girls—and their skin smooth and unblemished, with only the slightest traces of makeup here and there—not marred by tattoos of Steel Dragons or Blue Bamboo. It was a fragile victory—often temporary. Luyen was well aware that the smallest emotional incident in their personal lives could drive them from family and friends down into the underworld of the gangs.

"Don't do that!"

Luyen whirled when she heard one of her best assistants complaining loudly. It was a complaint laced with pain. She turned to find a group of young women sauntering into the center through a side door—four of Lui's gang girls. The leader was pulling along one of Luyen's high school sophomores, off balance, by her ponytail.

"Hey, knock it off!" Luyen dropped a stack of Tet flyers and rushed over toward the young women. They slid to a stop, but did not release the schoolgirl. "What's this all about?"

"She's coming with us!" A tall, slender girl with hair feathered to the sides in brown swirls thrust her chin out at Luyen. "No more of this Goody Two Shoes bullshit. Her big sister's with Steel Dragon"—she nodded to the shortest woman in the group, who stood in a defensive stance now, feet apart, hands on her hips—"and now she's with Steel Dragon, too."

The women's behavior sent a chill through Luyen. There seemed no desire on their part to preserve their heritage—or to even acknowledge it. None wore their hair long like Luyen, or naturally black. Most had dyed theirs a purplish brown, punk style. One girl even had bleach-blond curls. All wore black pants or miniskirts, and jean jackets dyed black, or smooth leather, also black. Garish makeup, accenting their eyes, was the rule. Luyen felt sorry for them. And the memory of her homeland.

Luyen's eyes dropped to big sister's legs. Aside from the miniskirt and halter top, she wore purple socks that rose up out of black high heels to mid-calf, giving a half-

sensuous/half-kinky cast to her lower curves despite the
tacky appearance. Typical gang attire. The oldest of the
group couldn't have been more than seventeen or eighteen. Unlike Luyen, she spoke unaccented English.
Probably born in the U.S.A., or a mere infant when
coming over on the boat.

"Why don't you let *her* decide whether or not she goes
with you." Instead of advancing further, Luyen backed
toward a table where her purse lay.

"She already had that chance," a second woman
hissed, pointing a forefinger at Luyen threateningly.
"And she made a wrong choice. She was supposed to
be at the pad this morning. She didn't show. We're her
escort."

"What will it be, Lai?" Luyen locked eyes with the
schoolgirl. "Do you want to stay with us? Or do you
want to drop out of school and go with *them*?" Luyen
made the word *them* sound like diseased rodents.

"I want to stay with you, Miss Vo!" The girl did not
hesitate in deciding. Her sister rushed forward and
slapped her.

"Then stay, Lai." Luyen's tone grew angry. "It's a
free country. That's why your parents came here—so they
could make their own decisions." Her eyes darted to the
leader of the female gang. "That's why *your* parents
came here, too. It's called freedom of choice. Are you
going to deny it to Lai and any of the other girls here?"

"You're so full of shit, bitch!" A third woman produced an obscene gesture that became a raised, clenched
fist. "There ain't no freedom in Little Saigon. There's
only Steel Dragon!" she yelled, eyes scanning the faces
of the other volunteers, now frozen throughout the center. "And don't none of you whores forget it!" She
quickly turned to face Luyen again. "You're C.S.O.
clown suit don't mean jack shit around here, cunt."

"Right." Luyen tensed. It was at times like these that
she wished she still carried her pistol on her hip. Like
Rachel Zamora and Beth Holly and the other policewomen at M.A.G. and Garden Grove P.D. Like back
during the war. But Vo Thi Luyen was "only" a Garden

Grove Community Services Officer now—a liaison between the police department and the Vietnamese community, temporarily assigned to Abel's M.A.G. task
force. And she had come to feel more comfortable sitting
behind a desk at the substation, compiling crime stats.
Hot dogs like Holly and Zamora could have the street.
C.S.O.s didn't make enough money to put up with all
the asphalt jungle jive.

Out on the street, life could actually get lethal. Now,
it seemed just as dangerous under the Cultural Center's
roof. Half the women standing across from her probably
carried switchblades in their pantyhose or Beretta's in
their bras—that much Luyen knew from experience.

And she could do without the cool, icy resentment she
saw in the eyes of many of her fellow countrymen—and
-women—Vietnamese who disapproved of her working
for the Blue Shirts.

In Vietnam, where the National Police Force had much
of its roots in the Binh Xuyen River Pirates Dynasty of
the forties, fifties, and early sixties, most of the *canh-sat*
officers were corrupt—or at least that was how the Saigon
news media and American press corps liked to portray
them. White Mice, they were called—as much because
of their tactics, perhaps, as the color of their shirts. Rodents to be despised and hated. Here, it was different.
She didn't think there was even one bad cop on M.A.G.
or the Garden Grove force.

Luyen ran her fingers along the bulge in her small
handbag. Commander Sanders would have her job if he
knew she carried the snub-nosed .38 Smith and Wesson.
But this was Little Saigon, and, even working supposedly
''safe'' assignments like the center or the substation, she
felt safer when she was armed. There was even talk they
wanted her working the street soon, partnering with a
blue-suiter during the upcoming Tet Festival. That would
make Luyen an even bigger target. The .38 gave her back
some of the confidence she had lost upon leaving South
Vietnam.

It had not always been like this, however. Luyen served
as a municipal policewoman for over five years before

the fall of Saigon. Her husband, also a *canh-sat*, was killed during street fighting along Newport Bridge on April 30, 1975—a day she would never forget.

Now approaching thirty-five, she still looked twenty-two. The long black hair and slender, lithe figure helped. Luyen had never remarried, electing instead to pour all her energies into her job. She was notorious for working countless hours of overtime without logging them. Abel never took her loyalty for granted, however, and made sure she walked out of the substation with a hefty paycheck every two weeks. He knew where the money went: Luyen had been trying to get the surviving members of her family out of Vietnam for over thirteen years now. Luke Abel would never forget when, over lunch, she had told him about their plight. Tears in her eyes, she confessed that she could no longer remember what her mother's face really looked like.

"I'm going to give you . . . young ladies . . . ten seconds to vacate the premises," Luyen said after she reached the table with her purse on it. She leaned back against the edge of the table, without touching the handbag.

"And if we don't?" The woman at the front of the group reached down into her halter top and produced a butterfly knife. With an impressive swirl of both wrists, she slammed the chrome handle from palm to palm, end over end, until a long blade suddenly appeared. Then, she started advancing toward Luyen. "Then what? You gonna call the pigs on us, *sister*?"

Luyen felt the chill return. How far could she go with these girls? True, one had a knife, but would she actually be exonerated if she drew her revolver and began shooting? What if innocent bystanders were wounded? What about the mental trauma her girls would surely suffer after witnessing a shooting right before their eyes? What about the trouble she would find herself in for carrying a concealed weapon—something C.S.O.s were not allowed to do.

The woman was face-to-face with Luyen now, but she lowered the knife. "I suggest you just keep your motherfucking mouth *shut* from here on out!'' She bared her teeth and twisted her face to one side. "Lai's coming with us, and if you try and stop us—''

"If she tries and stops you . . . *what*?''

Every head in the room turned to find Lieutenant Abel, Sergeant Thornton, and Detective Zamora standing in one of the doorways. His 9mm automatic extended at arm's length, Thornton had taken a deadly bead on the girl with the butterfly fighting knife. But Abel's hands were empty as he strode up to the young woman, twisted the glittering blade out of her hand, and, with a rough backhand swing to the forehead, knocked her off her feet and onto her bottom with a dull thud.

The other gang girls ran over to lift her up, then headed for the door. "You'll pay for this, pig cocksucker,'' the girl screamed just before they walked out.

"Yeah, tell Lui to put it on my bill.''

"I see they got the windows repaired.''

"I like the mirror tint.''

"Makes it harder for shooters outside to hit their target sitting on the *in*side.'' Glenn Thornton chuckled.

"Reminds me of Saigon, where the blood and chunks of flesh were mopped up after an early-morning open-air café bombing, in time for the noon crowd.'' Abel winked at the somber-faced woman sharing the isolated corner table with them along the back wall of Pho-75, but Luyen did not respond.

"Aw, come on, honey.'' Rachel reached over and patted her wrist. "Don't worry about it. It's over. They had knives. There was nothing you could do, for crissake.''

Luyen remained silent, staring down into her glass of ice coffee. Abel understood. She was suffering from loss of face. Had the two M.A.G. agents not shown up when they did, she might have gotten her ass whipped.

Glenn tilted his head to one side in a sorry attempt at making Luyen laugh. It didn't work. The frail-looking woman stared down into her glass, then glanced at her watch. Abel and Thornton both watched her stir the bean

sprouts in her bowl of *pho* noodle soup around without
lifting them up.

Abel glanced toward the door as two women entered
the restaurant with anxious looks on their faces. Anxious
for a good meal, that is. He noted that both were white,
in their fifties, typical suburban tourists. That they were
venturing down into Little Saigon for some Vietnamese
food warmed his heart. That was definitely what they
needed more of along the Bolsa Strip: better community
relations.

The Pho-75 Restaurant was more than a soup stall. It
was, in fact, a huge restaurant with a small counter bar
tucked away behind a man-made concrete stream of giant
gold-and-orange fish. Most of the clientele were Asians,
but every officer assigned to the district was well aware the
owner served some of the finest Viet-French cuisine in
town, and the prices were kind to a policeman's wallet.

Though the waitress recognized Thornton, and un-
doubtedly knew Luyen from community gossip, the officers drew little attention, for they were all out of
uniform and sitting at a dark corner table. The lieutenant's back was to the wall. As always.

Besides the housewives, Abel's group of four and a
table of six schoolgirls seated against the far wall were
the only other customers in evidence at the moment.

Until the black Nissan four-door pulled up in front.

Thornton's and Abel's eyes instinctively focused on the
car's front license plate. Luyen was still staring down
into her melting ice cubes. "I hate Tokyo-san sedans
with black tinted windows," Thornton growled.

"Mellow out, *amigo*," Abel spoke softly. But when
four Vietnamese gangsters, wearing raincoats that fell
just below their knees, emerged from the vehicle, he said,
"And *I* hate jerks who wear rain jackets when it hasn't
rained all day."

"Know 'em?" Thornton asked Zamora. When she
shook her head in the negative, he glanced over at Luyen.
"How 'bout you, darlin'?"

"I don't think so." Officer Vo forced herself to participate . . . to concentrate on faces . . . a scar here, a tattoo there. But nothing recognizable. "Probably just some fresh meat for the Steel Dragon gang." All four wore black sunglasses, making identification difficult in the dimly lit restaurant.

"None of 'em ever been popped by me," Abel decided after a careful examination. Then some familiar body language swagger caught his eye. "At least, I don't think so. . . ."

"Seems I've seen that middle mug on a wanted poster somewhere before, though." Thornton's uncertain words came out slowly. Glancing toward the bar in the distance, Thornton looked as though he wanted to start breaking beer bottles.

The four youths—all in their early twenties, with hair slicked straight back—brushed past the menu-toting waitress and headed straight for the old papa-san seated behind the cash register.

"Somethin' numba ten's goin' down here," Abel whispered as he slowly reached under his sports jacket.

"Maybe they're the old man's numba-one *sons*." Thornton sighed deeply.

"And I'm the Virgin Mary," Luyen replied.

"Check out the tattoo on that one punk's wrist," Thornton observed, as the youth reached up and shook the papa-san's concentration from the magazine he was reading.

"You're right." Abel nodded. "Steel Dragon gang?"

"Hey wait a minute." Thornton's memory kicked in. "The big kid with the tattoo is Brass Balls himself."

"*Our* Brass Balls?" Abel's eyes lit up with anticipation. "The prick shaved off his goatee." Brass Balls was Lui's driver. That probably meant the gang leader was somewhere nearby. The lieutenant hoped he was right outside the restaurant's swinging front doors. "I thought he was still in county jail."

"No such luck. Bailed out before the ink was dry on my report."

"Well, it looks like he's not wasting time going after new opportunities."

One of the young men unleashed a low-keyed but obviously hostile torrent of Vietnamese at the papa-san, who lifted his hands up as if helpless to comply with their demands, and both Abel and Thornton started to rise from their chairs.

"Stickup?" Abel whispered to his partner. Thornton shook his head. The papa-san was waving his hands as if to gesture that things were beyond his control—not because a gun had been produced.

"Don't quite have a robbery's ring to it." Thornton drew his own weapon, however. One couldn't take members of the Steel Dragon clan lightly. "Raincoats usually means sawed-off shotguns underneath."

"A Viet gang-banger favorite," Abel had to agree. He felt his heart start to race, and wondered if the adrenaline flow had had time to abate since leaving the earlier shooting scene.

Suddenly, a woman in her early fifties rushed out from the back kitchen area, exchanged muffled words with the papa-san, then slapped the nearest youth and began cursing at them in heated Vietnamese as she tried to shoo them from her establishment.

The four men stood their ground—upper torsos leaning back slightly with each assault, but black boots firmly planted and unmoving. And then the one they knew as Brass Balls threw a punch that flattened the woman's nose. Blood splashed on the wall and counter behind her.

"Let's go," Abel said, making eye contact with his partner. Thornton and Zamora nodded with obvious irritation.

"Luyen, if we start bustin' caps, get the cavalry over here on the double, understand?"

The C.S.O. stood and made her way to the phone in the back.

≡ CHAPTER 6

"POLICE!" ABEL GRABBED the nearest gang banger and threw him up against the wall. "Assume the position, assholes."

As if to verify his partner's authority, Glenn Thornton was right behind the lieutenant, gold shield and ID card out for all to see. "Well if it ain't our lifelong buddy, Brass Balls," he proclaimed loudly, basking in the punk's expression as his eyes, registering shock over the bust, shifted back and forth from the undercover detectives, to the injured woman sitting in the middle of the floor, and back to Abel and Thornton again. Zamora dropped to one knee beside the assault victim, while Luyen wavered by a pay phone, gauging the situation.

Then, the young hoodlum's chest expanded importantly. He liked the nickname jailers had assigned him several years earlier when he took half a dozen of them on after refusing to submit to a strip search. That had been shortly after his first misdemeanor arrest. The handle had stuck, and even Lui's other gangsters sometimes used it with a certain degree of awe. Though Brass Balls was now into felony seven-ups, or crimes that carried a minimum seven-year prison sentence, he still managed to do small time in the monkeyhouse every once in a while.

The three Vietnamese standing behind Lui's driver did not protest or resist. They simply shrugged, turned and faced the wall, and leaned against it—arms and legs spread.

His automatic trained on the unruly subjects' backs, Thornton's feet shifted from side to side nervously as Abel commenced with the cursory frisk. His fingers had barely touched Brass Balls's collar, lifting it up, when the wiry hoodlum sprang back away from the wall and whirled, bending to the side as he did, and connecting with a hard kick to Abel's ribcage.

The air knocked from his lungs, Abel dropped into a crouch—just in time to catch another heel against the left temple as Brass Balls swung around in the opposite direction.

"Fucking punk!" Thornton yelled, lunging forward in an attempt to bring his pistol butt down on the suspect's head, but Abel had already recovered. He grabbed onto the gang banger's hair and yanked his face down onto the floor.

The M.A.G. lieutenant's knuckles came down against Brass Balls's jaw only once before the strong Vietnamese squirmed free and brought a knee up into Abel's belly. "Christ!" Abel began punching, but those few blows that landed didn't seem to be having much of an effect.

"Is this fucker on PCP or something?" Thornton produced a lead sap and rammed it against the suspect's lower back—aiming for the kidney—without results.

"I don't know, but—"

Thornton wasn't in the mood for experiments. He jammed the barrel of his pistol against the gang member's ear. "Knock it off, asshole!" he commanded, as Zamora rushed up to cover the other hoodlums.

Sighing loudly, Brass Balls finally complied.

Abel's chest was heaving. He felt as if he had cuts and bruises on his cuts and bruises. He resumed frisking their prisoner as Thornton placed handcuffs on him, then searched the other gang bangers as well.

"Clean," he pronounced sixty seconds later, stepping back away from them. "All of the lowlifes."

"Just makes you wanna vomit on a Vietnamese, don't it?" Thornton sneered. Shifting his comments to Brass Balls, he added, "You're gonna ruin your reputation, kid. No hardware for Glenn to confiscate today?"

"What did we do, Officer?" Speaking with mock innocence, the youngest, smallest member of the group turned a baby face to Lt. Abel. He and Thornton immediately remembered the youth now: One of the vice detectives had popped the kid two or three dozen times for narcotics sales—his age was the one thing that saved him from the big house. He was fourteen.

"Assault, for starters." Abel looked over at the elderly couple discussing the roust in guarded whispers, then at Brass Balls. "Then, assault on a police officer and extortion."

"Extortion?" Brass Balls laughed as he was hustled to his feet. "Can you show me a—"

"No one gave you permission to relax!" Thornton slammed the gang member back up against the wall again.

"Can you show me a . . . complainant?" he persisted.

Abel turned to face the owners. They were already beginning to look as if they had other matters to attend to. "Don't tell me, papa-san," he growled. "You're not going to press charges! Even though he decked your wife there."

"He no speak Engli—" the woman began, wiping blood from her nose and lips.

"Don't feed me that line," Thornton cut her off. "I've been in here before when he was singin' like a bird in pidgin English to some tourists from Australia. He speaks the lingo like an ABC."

"We ethnic Vietnamese." The woman waved a reprimanding finger at him. "Not American-born Chinese."

"What was Lui's boy here arguing with you about?" Abel cut in. "Was he threatening you, Mrs. Nguyen?"

"He no threaten!" Her eyes pleaded. "He ask my

husband about busboy jobs for his friends here! That all!''

''None of these punks has ever washed a dish in his life! Does he always get into a shouting match over minimum-wage jobs? Does he punch defenseless women out over that kind of dispute?'' Thornton rocked back slightly on his heels, preparing to pounce. He and Abel were both watching Brass Balls closely. Staring over his right shoulder, the gang member's eyes were, in turn, trained on the old man's. ''I heard the word 'money,' *tien bac*.''

''He tell them we no can hire new people now. No money. That's what he say. No money for hire them!''

''Why don't you *peace* officers go out and harass some of the white boys who've been moving in on our territory.'' Brass Balls cautiously pushed back from the wall again. Thornton pushed him back quickly.

''White boys?'' Abel asked, brows coming together slightly now.

''Yeah. The Rebs, Mercs, or whatever that valley boy-san crowd is going by these days. They all look the same to me, cruisin' Bolsa in their Mercedeses and Rolls Royces, callin' us chinks, and challenging us to fight. But you *knowwww* fighting is against our religion, right, Lieutenant Abel?'' Brass Balls locked eyes with the M.A.G. detective and sneered.

''This is your last chance,'' Thornton told the restaurant owners. ''Either you prosecute, or we're going to have to kick 'em outside and cut three of 'em loose.''

''Not countin' Brass Balls, of course.'' Abel patted the side of his prisoner's face with mock affection.

''No trouble,'' the papa-san said softly. He looked like a beaten man. Beaten and humiliated, but safe—so long as he refused to cooperate with the police, the blue shirts. His number-two wife's broken nose didn't count, of course.

''Have it your way. Okay, assholes, outside, now!''

''Outside?'' one of the other punks protested defiantly. ''We were just about to sit down for a bowl of *pho* noodle soup, gentlemen. Care to join us?''

"Move!" Abel pointed toward the door.

Grinning like the juvenile delinquents they were, the three younger gang bangers headed for the restaurant's entrance. Handcuffed, Brass Balls stood his ground, if only momentarily. "I'm serious, Lieutenant," he said. "Those Rebel jerks are cruisin' for a bruisin',' and we will most seriously respond with more than knuckle sandwiches, if necessary."

Abel turned to face his partner. "Looks like our boys's been attending ESL classes." Thornton folded his arms across his chest as he stared at the gang banger. But Glenn doubted that Brass Balls had ever attended an English as a Second Language class. Stealing stereos was more the young hoodlum's style.

"At least he doesn't talk like a valley girl."

"Okay, fine." The young hood turned and started for the door. He knew the routine: Go directly to jail; do not collect extortion payments today. Maybe tomorrow, when the Man's not around. "But blood is gonna flow in Bolsa's gutters, *Officers*."

"Well, Buddha bless me!" Thornton's grin grew ear to ear as they stepped outside. Despite the Nissan's black-tinted windows, Lui's strained countenance was now clearly visible as the gang leader sat motionless in the backseat. "Let's see the little shit talk his way out of this one."

Dust swirled about the black Maxima as a marked patrol car pulled up into the restaurant parking lot. "Greetings and salut*asians*." One of the local patrolmen alighted from his black-and-white. "Just happened to see that Nissan sittin' in the shade over there and smelled trouble brewing."

"Make yourself useful." Thornton had collected identification from all four gang members. He handed the driver's licenses to the officer. "Run me some clearances and list the plate on that Nissan sedan over there."

"I think it's time we heard what Mister Lui has to say about all this." With a businesslike gait, Abel walked over to the Nissan. Pulling a sap from his back pocket, he tapped the glass. They were light taps, but the lead-filled sap was heavy. Thornton flinched. The glass sounded as though it might crack at any moment, but Abel kept tapping away. Finally, the electric window dropped.

"So we meet again, Lieutenant." Lui managed to keep a straight face. He seemed to have temporary control of his temper this morning. "Too bad."

"Nice to see you, too." Abel smiled down at the gang leader, but Lui kept his eyes averted.

"What can I do for you?"

"You can start by getting out of the fucking car!" Abel reached in, flipped the locking lever up, and jerked the door open. He grabbed Lui by the front of his black silk shirt and dragged him from the vehicle. "I believe we had some unfinished business to settle: You were of the inclination to burn down a house I don't own, and rape a wife I don't *got*!"

Thornton watched Lui fly up against a wall of the restaurant and grab hold of the cracks between the bricks. "I'm clean, Lieutenant." The anger was evident in his voice but, unlike his driver, Lui did not resist.

Abel patted the drug czar down, then whirled him around. "Gimme your driver's license," he instructed. "I wanna make sure your no-account ass isn't revoked. I'd hate to have to tow this crate and write you up for driving under suspension or whatever the computer throws back at me."

"I wasn't driving, Lieutenant. It's not my car." Frowning, Lui turned away, folded his arms, and stared at traffic passing in front of the restaurant, while the patrolman began running Vietnamese names through the national crime and info computer and DOJ's data network.

"He got that right, Lieutenant," the patrolman yelled out. "The vehicle is registered under something called 'The Vietnamese Youth Club.' "

Abel looked at the gang leader skeptically.

"We're trying to get respectable, Lieutenant. We've paid our debt to society. . . ."

"And who paid for this car?" Thornton cut in curiously. "No jobs, no other income that *we* know about.

I suppose some wealthy warlord back in Laos left it to
you in his will.''

''Rich parents.'' One of the youths threw his chin out
at the detective sergeant from a safe distance.

''. . . Now we're just trying to make some positive
contributions to the community,'' Lui continued.

''That better not include shaking down shop owners
and restauranteurs along the Bolsa Strip, Lui. I'm gonna
be watchin' you and your crew like stink on shit.''

Lui's smile faded. ''You don't need to put it *that* way,
Lieutenant. You should show some respect. We intend
to someday become upstanding members of the business
community, and then you'll regret—''

''I just want you to know I'm going to pin that Pho-
75 window smash on you, Lui—if it's the last thing I
do.''

Lui's face went blank. ''The *what*?'' he asked. He
locked eyes with the lieutenant and somewhere in their
deceptive depths Abel read confusion, even innocence.
''We're not into that kind of shit, Lieutenant. Popping
balloons at the school prom is more our style, you
know?''

''Yeah, I'll bet. . . .'' Abel thought of Victor The Vet,
and his mention of a big silver car. The M.A.G. lieutenant had a complete roster of Steel Dragon's current motor
pool—clean, stolen, or otherwise—and there wasn't a silver car, van, or truck on it. Which didn't mean didly in
Little Saigon.

''They're clean, Lieutenant,'' the patrolman said, returning to the group, without releasing their IDs. ''No
wants or warrants, no record found on the license check
for Mister Lui here.''

''There's something weird goin' down in Little Saigon''—Abel stared Lui down—''and I wanna know what
it is, kid.''

Thornton propelled Brass Balls over toward the patrolman. With his hands cuffed tightly behind his back,
it was all Brass Balls could do to maintain his balance as
he bounced off the cruiser's rear quarter panel, into the
officer's arms.

Thornton told the patrolman, "Book him for assault on a police officer."

"You got it, Sarge!" The officer hustled with enthusiasm as he ushered Brass Balls into the rear seat behind an iron grille welded to the front headrests. He buckled the prisoner in, then rushed around to the driver's door, got in, and threw the gearshift into drive, microphone already to his lips as he radioed in his unit's beginning mileage.

"Just tell those round-eye Rebs to stay out of Little Saigon," Lui warned. "Or it's going to be worse than the day Saigon fell. And we'll tell the blood-sucking news media maggots you had ample warning but chose not to heed it. And you *knowww* how the press loves to come down hard on the police, Lieutenant."

As the gang bangers were getting back into their sedan, Abel grabbed Lui's arm. "Listen up! I'm not working just a Chinatown beat anymore, sleezeball. Orange County's home sweet home again, *and . . . I . . . like . . . it*! My partner and I are color blind—just like the rest of the M.A.G. force. We don't care if you're white, yellow, black, or P.D. blue . . . you get out of line, and I'll issue you a one-way ride to the slammer at county."

"And if we don't play by your rules, Mr. *M.A.G.*?"

"We'll cancel your ticket," Thornton answered for his partner. "We're fair, but we don't put up with any crap, creep."

"You're sure dishin' it out today," Lui grunted.

"There's a new law coming down in Little Saigon, starting *today*." The M.A.G. lieutenant's false grin faded. "Abel's Law. You break it, and I . . . break . . . you."

"Got that?" Thornton moved to one side so that his shadow fell across Lui.

But the gang leader did not appear impressed or intimidated. "Then you better tell the same thing to whitey!" he said. "They think they can come down here and move in on our territory without any resistance from the people. Well, Steel Dragon don't slumber when there's intruders on its turf. Just remember that."

Abel did not respond to Le Van Lui's street speech. The words had taken him aback, somewhat, though his face and—most important of all—his eyes, remained emotionless. By the time he had composed his thoughts, Lui's gang had piled into their Nissan and were backing out of the parking lot. But the young hoodlum's words continued to reverberate in Lt. Luke Abel's head.

Turf challenge. It was the kind of animosity that laid siege to whole neighborhoods and could bathe Little Saigon in blood.

≡ CHAPTER 7

THE NEXT DAY, Luke Abel leaned over the radio console to get a better look at the data call Desk Sergeant Shelley was typing into the C.A.D. system—computer-aided dispatch. Shelley, a balding supervisor in his fifties, was typing the equivalent of seventy words a minute using only two fingers.

"Wish I could peck that fast." Abel chuckled. Which intruded upon Shelley's concentration. "Maybe I'd finally be able to finish the war novel I've been working on for the last twenty years."

"If you don't mind, Lieutenant *Hemingway* . . ." He erased a line of narrative and started over.

"Sorry." Abel noticed the paunch pressing up against Shelley's wrists. The sergeant had once been one hell of a street cop. Now, he was out of shape and had lost his sense of humor—probably from too many years sitting inactive behind a keyboard.

Abel patiently watched him type in the number 245— which lit up a bright PRIORITY ONE bar across his screen and got the other dispatcher's immediate attention. Abel glanced down at the phone bank. Five 911 lines were glowing. Three complaint takers seated nearby were taking calls from excited citizens reporting the same crime Shelley was entering.

Dialing 911 automatically registered the caller's phone number and address on the screen, as well. Abel squinted, and recognized the glowing green location: a pay phone near Bolsa and Bushard.

A 245 was Assault with a Deadly Weapon, and the primary dispatcher was already airing the call to an Area-2 unit in Garden Grove designated by the computer as soon as the location was entered into the system. Abel read along as Shelley typed:

RP STATES VICTIM WAS STRUCK WITH BASEBALL BAT BY ONE OF FOUR CAUCASIAN SUSPECTS IN A PINK MERCEDES . . . UNK LICENSE . . . LAST SEEN HEADED EASTBOUND BOLSA FIVE AGO. VICTIM IS ELDERLY V.N. MALE/DOWN & OUT/THE GUTTER NORTHWEST CORNER OF THE INTERSECTION.

Entering the 245 code into C.A.D. simultaneously generated a paramedic response from the Fire/Rescue Dispatcher seated nearby, and Abel could hear the sirens of an ambulance and assisting fire truck rolling from the stationhouse next door.

"Two units on scene," the dispatcher informed them. "Suspects have rabbited. They're asking for detectives and a coroner."

"Coroner?"

"Right." The woman nodded confidently. "Looks like the white boys zapped themselves a local down on Bolsa."

"What else have you got going?"

"Three five-ninety-fours on Bolsa, between Brookhurst and Bushard . . ."

"What kind of vandalisms?"

"Someone slashed up a bunch of expensive suits and dresses at the garment stores there. All three merchants report the suspects were Caucasian males in their late teens or early twenties. Fled on foot after leaving the damaged clothes piled up in the fitting rooms."

"Wonderful." Abel sighed in resignation. "What else?"

"Half a dozen four-fifteens pending . . . mostly down on Bolsa. All *those* at Viet restaurants."

"What kind of disturbances?"

"Verbals involving Caucasian subjects refusing to pay. Three walk-outs at the Pho-75 in the last hour alone."

"And just getting in a felony vandalism," one of the pretty department clerks added. "At the New Saigon Mall. Someone slashed the tires on over a dozen cars. Eyewitness advised the suspects were 'white men wearing rolled up jeans and some kinda army boots.' "

"Looks like you guys can use an assist out there today. Why don't you show me 'enroute' to that Agg' Assault down on the Strip . . . ?"

"M.A.G.-13 ten-76 Bolsa and Bushard," Shelley typed into the computer.

The lieutenant headed for the stairwell that would take him up out of the "hellhole," as veteran dispatchers referred to the communications bunker.

"If M.A.G.-fourteen ever codes in from that bomb-disposal run"—Abel paused—"advise him that I'm on my way over to—"

"Sergeant Thornton's already on-scene." The redhead flashed her perfectly straight teeth at him in a seductive Ann-Margret pose. "Bolsa and Bushard. He told me to have someone go into the Break Room and wake up your Sierra-Alpha."

" 'Sierra-Alpha?' "

"Sorry ass."

"Oh . . ."

"He was just walking across the street," the elderly Vietnamese woman told Abel in fluent English. "*In* the crosswalks, *with* the signal. But they could not wait. They honked at us, and called us 'chinks' and 'gooks,' and when I couldn't hurry him up—he needs a cane—when I couldn't hurry him up, they jumped out of their car . . . five of them . . . and they beat him with a baseball bat."

Abel stared over at the body lying facedown in the gutter—a paramedic's blanket covering the upper torso, a pool of blood collecting around the twisted left arm

and upturned hand. "They beat him *to death*!" the
woman was saying.

"Five of them? Not four?" Thornton sought clarification.

"Five." She seemed adamant. "I got their license
plate number." She showed him the letters she had
etched across the palm of her hand with a hairpin. MERC-
IT crisscrossed her lifeline in jagged red gashes that were
already beginning to scab over.

"Two-twenty-two aired it already," Thornton advised
the lieutenant. "It comes back on a Mercedes. Dispatch
has put out an interagency broadcast."

"I know—I just came from Communications."

"Morning, guys. . . ."

The two M.A.G. detectives turned to find Luyen and
Zamora standing behind them. Rachel wore jeans and a
blue sweater; Luyen was in her dark blue C.S.O. slacks
and blazer. "Hey, ladies!" Glenn seemed suddenly re-
juvenated. "What brings you down to the strip?"

"Sergeant Shelley notified us to come down and help
out Mrs. . . . Truong, is it?" Luyen glanced over at the
elderly woman. Her hair gray, and pulled back in a bun,
Abel judged her age to be in the late sixties. There were
no tears in her eyes, but her lower lip trembled continuously.

"Yes, thank you." She shuddered, unable to take her
eyes off the blanket covering her dead spouse. "Truong
Thi Tinh. I don't know what I'm going to do."

"We'll take care of you, Mrs. Truong." Luyen draped
an arm around the woman's shoulder. "Is it okay if we
take her over to our car?" she asked Abel. "Get her out
of the sun?"

Before he could answer, someone jumped forward,
camera clicking. Abel flinched, closing his eyes tightly
and feeling his temples begin to throb. He turned to find
a reporter and her photographer lurking behind him like
two vultures.

"Jesus!" He and Thornton both turned their faces
away from the news people. Turning to Zamora, he said,

"Notify Garden Grove to get with Mrs. Truong on composites as soon as possible."

"You got it, Lou!" Zamora flipped him the thumbs-up and smiled before turning to offer a looks-could-kill glare at the female reporter.

"What have you got here, guys?" The female reporter dropped into a squat beside the corpse and pulled the blanket back.

"No comment." Abel delighted in seeing the shock and revulsion register in her eyes.

"Please don't puke on our deceased person." Thornton went to work on the reporter.

"Jesus," she stumbled backwards but managed to regain her footing as she rose to lock eyes with Abel. "They bashed his brains out, Lieutenant."

"No comment." Abel grinned tightly.

"We monitored the call. Dispatch said something about all the suspects in this Asian bash being white punkers. Any truth to that?"

"No comment." Abel folded his arms across his chest and puffed his lips out at her.

The reporter sniffled, wiped her nose with the back of her hand, and scribbled something onto a clipboard.

"Come on, Abel." She stared into his eyes without blinking this time. "Why don't you tell me what's been going down in Little Saigon recently. Or do I have to get my hard copy from the gang bangers?"

"Sorry, no comment." Abel turned to leave.

"That's no way to treat the press," she yelled after him but refused to follow.

Neither Abel nor his partner bothered to voice a reply. To them, the news media were nothing but jackals. Every one of them: newspaper reporters, radio commentators, TV anchorpukes. All of them distorted the facts and loved to make real cops look bad.

The two M.A.G. detectives had not been back in their unmarked car for five minutes before a woman's slender hand shot through an open window and grabbed Abel's forearm. "Officer?"

Visibly startled by her undetected approach, Thornton struggled to maintain a straight face. "Yes, ma'am?"

"I work in shop down there." She pointed to a store-front brightly decorated with dozens of flapping red-and-yellow flags. "At Golden Buffy. We had some . . . customers. . . ." Her expression was pained. There was indecision in her eyes. "They knocked over statues and broke glass display case, then *di-di*—ran away. They hit my younger brother on way out."

"What time today did this happen, ma'am?"

"Oh, not today. Yesterday."

Abel and Thornton looked at each other.

"At first we not want to call you," the woman said, and Thornton's eyes returned to her attractive features. "But after poor Mr. Truong tonight, I was talk with my parents about it, when we saw you parked here, and well . . . everyone know Luke Abel Malibu."

" 'Just a coupla fag *cholos* . . .' " Thornton laughed.

"Huh?" the woman's lips became a puzzled crimson circle. Jet-black, silky hair fell to a waist wrapped in the traditional form-hugging *ao-dai* gown. She wore a little makeup, and her skin had an unblemished, almost chalky complexion that melted away most of Thornton's defenses.

"Oh, nothing, ma'am. Why don't you tell me what happened," he sought to ease her discomfort. "Can you describe them?" Thornton was automatically thinking of Lui's Steel Dragon boys.

"They were . . . white." Her eyes dropped toward her feet in apparent embarrassment.

"White?" Thornton was becoming visibly troubled by the sudden turn of events in Little Saigon. Spontaneous traffic altercations between Asians and whites was not unheard of along the Bolsa Strip, but planned criminal mischief by Caucasians was rare.

"I afraid so." The woman nodded. "Five of them. They wear army boots with the jeans tucked in top. They hair was cut very, short—like bald mens."

"Skinheads." Abel shook his head with contempt.

"How you say?" the woman tilted her head to one side.

Thornton pressed his hair back tightly. "Skinheads." He smiled.

"Ah, *skin*heads." She matched his grin. "They left in fancy car. Rich boys. A Rolls Royce."

Thornton got an idea. "A *silver* Rolls?" he asked.

"Same-same." She nodded again.

He and Abel exchanged puzzled looks laced with subdued excitement. "About what time did this happen?"

"In morning. Jus' after we open. Eleven o'clock."

"Bank *presidents'* hours." Thornton laughed with mock envy.

"I no understand." The woman's head tilted the other way.

"Nebbah mind," he said, leaning over to unlock the passenger-side door. "Why don't you hop in and we'll take you back over to your shop for a report. . . ."

The woman backed away. "*Hop* in?" Her smile vanished.

"Don't ya just love it workin' Bolsa?" Thornton laughed lightly as Abel prepared to pull out into traffic.

"I have put everything into this shop, Officer." The slender woman wearing a purple-and-black *ao-dai* stared up into Luke Abel's eyes. "My life savings. Twelve- and eighteen-hour work days. My family has sacrificed. And yet these . . . these *hoodlums* can get away with *this*!" She held up the slashed garments for Abel's inspection.

"Razor blade," Thornton proclaimed, examining the precise gashes that were so long the garment was unworthy of repair.

"Yes," tears were in the woman's eyes now as her husband joined her. "Razor blades."

"They could have cut our throats," the man was telling his wife as well as the two-detectives. "We were lucky."

Abel stared at the husband's one leg. The husband stared back, a warrior's understanding in the depths of his eyes. "You are a veteran," he said.

"Yes."

"How many years you stay Vietnam?" the woman asked.

"Seven."

"In my country, you were . . . police there, too?"

"Yes. An MP. An MP sergeant."

"Seven-hundred-sixteenth Battalion!" The woman nodded proudly. "Good men."

"Nebbah mind," the husband said. "Not our business. Please excuse my wife's curiosity. It was many years ago. Now we have new life. We only want to survive . . . to be left alone to run our shop, pay our taxes, raise our children. . . . We do not need this." He lifted a handful of silk shirts that had been slashed.

"We'll do everything in our power to locate the people responsible for this, sir," Abel responded. "You said they were in a pink Mercedes. Five white men in a pink Mercedes, right?"

"I have written the license plate down on that piece of paper," the woman said. "But they were boys. Only boys," she said. "Boys with so much hate in their hearts. It makes me sorry for them."

"What are they saying, Luyen?"

"Old man say American gentlemen drive up as they are crossing the street, yell at them, curse them and insult them because they were in the way—did not make it across the street fast enough. And when Mr. Ho here told them to please excuse their blatant stupidity"—eyes narrowing with muted anger, Community Service Officer Vo Thi Luyen's expression grew stern—"the Americans must have thought his smile too insulting."

"*White* Americans?" Detective Zamora stared at the bloody bump rising on Mr. Ho's forehead.

"Yes."

"Ask him if he wants an ambulance." Abel reached for a dash mike.

The assault victim obviously understood some English, for he was vigorously shaking his head from side to side now. "No, no ambulance!" he said. "Thank you. We leave now. We go home. Santa Ana."

"Can you describe them to us?" Thornton had his pocket notebook out now. "What kind of car were they driving?"

"Mercedes!" The shortest man in the group spoke up. His eyes sparkled in what Rachel decided could only be admiration. "Pink Mercedes."

"Did you get a license plate?" Luyen asked them in English.

"License plate?" The man was in his late sixties.

"Number," Luyen translated. "On the back of the car."

"Only some of it," the tallest of the four now bowed slightly upon speaking his first words. He held out a palm to Luyen. Across it were scribbled four letters: R-E-B.

Puzzled, Zamora's brows came together as she concentrated on the partial plate, but could make nothing of it. "Would you be able to identify these men?" she asked. Luyen translated.

"No problem," the man nursing a head contusion nodded. "No more silence. I talk in court, if you want."

"This no more Vietnam," the taller man agreed. "It America. This thing no can happen here. We talk police . . . to judge."

"Well, I don't know about that." She kept her eyes on her notebook. "But we appreciate your cooperation. Get their names," she told Luyen. "We'll make an appointment for them to have a follow up interview with Vinnie—if he even shows up."

"You think you will be able to find them?" the old man turned to gaze up at Lt. Abel.

"We're going to give it our best shot, sir," the lieutenant nodded respectfully.

"You no have to shoot," the man said. "Just put in jail."

≡ CHAPTER 8

IT WAS 8 A.M. when Luke Abel opened the three dead-bolts on the iron-frame door to his apartment and was immediately greeted by an irate, squawking sound.

"Yeah, and I missed you sorry fuckers, too. . . ." He walked past the large chrome bird cage, refusing to further acknowledge the presence of the three blue-and-white parrots clinging upside down to the front bars—their tilted heads shifting even further into comical poses as they followed his progress toward the kitchen.

As soon as he was out of their sight, the birds began squawking again. "Yeah, yeah . . ." Abel responded, grabbing an orange box of seed from beneath the sink. "I been busy, assholes. Too much fucking overtime. Lunch is on the way. Just fucking hold on to your feathers."

Never gonna get any sleep around here if they keep this crap up, Abel thought. When he returned to the living room, the birds went silent, but their little black eyes shifted about, following his every move.

When he opened the cage door, two of the parrots soared out like dive bombers. They raced about the room at blinding speed, darting around corners and between bookcases, shrieking the entire time. The first landed on Abel's shoulder and proceeded to peck gently at his ear.

The second plopped down right on top of his head, rolled through his hair, and bounced onto the floor.

"Real swift, Sherlock," he muttered.

The third bird had remained inside the cage, perched on the feed tray, experience gleaming in his eyes as he patiently waited for Abel to provide the seed. "Yeah, Dirty Harry ain't no dummy, is he?" Abel's finger rubbed the bird's belly before finally pouring food into the tray. Plumage expanding as Harry leaned into the physical contact, the bird tilted his head upside down and locked eyes with the seldom-seen detective. "Yeah, yeah, I know. . . ." Abel said. "Don't worry—it's me. Not some stranger. It's papa-san. It's Lucas."

The two other birds had returned to the cage door, but couldn't get inside because it was filled with Abel's wrist. "Settle down, you clowns!" He laughed as they playfully pecked at him, trying to get at the food while Dirty Harry flung seed out of the feed tray with obvious glee.

"Jesus." Abel finally retreated from the cage. "What you boys need is some feathered pussy—a woman bird-brain. Hell, *three* women birdbrains. *That* should keep you occupied while I'm gone, eh?"

"Fuck it!" Dirty Harry replied with a cranky rasp between beakfuls of seed.

"Christ." Abel shook his head in resignation. "Glenn better knock off with the English lessons." Last time his partner had been over to drink a case of Millers and watch old *Police Story* videos, he'd spent half the time trying to get the birds to say "Polly want a blow job?"

The birds had failed to latch onto *that* phrase, but Harry had been saying *Fuck it*! ever since *The Deerhunter* came out, more than ten years ago. Abel resigned himself to the fact long ago. He was too attached to his parrots to give them away or set them free. He was just thankful Sherlock and Bronson had never picked up on the ability to talk. Or talk back. Thornton was working on them, though.

"Xinh's gonna really *enjoy* you three pricks." Abel refilled their water holder with a frown. "The Good, the Bad and the Ugly." He reached inside and stroked Sherlock's shoulders gently. "All I can say is you better learn some manners before she arrives. . . ." *Before she arrives*. There he went again, talking as if he knew Xinh was still alive.

"Fuck it!" Dirty Harry replied with a twinkle in his eye.

Abel sighed, heading back into the kitchen for a beer. The birds went crazy when they heard him twist off the cap. The apartment filled with the sound of screeching again. "Okay, okay." He slowly walked back over to the cage. "Beeeeeer." He dragged the word out as if teaching a child how to say it.

All three parrots flew out of the cage and landed on his free arm. "You're a trio of spoiled brats—you know that, don't you?"

Harry squawked up at him impatiently. "Fuck it!" the bird said. "Fuck it!"

"Okay, okay . . . ." Abel gently tilted the bottle until a bubble of beer bulged at the neck. Dirty Harry pecked at the glass rim, waiting patiently for the beer to soak his beak.

After the other birds had their taste, Abel guzzled half the bottle down and walked into the bedroom. He glanced at the two dozen poster-size photos of Xinh gracing every wall in the room, felt a warm tingling sensation swirl down through his loins, and, for a moment, saw the two of them on the bed, naked and locked in a passionate embrace, arms and legs a tangle of perspiration-soaked flesh as they entered another hour of lovemaking. . . .

"I miss you, Xinh."

For an instant, as he stared up at the largest picture— Xinh sitting on the banks of the Song Saigon in her purple-and-black *ao-dai*, long hair flowing in the breeze, a huge temple obscuring the sunset in the background, the entire scene bathed in varying hues of warm crimson— he saw instead the last days of the Thieu regime crumbling away as the communists surrounded South Vietnam's capital.

He saw Xinh sitting alone in their apartment, heart frozen with terror, as a helpless Luke Abel, handcuffed

by red tape and petty bureaucratic bickering, waited in
Thailand for a flight back to Saigon while the VC fought
canh-sats on Newport Bridge.

Xinh. Abel had first met her when he was an MP in-
terrogator and she was a translator for the National Police. He'd almost married her. Not just some Buddhist
temple ceremony she'd been so contented with, but a big
get-together at the cathedral in downtown Saigon with
both Alpha and Bravo Companies of the 716th Military
Police Battalion in attendance—a military sword ceremony, Chaplain Hubler presiding, two dozen MP jeeps
waiting outside to give them a Code-3 escort to Vung
Tau, and all the rest. But she had refused to marry Abel
unless she could prove her love for him—that she was
not just looking for a meal ticket out of the Nam.

Xinh did not wish to leave her homeland. She hoped
they could someday settle down together, and live their
days out in Saigon. But they stalled too long, and Abel
was transferred to Thailand after the peace treaty of 1973
mandated that all American troops leave the Republic of
Vietnam. Hanoi continued to funnel men and arms south
of the DMZ, along the Ho Chi Minh Trail. Abel's tour
with the 281st MPs in Sattahip lasted two years, and he
was not allowed to leave the Kingdom of Siam to visit
the woman he wanted so desperately to make his wife.

Then Saigon fell, and he was unable to rescue Xinh
from the city before the communists came. The U.S.
Army had Sgt. Luke Abel chasing AWOLs and black
marketeers next door, in Thailand, and he couldn't get a
flight to Tan Son Nhut until it was too late. By the time
he reached their apartment on Thanh Mau, Xinh was
gone. He found the framed pictures of the two of them
posing together torn to pieces and sitting in a pile of
ashes along with the papers that allowed them to legally
live together, the box containing his army paycheck stubs
and ration cards—everything that could implicate her—
lying on the floor. Burned. Gone forever—insurance
against death squads and middle-of-the-night house
searches by the Cong. They had discussed it before. Xinh
did not want to be identified as a GI's woman. She didn't

want to be marched naked down the middle of Tu Do Street with the other "whores," a bayonet in her back.

And still the communists arrested Xinh. One of the neighbors must have squealed: Xinh slept with the round-eyes. She fucked an MP, the worse running dog of all. She was a GI whore.

He received one "message" from Xinh after Saigon fell on April 30, 1975. It was to inform him the "authorities" were sending her to a reeducation camp up in the northern jungles. She did not expect to be able to communicate with him, ever again. That was in 1975. He had never heard from her again. Somehow he held on to hope, though—a feeling she had survived the camps . . . a gut instinct they would somehow be reunited again.

Abel lit a *joss* stick every night, in Xinh's memory. He kept photos of her on all the walls in his apartment. They were a constant reminder of the woman he abandoned to a life of pain, suffering, and misery in Vietnam.

"Wait 'til you see this place, Xinh," he spoke up to one of the blown-up, *poster-size*, unsmiling faces staring back down at him, her eyes seemingly following him across the room. "They call it Little Saigon. It'll either make you feel right at home or wanna freak out—we'll have a ball."

He stared up at the photo he took the week Uncle Sammy was sending him to Thailand's 281st MPs, claiming he had been in The Nam too long, was squatting on the floor when there were perfectly good chairs in the room, and was eating *pho* and sugarcane cubes on Nguyen Van Thoi Street instead of hamburgers at Pershing Field's mess hall.

He reached over and pulled some small black chunks of licorice from a glass-covered candy platter sitting on the nightstand. He could hear his partner's routine verbal offer: "Have some more cordite, kid."

With the first bite, memories of misty, smoke-laced battlefields swept over him. Licorice did that to Luke Abel. The taste was similar to the lining left inside one's throat from several hours crouched amid drifting clouds of gunsmoke. Not unlike the way exhaust fumes from

trucks and buses made him think of Saigon instead of
L.A. smog, the smell activated memory cells that took
him right back to Vietnam and, still, the grin grew. Abel
had been chewing licorice, in lieu of tobacco, for over
twenty years now. Ever since Xinh had made him stop
smoking.

Old Saigon. Xinh. She would be just over forty now,
like him.

Suddenly enraged, he kicked over the nightstand and
walked into the apartment's second bedroom, which had
been converted into a den. The walls were lined with
countless books about the Vietnam war - some 2,000 at
last count. Tapestries from Saigon and Bangkok and
Phnom Penh covered the windows. Shelves were filled
with Vietnamese music casettes, all pre-1975. Over a
dozen photo albums—not that many, for seven tours in-
country, were stacked precariously in one corner. It was
where Abel came to be truly alone—isolated from the
job and the outside world. This room was his fortress of
solitude . . . where he could put on headphones and listen to Vietnamese music tapes over and over while reading the latest copy of *Indochina Chronology*, or writing
his weekly letter back to Saigon. Back to Xinh . . .

He couldn't mail them. He had no address—no proof
she was still alive. Hundreds of the notes sat in a soldier's footlocker at the M.A.G. substation.

Feeling drowsy, he checked the fridge and resisted
downing a beer, which would only increase the effects
of the fatigue he was feeling. Instead, he put on a pot of
coffee—choosing to open a fresh can despite the half-
filled container beside the percolator—simply because he
was in the mood to get a whif of freshly ground coffee
beans. Funny, how coffee had become his constant com-
panion of sorts, ever since he first began wearing a badge.
Or an MP armband. The leech-infested nightmares about
Vietnam still haunted him, though Abel had loved his
tours of duty overseas.

He had made it through only the first two pages of the
latest issue of *Indochina Chronology* when his head

slowly dropped to the desktop and Luke Abel began snoring.

Her screams brought tears to the edges of his eyes, but there was nothing he could do. Five men, M-16 automatic rifles slung across their shoulders, leaned over the long, metal table, jabbing the woman with wires . . . poking and prodding . . . attaching the battery clips to her nipples and the lips of her vagina. A hand shot through the muggy, smoke-filled room, signaling the weasel of a man seated behind an olive-drab metallic contraption, and the underground chamber was filled with the whirring of the field phone. And the woman's screams.

"She VC, Sergeant Abel! She VC whore fo' sure!" The canh-sat *appeared positive. "They come here from Hanoi, hunting cherryboys, from CHI-cago. We make her talk . . . one more hour under the wires . . . maybe more . . ."*

"I . . . not . . . VC!" the woman screamed, her chest exploding with the echoes of her cry . . . soul racing out after MP Sergeant Abel . . . ghost chasing him through the endless catacombs of the underground chamber. He ran into a dead end, stumbled through the dark, fell into a bottomless pit . . . right on top of Xinh. "No!"

Abel sat bolt upright at his desk. Soaked in sweat, he glanced around. There was a familiarity to his surroundings, yet he felt odd, out of place somehow. The green glow from the wall clock's digital display illuminated his framed commendations hanging on the far wall above the Doc Savage poster—a rare remnant from his high school days—and he knew he was safe. He was home, in his den, in California. Not Vietnam. It was the eighties . . . not 1968. Smoke curls drifted before his eyes, and he glanced over at the three *joss* sticks smoldering in the urn. The incense was still glowing. He had been off the street and asleep for a little over four hours.

"Ten-four, One-eleven . . . ten-eight."

Abel tensed, ready to spring but wanting to hide . . . disappear forever. The static-laced voice sent a bolt of

fear through him, but, just as quickly, he recognized the
dispatcher's voice . . . realized it was just his police
scanner. *Christ . . . must've turned the stupid thing on
in my fucking sleep.* He hadn't listened to the police radio, while off duty, in years.

"Request Ten-twenty-eight, Ten-twenty-nine on a
white Thunderbird, California personalized Zulu X-Ray
Bravo seven one four. . . ."

He slid off the chair and started toward the bathroom,
ripping the radio's plug from the wall as he stumbled into
the hallway. He filled the sink with cold water and
splashed his face for two or three minutes, until his head
cleared, then checked his watch. The digital display was
set to military time: 1230 hours. Christ, he thought, only
a little after noon. That must fucking account for how
bright it is in here.

The music came to him, then. Distant, somewhere on
the ground floor. It had to be the girl again. The girl in
101—two flights below his. Her balcony window was always open, and he could hear Vietnamese music floating
up through it whenever he opened his own window. Mellow, soft rock songs from the sixties.

He shut off the water, doused the bathroom light, and
walked out onto his balcony, where he could hear voices
below. A one-sided conversation—the woman was talking on the phone. Laughing, giggling.

He stared down at the Bolsa Strip, several hundred
yards away. People were entering restaurants, driving to
bars—only now they were in Chevrolets or Toyotas—not
in the three-wheeled cyclos or blue-and-yellow Renault
taxicabs that had crowded Old Saigon.

Abel's apartment was on the top floor of a three-story
complex that rose up behind the Man Wah shopping mall
compound. He enjoyed it because it was not that much
different from his old apartment in Saigon—the sights,
sounds, and smells. It brought back the memories, too,
but he thought he had learned to live with those. The
dreams, returning again now, proved him wrong.

Massaging his temples, Abel walked back over to the
bed and collapsed across it. The phone rang less than

thirty minutes later. It intruded into his nightmares of back-alley prowlers and rooftop foot chases, and Abel rolled from the bed, onto the floor, searching for his fallen service weapon—the .45 he had dropped while chasing the black-marketeer from one dream to another, through the back alleys and tenements of Thanh Mau Street.

The phone stopped ringing before he could answer it—how many rings? Ten? Twenty?—and he focused on the clock again: 1300 hours. Trying to get back to sleep would be a lost cause for him—total exhaustion aside.

He checked the amount of cash in his wallet and decided the Can Tho Cabaret deserved to be graced with his presence.

≡ CHAPTER 9

"WE'VE GOT SOME of that imported German beer in today, Luke."

Abel glanced up from his note pad and forced a smile. "No thanks, Anh. Just the usual, thanks . . ."

"How's the street?" She reached down under the counter and brought up a frosty bottle of Miller's High Life.

Abel's smile remained intact, though the friendly sparkle in his eyes faded. "Still as polluted as ever, Anh. You're not missing anything. Besides, the scenery's nicer in here." His eyes dropped to the swells of flesh along the top of her sarong, then darted down the counter to inspect faces on the other patrons at the bar.

Anh Adams, Eurasian beauty and proprietor of the Can Tho Cabaret on Westminster Avenue, pinched Abel's cheek then set to work concocting a Singapore Sling for herself.

It was slow at the bar in the mid afternoon. A few off-duty cops were in evidence. Anh's dark eyes stared through him, for Lucas Abel did not feel entirely present and accounted for tonight. The beer helped. Abel glanced over at the shapely female members of the band as they helped the beanpole of a drummer carry his gear out from their van.

One of the off-duty officers watching the TV called for his tab, and as she left, Abel could not take his eyes from Anh's firm, bouncing bottom.

Anh Adams. Going on forty, but still looking twenty-nine. Widow of Garden Grove Police Officer Scott Adams, gunned down on the Bolsa Strip, 1978, while trying to take a car thief into custody. She had met Scott in Saigon, where he was an Army MP, serving with Abel. At the time, she was a twenty-year-old, struggling night-club singer, still innocent and idealistic—a writer of peace songs and ballads about lost loves and loneliness caused by the war.

Every time he looked into Anh's kind, trusting eyes he saw the reflection of his old partner. . . .

He could still remember Scott Adams clearly. They had been MP partners in Saigon for nearly two years. In that time, according to Scott, they had survived sixty-eight rooftop sniper attacks together. And Scott would know—the buck sergeant kept copious notes on everything he witnessed in The Nam. He could envision their patrol jeep careening down the narrow, winding maze of alleys behind Tu Do Street, enroute to a Shots-Fired call or Ten-100, MP-Needs Help!

Luke was forever warning Scott to slip on his helmet and flak jacket, but the younger military policeman rarely complied. "I'm our lucky charm, Gus!" he'd always reply. "Nothin' can happen to me so long as we're partners! My Tarot card reader at Le Loi park *guaranteed* it!" Anh had been his fortune-teller back then.

Scott Adams had survived Vietnam. He just didn't foresee the world of hurt he'd encounter on the streets of Little Saigon. The eleventh anniversary of his murder was approaching: April 30, 1978, which also happened to mark three years since the fall of Old Saigon. It was a date Anh would never forget.

Abel could still remember every detail of that call. Adams had made a traffic stop on Bolsa—only a few blocks down from where Luke himself had pulled over some suspected gang bangers—and declined a second backup car. Less than a minute later, the dispatcher was

airing a felony code over the radio. The car Scott had
stopped was hot. And Abel could hear shots ringing out
down the block now.

Abel rushed to his idling unit and left a carload of
bewildered punks and a cloud of burnt rubber at the scene
of his own traffic stop. Ahead, beyond the drifting,
ground-clinging blankets of mist, lazy beams of blue-
and-red light lancing through the fog marked the spot
where Patrolman Scott Adams lay in the middle of the
street, on his back, unmoving, steam rising from the
gaping wound in his chest. He never did learn to wear
his bullet-proof vest.

They had never apprehended his murderer. Not even
identified a suspect, which, to Luke Abel, was the ulti-
mate insult. Somewhere out there, the puke was probably
sitting in a gang safe house, bragging about the shooting.
Or he might just as well be in a grave—one of the name-
less ten thousand vicious criminals American lawmen had
put into the ground over the last decade.

Anh Adams had used the life insurance money to buy
the Can Tho Cabaret. It had now become a cop bar of
sorts. Anh sang every night, always bringing tears to her
patrons' eyes with stirring, heart-wrenching songs from
the City of Sorrows. Songs she had written herself. Songs
dedicated to Scott, the only man she had ever slept with—
then or now.

The counter could accommodate about a dozen serious
drinkers, and was staffed by Anh's beautiful young
daughter when Anh herself joined the band as vocalist.
Recently, some Vietnamese New Wave bands appeared
at the Cabaret and, strangely enough, Abel and his crew
enjoyed their music.

A clicking buzz and grinding whirr behind Abel made
him think of VC boobytraps and tunnel tripwires, but he
didn't flinch . . . didn't drop to the beer-slick floor, seek-
ing cover. The jukebox kicked in with "Still in Saigon,"
and the two cops sitting at the bar—both Nam vets—sang
along with the Charlie Daniels Band. They lifted their
glasses of "33" to Abel, and he returned the salute with
his Miller's.

"Figured I'd find your sorry ass down here." Someone with quarters jingling in his pocket was patting Abel's shoulder from behind. "Your goddamn answering machine was turned off."

Abel recognized Glenn Thornton's clasp instantly. "Needed some alcohol in my system to slow me down." Abel laughed lightly.

"Don't I know it." Thornton asked Anh for a Miller's as well.

"Another beer, Gus?" Anh Adams was one of the few friends who still called him by the name Scott had given him.

"We have to be going," Thornton answered for his partner.

"We do?" Abel cocked an eyebrow. "I'm off duty, chump."

"Not anymore, *chump*."

"I heard about the problems on the Bolsa Strip," she said. "I'm sorry those punks are getting out of hand again."

"Why should you be sorry?" Abel asked her half heartedly. "You have no control over scum the likes of . . . well, I can't tell you their names right now, Anh, but—"

"People . . . the old-timers who come in here," she said, "they tell me this town used to be a quiet place . . . that the Vietnamese really screwed Garden Grove and Westminster up. Santa Ana was already lost." She winked. "But really . . . I'm sorry those few who live by crime make such a bad reputation for the rest of us, Gus. I wish I could ship them all back to Saigon . . . I really do. Some of them belong in the tiger cages on Con Son Island. . . ."

"The 'old-timers' have been feeding you a line of shit, Anh. Garden Grove and Westminster have got a combined population of three hundred thousand. Even an unchecked onslaught of immigrants wouldn't be able to change the atmosphere of a metropolitan area that much."

"Well, try telling that to the 'good ole boys' across the street at the VFW."

"Aw, they're not happy unless they're bitchin' about something." Abel winked back. "Last week it was taxes. Next week half of 'em will be dead from booze, broads, or both."

"Speaking from personal experience?" Thornton's laugh came across shallow.

"I'm a card-carryin' member." Abel's eyes shifted from his partner's to Anh's. "But I still spend all my money *here*."

"Sweet talk will get you everywhere, Gus." She popped the cap on another Miller's, set it in front of him, and disappeared.

"What's the word?" Abel turned to face his partner again.

"About the gangs?" Thornton asked, and when Luke nodded at his own reflection in the long mirror hanging behind the bar, "Brass Balls made bail."

"That's all? I expected as much."

"He wanted me to give you a message," Glenn said dourly.

"Let me guess. . . ."

"He wanted you to know he's going to find out where you live, burn down your house, and rape your wife."

"Why do they always think this lousy job pays us enough to buy a house?"

For some reason, Abel's tortured laugh brought a terrible sadness over Anh Adams.

"Have another." Anh Adams reappeared just as someone leaning over the jukebox paid the Charlie Daniels Band another quarter to sing "Still in Saigon" for the fifth time that afternoon. There were two unopened beer bottles in her hands.

"We really *do* have to be going." Abel placed a ten-dollar bill on the counter. "Two's my limit, on the job . . . and I'll drink *his* on the way to the substation." He tried to take Glenn's beer bottle away.

Anh pushed the note back to him. "You two *know* you can't buy anything in here." She waved a finger at Abel.

A telephone behind the bar began ringing, and Anh scanned faces left and right. "Who's not here?" she called out.

Nearly everyone seated at the counter raised his hand.

"Ten bucks says it's for the lieutenant." A patrolman from G.G.P.D. sitting at a nearby table with four bar girls directed a casual salute in Abel's direction.

Anh had already answered the phone. "Don't bet against him," she said with apologetic eyes as she handed Luke the phone.

"Abel here."

"It's Shelley over at Dispatch, Lou. Figured I'd get you at the cabaret. Hey, some guys from L.A.P.D. just came screamin' up to the Commo Center, lights and siren."

"L.A.P.D.?" Abel was suddenly alert. "*Here*? In Orange County?" He was thinking of Steel Dragon and Blue Bamboo and a Chinatown connection of some sort.

"Right. You know how crazy those clowns are. Anyway all they did was drop off a message. It's sealed, and has 'Abel's Eyes Only' scrawled across the top. Looks like a telegram."

"Do you notice any name tags?"

"You know those guys, Lou—they don't never wear name tags. But the guy said he was your old partner. Took me a while to track you down. I had one of my people run it over to your M.A.G. substation already, slip it under the door—in case you were in there and just not answering the phone."

"Thanks, Shelley! I'm on my way over there now!" Abel knocked over his beer bottle on the way out.

Thornton knew better than to show open interest in his partner's personal affairs. Official business would have been sent through the teletype for all to see, or simply through a C.A.D. computer relay.

He busied himself at one of the glowing consoles, but he was watching Abel's every move out of the corner of one eye.

The M.A.G. lieutenant ripped open the L.A.P.D. envelope and read the tissue-thin slip of paper inside.

There was nothing from his "ex-partner" or any of the other guys back at the old division. Simply a telegram, addressed to Los Angeles Police Department Headquarters, California. He had always told Xinh that joining L.A.P.D. was his dream. The dream had lasted slightly over a year, the job nine more, before burnout drove him south, away from the ghetto, into the barrio, and finally Little Saigon.

She remembered.

≡ CHAPTER 10

ABEL'S EYES FLUTTERED up to lock on his partner's, as if he were reading some Top Secret, sensitive material he should not have access to, but he remained silent, and forced himself to read the brief message.

> Lucas, I hope this reaches you. I am out. Our boat made it to Thailand after many weeks in the South China Sea. I am safe. I was not hurt. The camp is called Songklai. I have been here five months, two weeks now. I hesitated contacting you. It has been so many years. I did not want to interfere in your American life. My name has been placed on a manifest roster for California, USA, leaving in two weeks. Maybe destiny will bring us back together. Maybe not. I kept your name. Even in the camps. I never stopped loving you, Lucas.
>
> Xihn Thi Le Abel.

He glanced over at his partner, but still balked at saying anything—he didn't want to jinx Xinh's chances. The telegram was dated one week ago. She would be arriving before Tet.

"So are you going to lay it on me, or not?" Thornton could wait no longer.

"Oh, it's nothing," Abel folded the telegram up and placed it in his shirt pocket. He wanted to make sure this was not all just another in an endless series of dreams before he made any decisions. "Just those clowns up at L.A.P.D. jerkin' my chain again. It's a rookie recruit application."

"Looks like a telegram to me. Anything important?" Thornton was thinking of dead relatives.

"Let it lie, Glenn."

"If you say so." He resumed dipping Oreos into his lukewarm coffee.

Abel glanced at the footlocker stacked behind his desk, filled with his unmailed letters to Xinh. Now, they would no longer be necessary. That part of his life was over. Fourteen years after the Fall of Saigon. Xinh was free. Out. Still an ocean away, but now breathing the air of a new country. Thailand. Kingdom of Siam. He could now get on with the next phase of his life. Fourteen years late. The thought made him feel nineteen again.

He forced himself to walk over to a flask beside Glenn's desk—time to pretend nothing was askew.

"The coffee sucks," Abel informed his partner, pouring the cold contents into a mug bearing a blue-and-silver decal of the L.A.P.D. badge. The inscription FEEL SAFE TONIGHT was above the police shield. Below it, the words, SLEEP WITH A COP. He sat down at his desk, unlocked a drawer, and removed a tray lined with spent .38- and .357-caliber slugs.

"If you're actually going to drink that shit, you need some of these." Thornton offered his box of cookies to Abel.

"No thanks. I don't even taste it anymore." Abel smiled as he took a sip.

Not failing to notice the first genuine smile on his partner's face in weeks, Thornton reached into his shirt pocket and threw Abel a small vial of caffeine pills. "They're better on the stomach lining," he explained.

Abel caught the vial, opened it, and washed two caffeine pills down with the papercupful of old-and-cold brew. "Hey, Vinnie still *sick*?"

"Ain't sick of pussy. I heard he's pokin' some cocktail waitress from the cabaret," Thornton said matter-of-factly as he wrestled with the computer codes. "Fresh meat'll make a man forget his priorities, ya know?"

Abel's eyebrows rose slightly. "*Our* Vinnie Verdugo?" he asked between rejection beeps from the computer. "The man with the 'No Gooks' bumper stickers on his car?" The sticker actually depicted a squinting Asian behind a steering wheel, surrounded by a red circle. The foreign driver was wearing a straw conical hat, and there was a red diagonal slash across his face. It was the current rage among Orange County bigots.

Thornton was frowning now. He looked as if he were about to punch the dust-caked computer console. "Same-same. Zamora told me he had the hots for that recent-refugee with the Barbara Eden boobs."

"That explains it."

"Hey, she can ring my ding-dong any day." Thornton had his 9mm automatic out now. He was pointing it directly at the glowing console, but hesitating—as if waiting for his partner's mandatory request that he holster the weapon.

"It'll only mean more paperwork." Abel finally forced the words out.

"But it just might be worth it." Glenn kept the pistol in a two-handed combat grip. His toothy grin had grown ear-to-ear.

"What's up, fellas?" The door flew open and Luyen walked in. Her spirits also seemed to have ballooned. Time "healed most wounds," even loss of face, Abel decided.

"Not much." He was standing in front of a wall map bristling with multicolored pins now. Little Saigon's two-mile-square business district was decorated with blue pins for robberies, black for homicides, yellow for burglaries, and red for arsons. "Just trying to make some sense of this recent rash of aggravated assaults—not to mention the murder of that unarmed old man—and figure out why all the suspect vehicles had personalized plates with the letters MERC somewhere in the message.''

"We're looking for a Porsche, been used in bookoo strong-armed robberies,'' Thornton told her, offering the box of Oreos, which Luyen declined with an expression of mock disgust. "Got a partial plate on it of M-E-R-C something or other. Then that silver Rolls involved in the Bolsa murder had plates that read R-E-B-E-L. 'No Record Found' in the DMV motor vehicle computer, however.''

"Probably a recent listing,'' Luyen sat down at her desk.

"Well, sounds like that wanna-be-vet Merc gang,'' Abel said. "I just spoke with Dispatch. They're still working a backlog of cold assaults and burg's in Little Saigon—white on yellow.''

"Speakin' o' white on yellow''—Thornton leaned back in his chair and balanced his running shoes atop the computer console—"my old lady's been doin' a lot of complaining about these long hours we been keepin,' Luke. When we gonna slack off? This Seven-P to Three-A shift is killing my love life, and I haven't had a day off since the Porsche bandit stakeouts began.''

"But I bet your wife loves the overtime on your paycheck,'' Abel reminded him.

"Yeah, I guess you're right. Aw, she'll get over it, and screw her anyway, if she don't,'' he expanded his chest bravely, then let the air out in an embarrassed flutter after Luyen stared him down. "Besides''—he sought to save face in true Oriental fashion as he glanced back over at the attractive C.S.O.—"wives are like used cars: When they get old, you trade them in for a newer model.''

"Why are you looking at me like that?'' Luyen lifted her chin.

"Are you available?'' Thornton went through this with her at least once a month.

"I'm probably five years older than your Korean gymnast,'' Luyen reminded him.

"But *she* don't know how to make *nuoc-mam*, dahlin.' '' Thornton batted his eyelashes. "Besides, you know what my favorite Viet custom is, don't you? Viet men can have as many wives as they can support. Maybe you could be my Number Two wife!" He glanced over at his partner for approval, but Abel dismissed Glenn's antics with a side-to-side headshake.

"That was Vietnamese custom in *Vietnam*," Luyen corrected him as she busied herself with a stack of paperwork. "Not America."

"That's not what all the ex-Arvins at Can Tho Cabaret told me." Thornton folded his arms across his chest in victory.

Luyen laughed, and the carefree sound warmed Abel's heart. "If they had *any* wives here, they would not be spending their evenings at Anh Adams's nightclub!" she maintained, rising from her desk and walking back toward the restroom.

After she was out of earshot, Thornton told Abel, "Speakin' of Viet pussy, I'm continually amazed you haven't broken down and shacked up with one of these Bolsa girls, Luke. Hell, you take Luyen—she's constantly got the roving eyeballs for you, ya know."

"I *heard* that!" Luyen called out from behind the closed door.

Ignoring her, Glenn continued. "What has it been now, ten, fifteen years since you left Saigon? That's a long time, brother. . . ." He smiled despite the general knowledge that Luke Abel could chase thigh with the best of them at the weekly departmental "choir practice" where booze replaced hymnbooks.

Unable to remain silent a moment longer, Abel removed the Cop-O-Gram from his pocket and handed it to Glenn as Luyen returned from the restroom, hovering over Thornton's shoulder like a curious butterfly, sensing a juicy tidbit of potential gossip unfolding.

"It's from Xinh. She's out." His word were a cautious whisper.

"Xinh? *Out*!?" Thornton rushed across the room and embraced his partner before even reading the telegram.

"She escaped by boat, God only knows how long ago!" tears were streaming down the M.A.G. detective's face. "She just made it to a refugee camp in Thailand six months ago."

"And she just *now* cabled you?" Luyen's smile faded somewhat as she read the fear in her lieutenant's eyes. Though he often discussed his MP days back in Old Saigon, reminiscing about lost loves was taboo with Abel.

"That's great, Luke! That's really fuckin' great, man!" Thornton was slapping Abel on the back and dancing around the room with Luyen now, to the tune of police scanner transmissions.

"I'm not sure what I'll say to her. After all these years. I'm just not sure how I'll react . . . if she'll still love me . . ."

"Don't sweat it, brother! She cabled your sorry ass, didn't she? Just go with the flow! Everything will fall into place. Trust me."

"I just hope I live to see the day she arrives at LAX airport." A shudder tore through Abel's frame. "This Tet business is getting . . . eerie."

"Mellow out, partner. Everything will work out fine."

"Maybe I should fly out to Thailand and meet her. Take some leave of absence. Tell Sanders to take this badge and shove it where the sun don't shine."

It was Luyen whose warm hand brought an unexpected comfort as she draped it over his shoulder. "She will be all right. I went through, many years ago, what your woman is going through now. The best thing to do until she gets here is busy yourself with work. It will make the time pass faster. There is nothing else you can do. Cable her back, then resume your routine. They do not allow visitors at the refugee camp.

"Now tell me more about this black Porsche and the purse snatcher everyone's so hot-on about zapping. I've sent teletypes out to every P.D. and sheriff's console in the quad-county area about your MERC plates, but no one's bothered to reply yet."

She opened a thermos and poured Abel a fresh cup of hot Viet-style coffee made with just the right amount of French cream.

"Not even the L.A. Sheriff's CRASH unit?" Thornton asked.

"Nope. Zilch."

Abel quickly updated her on the latest information they had about the Porsche bandit—which was practically nothing—and pointed to a new stack of reports in the middle of her desk. *"Those,"* he said, "are the latest white-on-yellow assaults that have gone down on Bolsa. Get 'em into the stats computer as soon as possible. We're gonna cruise the strip, check for trouble."

"Right." Luyen flipped on her console. "I'll keep you posted if anything turns up."

As they reached the second-floor stairwell outside, a chorus of electronic wails in the distance caused Thornton to cup an ear. "You hear that?"

"Sirens. A lot of them. Comin' our way—but from where?"

"It's definitely music to my ears, but I dunno," Glenn said.

"L.A. Sheriff's got 'emselves a chase!" Luyen called out through a window. "A Porsche! I just heard it on the scanner."

"Let's go." Abel grinned, the rush of adrenaline making him suddenly feel twenty years younger again as they ran toward the 1974 Malibu.

"Clear on the right!" Thornton was advising, as Abel kicked over the engine. The souped-up 440 rumbled to life and the lieutenant rammed the gearshift into reverse.

"Ahhh, but I fucking *lovvvve* the smell of rubber burning in the afternoon!" Thornton sighed as the car's rear tires screamed in protest. They lurched backwards through a cloud of blue smoke and, in a single motion, Thornton had placed the red revolving light on the roof of the car and flipped the radio console's siren selector to WAIL.

"Who loves ya, mamma-san?" He glanced out the passenger side window and locked eyes with a startled old woman carrying two water buckets suspended from a pole across her shoulders. The woman produced a black-toothed smile, and, in precise English, replied

"Good evening, Officer." Thornton laughed aloud this time, saluting her with genuine respect as Abel "speed-shifted" the automatic into Low with a downward swipe of his wrist.

"There they go!" Thornton pointed west, down Bolsa, as a black Porsche, followed by several black-and-white sheriff's cars, roared through an intersection, south-bound. Sparks flew from undercarriages as the vehicles slammed through the dips.

"I'm gonna take Brookhurst south and cut 'em off!" Abel yelled. He punched the Malibu into overdrive in hopes of bringing their speed back up to par, and heads turned in their direction for half a block as the powerful engine roared. The four-barrel 440's growl brought another frown to Abel's face. "Jesus!" he muttered. "Did you turn the air-filter cover upside down again?"

"Makes this crate sound *badddd*." Thornton did not glance over at Abel as they zigzagged down a maze of side streets, coming out ahead of the chase, which they could hear but not see. "Gives it more air, too, chump." He sensed the disapproval emanating from the usually laid-back lieutenant. "More punch from the pistons. On your right!"

Abel's eyes locked onto a black Porsche heading toward them at a sharp angle down a nearby sidestreet. "It's *him*!" Thornton shouted, pointing at the Porsche's front license plate growing like some blurred image in front of a zoom telephoto lens. "The Porsche bandito! The hairball we've been trying to locate for the last—"

Abel swerved to the left as the 911 Cabriolet slid sideways through the intersection right in front of them and quickly sped away. "What the fuck's he trying to do!?"

"*Look out!*" Thornton yelled as a speeding sheriff's car failed to make the turn and skidded through the intersection in a complete one-eighty, heading straight for them in a broadside skid.

≣ CHAPTER 11

THE SHERIFF'S DEPARTMENT unit's left front bumper missed their Malibu's right rear quarter panel by only a few inches.

Abel fell in pursuit behind the Porsche 911 even as the out-of-control sheriff's unit was still sliding in tight circles through the intersection behind them.

Thornton reached forward and switched radio channels. "Command, this is M.A.G.-thirteen . . . do you copy?"

"Send it, Sergeant," a female's voice responded on the Orange-North channel.

"Be advised we're in pursuit of a black, nine-eleven turbo, now westbound Bolsa from vicinity Brookhurst . . . possible two-eleven/robbery suspect . . ." A loud, hi-lo siren was suddenly blaring in his ears from behind, and Abel glanced in his rearview mirror to find that the black-and-white sheriff's unit had recovered, rejoined the chase, and was now riding his bumper.

Thornton concentrated on the white-and-gold tags rapidly growing smaller in front of him. "California personalized plates Mike-Echo-Romeo-Charlie-slash-Uniform. . . . Driver appears to be Caucasian . . . late twenties or early thirties . . . wearing multicolored

T-shirt. . . . And he looks like a real hard-core sleaze-bag *skinhead*!''

Abel growled as he swerved in and out of several slower-moving vehicles. ''Don't these people know how to pull over when they hear a siren?'' he demanded.

The uncoordinated radio procedures of police agencies in Los Angeles and Orange counties as two forms of chatter clogging the interagency pursuit channel didn't help much either. Most Orange County departments used the military phonetic, while those in L.A. were happy with a shorter, civilian dialect.

A private tour bus pulled out in front of them from the Man Wah supermarket complex. The Malibu's left-side tires screamed in protest when Abel swerved hard to the right.

As soon as they were roaring along a straightaway again, Abel—steering with one elbow to leave his hands free—reached inside his bomber jacket and drew out a Colt .45. He flipped its left-side safety down with his thumb, then pulled back on the slide slightly, checking to ensure a hollowpoint was seated in the chamber where it was supposed to be.

Unlike most more cautious .45 owners, the cop had been carrying his service pistol ''cocked and locked'' since his rookie days on the streets of Saigon. To Lucas Abel, a .45 with no ''live round'' in the chamber created enough of a delay during gunplay for your opponent to cancel your ticket.

''What the hell's he *doing*?'' The smile had faded from Glenn Thornton's face. Their Porsche driver was ramming slower-moving cars now. Abel's forearms tensed as he prepared for any sudden evasive maneuvers—he anticipated the driver would swerve down one of the numerous side streets at any instant. But the Porsche continued westbound along the Bolsa Strip, gaining speed.

''Jesus!'' Thornton ducked as the Porsche's black-tint rear window suddenly exploded, leaving jagged shards along the frame.

Their patrol car was showered with fragments of glass as the other driver fired two more rounds back over a shoulder. He was holding a long-barreled revolver upside down. Puffs of gray gunsmoke billowed from the additional craters opening up in what remained of the safety glass.

All three rounds missed their Malibu, and Glenn Thornton's eager smile returned. "Well, All RIGHT!" he yelled. "It's party time!" And before Luke Abel could reply, his partner was leaning out the passenger's-side window, preparing to rapid-fire back at the Porsche with his Sig/Sauer P226. But they were approaching a residential area. He would have to wait for the right chance.

Trigger-happy sergeants did not keep their stripes long.

Abel's adrenaline went into overdrive. He could taste the gunsmoke in the air—it was already leaving a licorice-like lining along the inside of his throat, as if he'd just spent the entire afternoon out qualifying on the pistol range.

Rain clouds had converged over the Bolsa Strip now. They seemed to press down on Abel like the monsoon blankets that haunted Gia Dinh Province.

A Cal-Edison gas truck swerved out of his way at the last moment—losing two hubcaps as it struck the raised concrete curb. A slender woman in a gossamer-thin *ao dai* had to jump back out of the vehicle's path.

Thornton pulled back on the Parabellum's slide slightly to ensure a bullet was ready and waiting in the chamber.

Steam was beginning to pour from under the Porsche's engine compartment, but the vehicle wasn't losing any speed. A chorus of Yelp and Hi-lo sirens erupted behind them, and Thornton turned to find that four or five more sheriff's units and a California Highway Patrolman had joined the chase.

"He's gonna run that black bitch right into the ground!" Abel switched the siren toggle from Wail to Yelp as they approached heavy traffic again.

Thornton pulled a white spotlight from the Malibu's floorboards and laid it across the dashboard while Abel flipped the headlights to bright—they needed to give out all the warning possible. Unmarked units had their pros and cons. High-Speed chases were at the bottom of the list of don'ts, but nabbing a seven-ups suspect—felonies punishable by hard time in the slammer—was worth the risk in Abel's book of laws.

"Son of a bitch!" Thornton dropped low in his seat. The Porsche driver was firing back at them again—four shots from what appeared to be a blue-steel Colt Python .357 magnum boasting a six-inch barrel. The bullets missed their car but, in his rearview mirror, Abel saw the sheriff's unit closest to his back bumper brake hard just as its windshield exploded.

"Bad Boy scored a hit on the deputies!" Abel yelled.

Thornton turned just in time to see the sheriff's unit swerve to the right, its front end dipping sharply—as if the driver had stomped both feet down on the brake pedal. There followed a noisy, sideways skid of several dozen yards before the vehicle smashed broadside into an illegally parked Volvo stationwagon.

"Jesus!" Thornton was seated upright again as he watched the sheriff's unit fly across the Volvo, spiraling over and over like a giant black-and-white football.

"Get on the horn and call it in!" Abel motioned toward the microphone clipped to the dashboard. "Have Dispatch start an ambulance."

"We going to pull over and check on him, Gus?" Thornton fixed a semi-accusing glance on his partner.

Luke did not hesitate as he continued the pursuit, but his mind was flashing back to the first academy he ever attended—the Army Military Police School in Fort Gordon, Georgia, over twenty years earlier. He could still see the drill sergeant's face reciting the first rule in pursuit: Never stop to check on a fellow MP! Other men will arrive to check on him. YOU continue the chase! At all costs!

Abel glanced in his rearview mirror to find that one of the sheriff's units had skidded to the side of the road to assist his fallen brother. He let out an audible sigh, then told Thornton, "Disregard, my last."

"Already done!"

Up ahead, the dips at every intersection were filled with runoff water from the many storefronts, and he watched small geysers shoot up on either side of the Porsche as it plowed through the cement hollows in excess of eighty miles an hour. A lone sheriff's-department car appeared two blocks down the road, sliding onto Bolsa from a side street—his emergency overheads flashing brightly. "No!" Thornton muttered out loud—it was obvious the deputy was going to attempt to cut the Porsche off.

"Jesus!" Abel leaned hard into the steering wheel, jerking it to the right as the sheriff's car hydroplaned through the dip up ahead and suddenly swerved toward them. The black-and-white sideswiped the Malibu going in opposite directions, but neither driver spun out.

"That was about as close as it gets, Gus!" Thornton let out a loud sigh.

"I don't get paid enough for this shit," Abel glanced in his rearview mirror in time to see the sheriff's unit overcorrect, fishtail through another water-filled dip, spin around in a complete one-eighty, then bring up the pursuit's tail behind the other units.

"M.A.G.-thirteen . . ." a male dispatcher's husky, businesslike voice blared up at them from the torn and shredded floor speaker.

Thornton keyed the transmitter with his knee and yelled down a preoccupied but to-the-point reply into the microphone without removing it from its dashboard clip. "Westbound Bolsa approaching Magnolia!"

"Be advised, no wants or warrants on your plate."

Thornton didn't waste time with a verbal reply, but merely nudged the mike key a couple times with his knee again in acknowledgment. "Well, at least the dumbfuck's drivin' his own crate." Glen winked over at his partner. "MERC-U!" he translated the personalized tag. "Sounds like MERC material to me, Luke. You'd think they'd use a stolen car for their games of death. Felony stupid, man."

"Probably hasn't made the hot sheets yet," Abel countered with a routine caution gleaned from years of experience. He glanced in his rearview mirror. There were no longer any sheriff's units assisting him. "What the fuck?"

Instead, a semi-truck loaded-down with beer had pulled across the roadway from a shopping center parking lot at the northeast corner of Bolsa and Magnolia.

The sound of several sets of skidding tires reached his ears, then a triple-thump series of grinding, metal-against-metal impacts and the wind-down of four or five electronic sirens.

"Switch that sucker to the white channel, Glenn!" Abel's fist motioned down in the direction of the radio console's green Power light.

"We're too close to Santa Ana," Thornton argued but reached toward the channel selector anyway. "It'll bleed onto their net!"

"Then make it the blue channel, damn it!" Abel snapped. "Just see if you can get us some backup!"

"M.A.G.-thirteen to any M.A.G. units in the area, Bolsa and the Four-oh-five Freeway." Thornton nodded as he removed the mike from its dashboard clip and depressed the transmit lever.

Abel watched the green bulb dim as a brighter Transmit light glowed red. "Negative!" he told Thornton, temples throbbing as they leaned into another hard swerve through slower-moving vehicles. "I want *marked* units in on this before we stack it up against some vanload of senior citizens from San Clemente. No M.A.G. slicks!"

"M.A.G.-thirteen, this is Forty-seven-two-seventy and Two-seventy-two. . . ." another voice cut in on the net before Thornton could request cover cars. ". . . Be advised we're setting up at the San Diego freeway, northbound on-ramps. Two CHP units are waiting on the south side in case your subject rabbits the wrong way down the Four-oh-five. . . ."

"Westminster PD?" Abel glanced over at Thornton as he let up slightly on the gas pedal for the first time in a dozen blocks.

"Roger *that*!"

Abel gave the straining motor's oil a couple seconds to recirculate, then stomped down on the pedal again.

The Malibu kicked into overdrive and began gaining on the Porsche now.

"She's smoking bad, Gus!" Thornton observed, a rigid forefinger pointed at the Porsche's spinning rear tires. Plumes of black debris billowed from the coupé's undercarriage as they approached a gently sloping hillside composed of vacant lots and abandoned buildings.

"Pop a half dozen or so hollowpoints up 'er ass!" A sly grin appeared on Abel's face for the first time. "Aim for the blacktop behind the rear bumper. Ricochet some lead into the tires or up under the chasis!"

"You got it!" Thornton leaned out the window, fired nearly a dozen shots of Parabellum punch after the Porsche, then abruptly dropped back into the Malibu, covering his head.

The Porsche was burning rubber on hot blacktop as it lurched into a front-end dragging skid, and in the blink of an eye, the fifty or so feet separating their two vehicles shrank to five.

Abel was practically standing on the Malibu's power brakes, attempting to avoid a rear-end collision, and, just when it appeared they would collide anyway, the Porsche veered suddenly to the right, left-side tires squealing like a banshee as it roared off down a side street.

"Son of a bitch!" Thornton yelled, lowering his pistol as they entered a residential neighborhood.

Abel gritted his teeth, leaned hard into the steering wheel, and followed through with a fishtailing show of spinning tires and flying gravel.

"Uh-ohhhh." Thornton frowned in anticipation as two red lights lit up on the Malibu's dashboard panel: Temperature and Oil.

"No sweat." Abel was the one grinning again now. "The old boy always overheats when I run 'im hard. Tryin' to tell me he wants to stall out, but he eats this shit up with a passion!"

"Ch-ch-checked the—" Thornton's palms were braced against the dashboard now. His eyes were no longer bulging, as they raced to keep up with the accelerating

Porsche, but his knuckles remained bone white. "Ch-checked the oil recently, Lucas?"

"Bi-weekly, bud. Lucky Lucas leaves nothing to chance. . . ."

"Abel's Law Number Forty-one: Real Cop don't hit the street without first sweet talkin' his squad car from stem to stern. . . ." Thornton nudged his partner with an elbow as they rounded a curve and proceeded down another narrow street—this one filled with juveniles on skateboards.

"Your present Ten-twenty, M.A.G.-thirteen?" The dispatcher interrupted their shop talk, requesting a location. "Come on, Lieutenant Abel . . . talk it up. . . ."

"Think it's about time we called in our last-known-direction-of-travel?" Abel smiled over at the detective sergeant seated beside him.

"Trouble is, I don't even know where the hell we *are!*" Thornton produced an expression that seemed sufficiently bewildered, but Abel knew the deadpan mask was feigned.

"Call it in, Sergeant!"

Thornton glanced out at a pole rising up from a corner of the intersection they were passing through. "The goddamned gang bangers are stealin' *street signs* again, Gus!"

Abel nodded. It was not uncommon for the local punks to make off with their favorite signs now and then—especially along turf borders. City maintenance crews usually had them replaced soon enough. "I don' wanna hear excuses—you should have every back alley and side street in this county memorized by now, goon," he finally taunted his partner.

"*Shee*-it, *partner*." Thornton kept his eyes on the speeding Porsche. "Did you see that flash of red!" he pointed at a blur of movement on the passenger side of the Porsche.

Before they could get a closer look, a station wagon backing out of a driveway up ahead was nearly broadsided by their Porsche driver. Abel imitated his defensive driving style, and missed the station wagon's rear bumper by inches as the housewife inside stomped on her brakes just in time.

Abel scooped up the microphone with his gun hand while maintaining control over the shaking steering wheel with just his left. "M.A.G.-thirteen is now headed northbound on Van Buren from Bolsa, Dispatch . . . into Midway City. . . ."

Abel's nostrils dilated slightly as the odor of overheating brakes reached him. The brake pedal was going nearly to the floorboards everytime he used it now, but he couldn't remember a chase in which this didn't eventually happen. In his book, it was just a minor inconvenience.

"We got the bastard!" Glenn slammed a meaty fist into the palm of his hand as the black 911 skidded onto the dead-end street.

Calling in the street name to Dispatch as the Porsche driver executed a sharp U-turn directly in front of them, Abel then rammed his heel down onto the brake pedal again and jerked the steering wheel hard to the left—this time hoping to bring the Malibu around in a sideways skid to the right, blocking the Porsche's exit, but the driver swerved and blazed past Thornton's window using the wrong side of the road for an exit.

"You lowlife *scumbag*!" Gritting his teeth, Thornton brought the 9mm automatic's front sights down to bear on their suspect driver as the dazed-looking man flew past.

But suddenly he resisted pulling the trigger.

A small child was standing on a stoop directly behind where the Porsche had been. He was waving a squirt gun at Glenn as his mother tried to drag him into their house. Soon, they were both obscured by the rolling clouds of smoke and steam left by the bullet-riddled Cabriolet.

In seconds, Abel had the Malibu riding the Porsche's rear bumper again.

"We've gotta stop this bum!" Thornton yelled as the Porsche driver glanced back over a shoulder, made several moves as if preparing to fire back at them again, then narrowly missed running down two young Vietnamese schoolboys on bicycles.

"Right." He jockeyed for position alongside the Porsche's right-rear quarter panel. They were fast approaching the 405 Freeway again, at eighty-plus miles per hour.

"Hate to see such a beautiful machine bite the dust." Thornton did not sound sincere. The edges of his eyes were laced with envy now: Luke Abel's side of the patrol car would pass nearest the suspect vehicle when M.A.G.-thirteen made its move.

As the Porsche driver glanced back frantically over first his left, then right shoulder, Abel gunned the Malibu, bringing it up alongside the 911 turbo for the first time. A blatant violation of pursuit policy, granted, but rules and regulations were for rooks.

Steering with his right hand, he locked his left arm straight out. The .45 automatic's blue-steel barrel scraped against the Porsche's passenger-side window, and the auto thief's eyes bulged forth like boiled eggs as the two cars raced down along the Bolsa Strip. It was Abel's first good look at the driver: a Caucasian male in his late twenties, with circles under his eyes wearing a multicolored Whitesnake T-shirt. The kid's hair was close cropped, shaved down closer than a crew cut.

Bouncing out-of-sight on the passenger's side was a redheaded female, trying to hang on for the wild, bumpy ride.

Without explanation, Abel's gun hand dropped slightly, and, with the .45 barrel now pointing at the Porsche's right front wheel well, he commenced firing off round after round on semiautomatic.

"Jesus, Gus!" Thornton yelled as six hollowpoints ricocheted off the wheel rim and, an instant later, the Malibu struck a pothole, jarring both detectives and nearly knocking the Colt from Abel's fingers.

Then he saw the reason for his partner's change of tactics: On the north side of the street, at Chestnut, several schoolchildren were waiting at the light for a Walk signal.

≡ CHAPTER 12

SPARKS AND SHATTERED glass exploded from the Porsche's passenger-side window as the driver fired off a cylinderful of hotloads at the two detectives. Abel braked just in time, and the Malibu's front end dropped harshly as its front wheels froze into a skid and the school children up ahead scattered for cover.

"Bastard must have some speed-loaders lyin' in his lap, Gus!" Thornton was climbing out his window again, preparing to fire only as a last resort, but one of the suspect's six bullets had scored a hit on the Malibu's left front tire. They were soon riding on a rim, their speed half what it had been only five seconds before. Sparks began flying out from the wheel well like a giant, golden funnel.

"Screw it." Abel slammed a fist down on the steering wheel as he guided his unit over to the side of the road. "We got the hairball's license plate, and if it's a steal, the lab can lift some latents—his paws were all over that dashboard. And we can ID the puke."

"Yeah, fugitive detail can pick him up later. I'm getting too old for this crap. . . ."

The Malibu came to an unceremonious halt beside a garbage truck, its left-front quarter panel listing like a troubled ship at sea.

"Hey, Luke! Check it out!"

Straight ahead, about two blocks up the street, the Porsche was coasting to a stop. "Let's go!" Abel was already out of their Malibu and ejecting his .45's spent clip. From beneath his bomber jacket he pulled a spare ammo magazine and slammed it into the pistol's hollow handle.

The Porsche driver flew from his vehicle like a terrified jackrabbit, sprinting down Bolsa in an almost comical zigzag pattern. "The goofy fuck must think we're gonna waste him." Abel's chest was already heaving as they frantically gave chase, fists pawing at the muggy air.

"I *am*!" Thornton suddenly skidded to a halt. His pistol was up. His broad torso was down in a combat crouch: both arms rigid, elbows locked tight, right hand gently squeezing the 9mm's trigger, left hand motionless and palm up—the automatic's butt cupped in it. But the skinhead jumped a barbed wire fence and disappeared into a sprawling apartment complex. The M.A.G. sergeant watched helplessly as the perp raced over a low-rider Monte Carlo, into a maze of shoulder-high hedges.

"Fucking track star or something," Abel muttered, slowing to a pained walk. Behind them, a blue '89 Plymouth skidded sideways around a corner, tiny red strobe flashing on the dashboard.

Detective Zamora.

Ramming the gas pedal to the floor, she raced past them, crashed through the hedges, and nearly ran the suspect down. Chest heaving, he backed against the Monte Carlo, hands in the air, blood streaming down his face as the sheriff's units began roaring up to the scene, bringing with them a chorus of ear-splitting audio sensations to add to the adrenaline rush—several of the deputies left their sirens yelping as they jumped from their cars.

"There's someone in the Porsche!" an officer who hadn't even bothered to get out of his patrol unit warned the others.

Abel and Thornton both glanced over at the bullet-riddled Cabriolet. In the backseat, a dazed woman in her late teens or early twenties was rising up slowly from the floorboards. Her red hair was dyed purple along the edges where it flared straight out, stiff and brittle. Her face was caked with blood.

"Knew I should have made a career out of the military," Lt. Lucas Abel muttered.

"Where do you want us to take it?"

The four of them turned to find a City Yard tow-truck driver coasting to a stop. Abel's two-door Malibu was up on the hook—both front tires shredded beyond repair.

"Be gentle, Eugene," he told the tall, lanky, and bespectacled driver. "Replace the front tires, the brakes, and get it running, then park it outside the Bolsa substation, will ya? And leave the bullet holes the way they are."

"No sweat, Lieutenant." The city mechanic saluted them all with a frayed cigar butt. "Souvenirs?"

"Sort of."

"Right. Except for the bullet holes, I'll have 'er sittin' pretty and polished, like a virgin waitin' for her wedding night, before you and Sergeant Thornton even finish your reports. . . ."

"Thanks." Abel's eyes had shifted to an officer standing between the handcuffed female and the bullet-riddled Porsche. He was holding up several rifled purses, taken from the Cabriolet's backseat.

"Keep the prisoners separated," Abel directed, as Zamora attempted to hustle her prisoner over to the Plymouth before the angry deputies—their adrenaline still racing with the chase—could "subdue" the kid with their fists.

Zamora glanced back at the lieutenant. "I'll radio for a paramedic team to meet us at the substation. His wounds are minor."

"Don't forget we want to talk with this scumbucket after you book him." Thornton leaned into the back window for a better look at the prisoner.

The prisoner was now screaming incoherently and bashing his face against the door frame.

Zamora reached in and shook a no-nonsense forefinger at him. "Behave, dick-breath, or I'll snip your love muscle in two—at the *root*."

"I love it when she talks dirty to her perps," Thornton told Abel.

"Well, if it ain't lover boy." Abel rocked back on his heels as another Plymouth coasted up to the scene. " 'Bout time you rejoined the action."

Vinnie Verdugo. Detective Sergeant, assigned to M.A.G. since its inception. As cynical and pessimistic as they come. Twenty years on the street, the last five with the Asian gang task force. An East Coast transplant with a heavy Brooklyn accent, Verdugo was forty-one, blond, sported a thin but agile, wiry frame and a mean reputation among the back-alley denizens as a liberal distributor of urban renewal with his fists.

"Yeah, so screw you, Luke," he muttered with an icy grin. You could tell he hated the job but had nothing better than nightsticks and sap gloves to fall back on.

"How 'bout a lift back to the substation?" Thornton asked.

Verdugo stared at the sleazy-looking redhead leaning against the Porsche. "Is she gonna be in my car?"

" 'Fraid so."

"You got a deal." Verdugo's smile slowly grew.

Bloody spittle flying from the prisoner's lips splashed against the holding-cell wall. The crimson spray reminded Lucas Abel of the bloody backroom interrogations in Old Saigon. He closed his eyes slowly and lowered his head in resignation.

His ears accepted, sorted out, categorized the sounds closing in on him: a crackle of static-laced transmissions from someone's police radio, iron-bar doors slamming shut in the distance, the prisoner groaning softly a few feet away—on the other side of the angry policewoman . . . groaning between the defiant snickers. Groaning and cursing.

"You're still a goddamn dyke," the prisoner mumbled, his head lowered also, blood dripping from his swollen nose. Swastikas adorned the punker's wrists and forearms. Across his biceps the words WHITE PRIDE were emblazoned—in dull red, as opposed to the more traditional black and blue.

The man was in his late twenties, Abel decided. Medium height, slightly underweight but the muscles along his arms and neck tightly wound—dark flesh, firm and hard. Abel had seen the look before: ex-con to the core.

Over the multicolored T-shirt, he wore a tattered jean jacket with the arms cut off and a rebel flag sewn onto the back. On his feet, army jump boots, highly polished, with the jeans 'bloused,' or tucked inside. Scars crisscrossed both wrists.

". . . Nothing but a goddamned, fucking bull dyke."

"Put a cork in it, hairball." Rachel Zamora wiped smeared steaks of cherry-bright red from the back of her hand.

Rubbing his temples gently, Abel concentrated on the police scanner located somewhere back in the detectives' cubicles: this other female's voice more soothing, almost sensuous as it dispatched units to a dead-body call down on the Bolsa Strip. He tried to ignore the policewoman standing a few feet away—her back to him and his partner. Her vicious response to the arrestee's verbal taunts had not startled Abel. He just did not care anymore.

"You want a piece of this fucker, Lieutenant?"

Abel glanced over at Zamora. His eyes dropped the length of her finely sculptured figure then rose again, resting briefly on her haunches as he ran the words through his head a second time, digesting them, groping for a response while he climbed out from the dark abyss of memories. Over three years now in Orange County and he still found it difficult to shake the short, silent flashbacks that continued to haunt him.

"Well, Lieutenant Abel?" The policewoman's words probed the fog again, summoning him home from that devil's slayground deep in his mind. "You can use my sap if you want."

"Naw, Rach' . . ." Thornton answered for his partner. "We only beat our meat, but thanks for thinking of us."

Detective Zamora cast them both a playful grin over her shoulder. "Yeah, right," she said, chin lifting slightly in the direction of her arrestee's accomplice—the seventeen-year-old Valley Girl with red-and-purple spiked hair.

"Glenn tells me you and the dicks in Robbery think we got the right cats here on those strong-arms," Abel said.

"Samo-samo, Lou." Zamora nodded without making eye contact. "Knocked a poor old Viet mama-san off her feet over on Bolsa. Just before your chase. She's the one sitting out in the lobby. ID'd this puke's ass as we were transferring him to the holding cell."

"It won't fucking hold up in court!" the man shouted. "The old bag opened her mouth before you could even pop a photo lineup on her, man! I'm *outta here* in the time it takes you to fart Dixie."

"Bookoo brave." Thornton smacked a meaty fist into the palm of one hand. The impact made a crack not unlike a balloon bursting. Abel said nothing as his partner continued the sarcastic taunt. "Robbin' old ladies of their pocketbooks. Maybe you should pick on someone your age, hero. . . ."

"I busted some caps in your direction, didn't I pig?" the prisoner sneered.

"Yeah, and *that* oughta keep you behind bars for a while, if nothing else does."

"And don't forget the forty or fifty *stop-signs* he violated." Abel's chuckle was dry and lifeless.

"No-'count lowlife," Thornton growled.

Lt. Luke Abel grinned slightly. Then his eyes shifted to the arrest report.

BAXTER, HAROLD ALEXANDER. Aliases: "Stitch" and "Spitfire." D.O.B.: 13 October 1959 Age: 29. Last Known Address: North Hollywood.

"What brings you down out of the valley, Stitch?" Abel spoke in a somber tone. He did not look up from the paperwork but shifted his concentration to a glossy gray computer printout of CR hardcopy—Baxter's criminal record, his rap sheet.

"Still a free country, ain't it?"

"For honest folks," Thornton answered. He turned to Lieutenant Abel. "What'd you call him, Gus?"

"Says here his boyfriends call him 'Stitch,' " Abel muttered.

Abel's unblinking eyes scanned the hardcopy: nine years total at various California penal institutions since age eighteen, including Chino and San Quentin. Mostly assault and narcotics busts.

"Stitch?" Thornton moved toe to toe with the prisoner, and Baxter, still sitting on the iron bench, slowly looked up. "You a *seamstress*, or something, girl?"

The young woman standing in the corner spoke for the first time. "He *stitched* a cop ten years ago, asshole." Spittle flew from her drawn-back lips, and Abel's gaze returned to the droplets of blood oozing down the wall. "From throat to cock! When he was only eighteen!"

"Shut up, Queenie," Stitch yelled.

"Twenty bullets, man!" the woman thrust her chin out at Zamora. "A whole clip from an *M-16*, on *rock and roll*, baby . . . can ya dig it? Just like *Rambo*!"

Thornton's expression remained skeptical as he stared down at Baxter. "Sounds like a *career* criminal to me," he decided. "What you doin' out on the streets, sonny-boy?"

"Cram it, *dick*head!" Baxter's own chin rose defiantly as he started to get up, but Thornton's palms fell sharply onto both shoulders, forcing the prisoner back down onto the iron bench. "You ain't got jackshit on me. We both know that old chink bitch over on Brookhurst won't testify."

"Oh?" Rachel Zamora stopped filling out the fingerprint cards and turned to face Baxter. She leaned on one elbow against the ink shelf, unimpressed.

"Yeah." Baxter was suddenly getting his confidence

back. "So you might as well cut me loose, *puta*." His accent became Mexican, his tone insulting.

"Well, Strong-arm ain't zilch compared to Assault on a Cop." Fire simmering in her eyes, Zamora started to reply with another swinging backhand when a harsh buzzing from the intercom interrupted her. The booking room fell into a tense silence.

Turning slowly to face the intercom, Zamora slammed the palm of her hand against the transmit button. "What!?" she demanded, taking her anger out on the dispatcher.

"A carload of spoiled-brat skinheads are here to bail out their buddy, Rach'," an unoffended female voice on the other end replied.

Zamora's eyes met Abel's, and he stepped to the intercom. "Tell 'em he's being held for Two-eleven and Attempt-one-eighty-seven on a police officer, among other things," he said.

"I don't think he's getting out *this* week," Thornton added. "And I doubt even his Nazi pals can raise *that* kind o' bail on such short notice."

"Okay, Lieutenant." The dispatcher obviously recognized Abel's voice, and lines of suspicion twisted the edges of Baxter's eyes.

"There oughta be *no* bail on Chase-and-Shoot-Out cases," Zamora muttered as she busily scribbled across an evidence card.

"Where'd you get the Porsche, Stitch?" Abel asked. "Wasn't any registration in the vehicle, and somehow I get the feeling you're not a Cabriolet kinda guy. . . ."

"Oh," Zamora held up a slip of computer hardcopy. "Just got this back from Dispatch. The Porsche was stolen last night. From some of our less upstanding rich brats from Westminster. Probably the Mercs."

"White gangs stealing each others' wheels?" Thornton cast his partner a questioning look.

"You finished bookin' this creep, Rachel?" Abel pulled his jacket back, revealing his 1970-model Colt .45 caliber automatic pistol in a pancake holster. Handcuffs and a clip holder were also attached to his belt—all on the right side. The weapon was blue steel, the holster black leather. Two seven-round ammo magazines rested upside down in the clip holder.

"Sure, Luke, but . . ."

"Me and Glenn'll cart him over to the Monkey House for a session of truth-or-consequences while you finish your paperwork. I'll take full responsibility."

He had already jerked Baxter to his feet, removed Zamora's handcuffs, returned them to her, pulled his own set from their leather keeper resting behind the .45 gun butt, and snapped the "steel bracelets" across his prisoner's wrists without bothering to double lock them.

The intercom was suddenly buzzing again. "Yeah!" Zamora demanded impatiently.

"Now the lobby's full of county officers, Detective," the dispatcher advised. "They say they want a piece o' your prisoner back there. They wanna talk to somebody involved in the chase, and they wanna talk *now*. I think they're gonna go to town on the skinheads up here in another couple minutes if someone doesn't show. The exchange of insults is getting pretty heavy duty."

"Thanks. Stall 'em as long as you can."

"We can't release this skinhead to the deputies, Luke." Thornton appeared genuinely worried. "If we do, we'll never see him again until the judge hangs his no-account ass."

"Well, County *did* initiate the chase." Abel rubbed at the edge of his chin.

"From a strong-arm that occurred in the city," Thornton pointed out. "Which they didn't tell us about," he added hastily. "Which don't mean diddley-squat."

"Since they've got county-wide jurisdiction." The lieutenant nodded. "But you're right. Let's *di-di-mau* and *now*!"

"What about her?" Zamora motioned toward Baxter's female accomplice. Queenie backed farther into the corner as everyone's attention focused in her direction. "Strong-arm?"

"Accessory. She was in the car. She shares the penalty. Just keep her in the detention cell 'til you hear back from me," Abel decided. "We wanna see if Stitch here fits into our recent rash of agg-robberies down on Bolsa."

"You got it, Lou." Zamora clamped a hand down on Queenie's arm and guided her toward the holding cells.

"Hey, don't I get my *mug* shot taken?" the young woman protested. Abel and Thornton exchanged amused glances: She sounded seriously disappointed.

"After the gentlemen leave," Zamora replied.

"You pigs might as well ice me now," Baxter urged, " 'Cause when old Stitch gets out of the slammer, he's gonna come look you up."

"Can the crap and sell it to someone who gives a shit." Abel shoved Baxter gently through the shafts of harsh sunlight lancing down through the doorway from outside. "It's that brown seventy-four Malibu parked under the cherry tree, asshole. Get in."

A warm tingle flowed through the lieutenant's gut: Eugene did good, swift work. Two new, black radials gleamed under the late-afternoon sun, and he could spot only a few dents along the front end. In hot-pink crayon, the mechanic had written the word OUCH! over the string of bullet holes, but Thornton was already busy wiping it off with his elbow. Much of the side swipe damage was already sanded down.

Baxter stared at the jagged bullet holes, then his eyes fell to the old-style California license plates—gold letters glowing faintly on a blue background—and smirked contemptuously. *"Dinky-dau?"* he asked. "What the hell does *dinky-dau* mean?"

"It's Viet for *crazy*," Thornton, standing directly behind Stitch, whispered menacingly into the prisoner's right ear. *"Madman*-homicidal type o' crazy, sleazebag!" Baxter was stalling again, and Thornton gently planted the sole of one boot against the prisoner's butt and pushed, guiding him toward the unmarked investigator's car.

≡ CHAPTER 13

"YOU'RE CUTE, STITCH." Thornton grinned over his shoulder as they rode on Bolsa. "The queers at county lockup are gonna *lovvvvve* you."

Baxter stared out at the sea haze blanketing this stretch of Orange County, six miles from the Pacific Ocean. "No big thing," he muttered, unimpressed. "I been there before. Nobody messes with the Stitch. I got a rep, motherfucker—a *mean* rep." His eyes dropped to the shop signs obscuring each block-long series of storefronts. They were all in Vietnamese. "My lawyer was on the team that kept Charlie Manson from fryin'. He'll make pork chops outta you pigs."

"We've got some cops there that would like to . . . get your 'input' on the recent rash of strong-arms that's been plaguing Chinatown and Little Saigon," Abel said, ignoring the insults.

"Eat shit and die," Stitch said simply. When neither detective replied to the taunt, he glanced over at the driver, who seemed mesmerized by the cultural scenery flashing by outside.

Baxter stared hard at Luke Abel as the lieutenant locked eyes with a slender Vietnamese woman strolling down the sidewalk on the south side of the busy boulevard. She appeared as fragile as a porcelain statuette, yet confident as any businesswoman in Southern California—fearless despite the new country, the overpowering challenge—her head held high.

"Light's green, Luke," Thornton called from the backseat.

Abel checked his rearview mirror. A line of six or seven cars sat patiently behind his, waiting in silence.

Down the block, on the other side of Magnolia to the west, or east of Brookhurst, horns would have been blaring by now, but here in the heart of Little Saigon, no one wanted trouble. Especially the Asians. Not from a car filled with white men.

"Fucking gooks," Baxter hissed. "They killed my big brother, you know. The Imperial City of Hue. Tet, 1968. He was a Marine—gung-ho to the max. He had a future, but some zipper-head wearing a loincloth and tire-tread sandals blew him away. Motherfuckers. That's why we're here, man. . . ."

"That's why *who's* here?" Thornton's eyes narrowed.

"To represent the white race, brother. To take Orange County back from the yellow man!" Baxter shifted a shoulder as if trying to raise one of his handcuffed fists in a clenched salute. He began singing an off-key and out-of-tune version of "Born In The U.S.A."

Abel's eyes dueled briefly with the set staring back at him in the rearview mirror, but he said nothing immediately.

"The spics already got the San Fernando Valley nailed down, man!" Baxter continued. "And the niggers control most of L.A.—shit, they got 'em a jigaboo up there for mayor, don't they? Dude's got bacon in his blood."

"I'd shut your face, punk," Thornton said slowly, the anger evident in his tone, but Stitch Baxter didn't seem to notice.

"Orange County's all that's left for the white man," he retorted. "And now we want it back."

"You're dreamin'," Abel pulled back out into traffic.

"Maybe not."

"What *really* brings you down out of the valley and

into Little Saigon, anyway, asshole?'' Thornton lit a cigarette and slipped it between Baxter's lips.

Their prisoner inhaled deeply a few times and then, the Winston rolling to one corner of his mouth, eyed the M.A.G. sergeant suspiciously. Shrugging semi-gratefully for the smoke, Stitch Baxter decided to brag a little bit about his gang.

"We're formin' an Orange County chapter," he told them, "so 'the last gringo to *vamoos* out of Garden Grove won't have to worry 'bout takin' Old Glory with him,' you know?''

"And what's the name of your . . . 'club'?'' Abel countered for more information.

"The Rebs.'' Baxter managed to flex a bicep despite the handcuffs, and for the first time Abel noticed the Confederate flag tattooed to his arm.

"The *Ribs*?'' Thornton asked.

"*Rebs!*'' Stitch Baxter cringed. "Like *Johnny* Reb, you know?''

"We know.'' Abel's frown grew deeper. "And I want to tell you something, General Lee. We don't want any racial strife escalating down here in Little Saigon. Do you and I understand each other?''

"Ribs,'' Thornton whispered. "I like mine medium rare.'' He peered out at the traffic slowing to a crawl directly ahead of them. Vietnamese New Wave music blared from the open windows of one car.

"I've never heard of the 'Rebs,' '' Abel glanced over at Baxter.

"That's 'cause we keep a real low profile. We—''

"Well, we're just warning you.'' Thornton nodded slowly. "We've got enough problems brewing down here in Orange County without *you* punks addin' gas to the fire, *savvy*?''

"The annual Tet Chinese-Vietnamese New Year Festival is gearing up for this weekend, Baxter.'' Abel's tone turned somewhat cordial. "Your crowd's just looking for trouble down here.''

"It's still a free country, man. Ain't it?'' Baxter cut in. "Ain't that what my brother fucking *died* for, man?''

Abel seemed to ignore the ex-con as he continued. "Consider this a warning, kid . . . if your boys are in on any shit that hits the fan down on the Bolsa Strip this weekend, me and M.A.G. are gonna be on your case like white on rice!"

He turned to face the prisoner, and both men locked eyes as the Malibu cruised to a stop below a red signal light. "Well, that's mighty white of you, man. Mighty white, indeed! But maybe . . ." Baxter hesitated. "Just maybe I could talk to my boys . . . *if* you dudes cut the Stitch some slack."

"Slack?" Thornton frowned with obvious skepticism.

"Ease the charges, man. Let me make bond. Today."

"After we make a deal," Abel said, and Thornton's head whipped around as he looked at his partner. "Me and Glenn here just might consider droppin' the Attempt-Murder complaint if you help us out during the upcoming festival," the M.A.G. Lieutenant continued. "And tell us which one of your boys owns a silver Rolls."

"What about that deputy whose windshield I blew out?"

"Anything's possible. We'll have a little talk with him."

"And you'll cut me some slack . . . talk with the judge and—"

"*If* you order your Rebs to stay up in the Sci-Fi Valley and keep Little Saigon off the agenda until after Tet."

"No dice. I can't control 'em *all*, brother. We got some real radical dudes in our ranks. Like the guy who drives the silver Rolls Royce."

"Then we throw your no-account ass into the queer tank at county jail," Thornton threatened.

"I'm an ex-con, man. You can't scare me with that bullshit." But Stitch Baxter was not smiling.

"The bad asses in county just can't get enough of pretty white boys with *bookoo* tattoos." Reaching forward to massage Baxter's shaved head, Thornton went to work like a seasoned psy-ops agent writing propaganda leaflets in the Mekong Delta. "Especially the kind o' tattoos you're wearin' today, sport. Reminds 'em of their mamas.''

"I'm thinkin.' " Baxter slowly shook his head from side to side. "I'm fuckin' thinkin,' man. . . .''

"Don't strain anything.''

"And if I cooperate, you guys'll take me back to the PD and let me post bond?''

"You got it.'' Abel gritted his teeth. Making this deal actually hurt. "We'd appreciate your cooperation.'' Abel felt his stomach turn slightly at having to feign kindness to such a lowlife leach. "We want the Year of the Snake to arrive without . . . incident.''

"I'll try my best, man.'' Baxter suddenly sounded like a junior-high schooler seated in the principal's office during a verbal reprimand. "You know I'll have to be quiet, though. If any o' my brother Rebs figure out ol' Stitch is cooperatin' with the heat, they'll suffocate me with my own testicles.''

Abel flinched slightly. "Sounds like the games Charlie used to play back in The Nam,'' he said.

"So I heard.''

"Then it's settled.'' Abel pulled over to the side of the road and began executing a U-turn. "I'll hold off on the usual anti-gang pressure,'' he told Baxter. But his eyes were locked with Thornton's. "And you go back to your girlfriends and tell 'em to cool it until after Tet.''

"That's a a tall order to fill.'' Stitch's vocabulary had improved immensely. "But I think I can handle it.''

"Good.'' Abel nodded as he read his partner's mind and logged the silent protest. " 'Cause if you can't, the Rebs are history, and you're just another number at San Quentin.''

Abel stood between Stitch Baxter and Thornton as the Rebs gang leader emerged from police headquarters through a back door. "We're doin' this wrong, Gus.'' Thornton stood rigid in the middle of the sidewalk as Baxter's entourage escorted him toward the parking lot. "We can't just let the asshole walk so easy.''

"You know police work is getting more and more like

politics, bro'," Abel replied, draping his arm over his partner's shoulder. "You have to learn . . . the art of compromise. Baxter'll come through with info. Trust me."

Thornton's head slowly shifted as the gang members parted to walk around the two M.A.G. agents. His eyes came to rest on the lieutenant's. "I hope you're right, Luke."

"Compromise, Glenn." Abel started toward their re-paired Malibu. "You've gotta humor these gang bangers, make them think they're getting the better half of any deal."

"Yo, *Lieutenant*!" Stitch Baxter was calling to them from beside a silver Rolls Royce. Thornton ignored the Rebs leader, but Abel slowly turned toward the skinhead crowd and waited. He noticed the custom plate numbers.

"Someday you pigs ain't gonna have ol' Stitch to kick around anymore." His chin rose with his courage.

"Anything you say, kid."

"We Rebs is gonna catapult to the occasion and take over this town, man. We Rebs is gonna be *Big Time*!" Baxter had wrapped both arms around the shoulders of two of his buddies. "Soon, the white backlash is gonna vote ol' Stitch into the mayor's office . . . you wait and see. *Then* your fat asses are mine!"

Baxter was the last one into the Rolls and as Abel was formulating a reply, the gang leader winked at the M.A.G. lieutenant. Abel nodded, then turned his back. Maybe Baxter's split personality was all just part of the act. But somehow the wary investigator doubted it.

"Run a check with Dispatch on those tags." He handed a slip of notebook paper to his partner. "And request a listing from Motor Vehicles, too."

≡ CHAPTER 14

THE PAIN FELT good.

Water up to his waist, Luke Abel stared at the lagoon's edge, then out at the more distant sliver of ocean—its sparkling waves merging into a silver necklace of dancing pearls where the Pacific met the towering, castlelike clouds—clouds that reminded him of Xinh . . . clouds that stretched ten thousand miles back to the Far East. And Saigon, City of Sorrows.

Soon, they would be together again. . . . Sharing this white sand beach . . . He and Xinh.

He shifted about in the warm water, only to feel cool ceramic beneath his haunches now, and not sand at all. The self-induced fantasy was quickly fading as bolts of pain along his right arm—where Brass Balls had clipped him good with a karate chop at the Pho-75 nearly two days ago—replaced the heat lightning flashing on the tropical horizon.

But it was a pain he could handle—a pain that meant something. . . . It was a well-earned, almost precious pain. Not like the irritating, embarrassing pain brought on by sports accidents or even a clumsy act. These wounds had been inflicted by a felon.

He stared long and hard at the towering columns of cumulonimbus—*Dragon's breath* Xinh had always called the clouds, as they waded in the surf at Vung Tau, counting monsters on the horizon—but an incessant echo in the back of his head refused to go away and, slowly, the spell was broken . . . the vision began to fade away.

Lucas Abel sat in his bathtub, staring at a poster of some unnamed Tahitian atoll lost out in the middle of the vast Pacific.

The phone rang a second, and a third time, and still he refused to move.

Soon, he'd be a million miles away, where there were no phones. Tahiti, perhaps. Just he and Xinh. *Just the two of us on a deserted, white sand beach . . .*

"I know you're there, Gus. . . ." A husky voice followed the answering machine's message beep. His partner's. The slightest of pauses followed, then: "So pick up the goddamn phone. I know you're there. I just drove past and saw the Malibu under the carport."

A chorus of parrot squawks in the living room announced that Thornton's voice was recognized by more than just the undercover detective soaking beneath some serious bubbles. "Fuck it!" one of the talking birds called out enthusiastically. Dirty Harry launched into the torrent of expletives that Abel's partner had spent long hours teaching him.

". . . I'm gonna stay on the line until you pick it up. I know you've got this blasted machine set on *unlimited* message duration, you clown—so let's get with the program, *AND PICK UP THE FUCKING PHONE!*"

"Aw, Christ . . ." Abel muttered as he reached for a towel and Thornton began whistling his favorite cut from *The Good, The Bad and The Ugly* soundtrack so the machine wouldn't sense silence and terminate the connection.

"Fuck it!" Dirty Harry's excitement skyrocketed as Abel entered the hallway, dripping wet.

"Yeah, and you three juvenile delinquents better clean up your act!" the M.A.G. cop replied, refusing to make eye contact with the blue-and-white balls of fluff clinging upside down to the ceiling of their huge, chromed cage. Six beady little black eyes watched his every move in muted silence now as Abel picked up the phone. "Listen up, gutterbreath!" he greeted his longtime partner. "Xinh's due in this week from Bangkok, and my *bird*-brains over here don't possess a vocabulary any more extensive than 'fuck-it.' "

"Hey, hey, Luke Ol' Boy!" Thornton' smile carried over the phone lines. "Now *that's* class. But don't worry. I'll give Dirty Harry and his partners a crash course on feathered etiquette. How long do I have? When does Xinh get . . . uh, discharged from that Thai refugee camp?"

"They tell me Friday the third. Which means she'll be here Sunday morning. I'm keeping my fingers crossed, but—"

"I'm surprised you didn't take two weeks mental-health leave of absence and jet on over there to meet her at the 'prison gates,' " Thornton cut in.

"I tried. Sanders disapproved my paper work—said the upcoming Tet security precautions were too important to let me go right now."

"Uh, right. Typical Korean Fried Chicken attitude. But anyways—glad I got hold of you, chump!" There was no escaping it. His career. The job. His partner. The street. A twenty-four-hour cop he was not, but Little Saigon just would not let him alone. "The guys are getting together for a little choir practice over at the cabaret. They wanted me to drag your sorry ass over there."

Abel considered, then rubbed at his throbbing temples. "I think I'll pass, Glenn. I'm wiped."

"Tell me about it. But, hey—I seriously fucking suggest you take advantage of today's opportunities. Anh told me she's trying out floor-show dancers direct from Patpong Road, Bangkok. You know: topless-bottomless. Eventually. No telling when you'll be able to eyeball a shot o' fresh tit once Xinh gets here. Besides, we're on duty in a few hours, anyway."

"Well . . ."

"I'll pick you up in zero-five, chump. On the sidewalk in front of your carport. Be there."

Before Abel could protest further, the line went dead.

* * *

As they cruised slowly toward the Can Tho Cabaret, named for Anh's birthplace, a sleepy town of 50,000 on the Mekong Delta's Hau Giang River sixty miles southwest of Saigon, Abel scanned the faces of the women strolling in front of storefronts along Bolsa. Brave women, fearing little, even when alone, for this was America now—not Vietnam. The VC didn't rule the streets here. The cops did. That was one of the laws Abel brought to Little Saigon with him.

The M.A.G. lieutenant had been trying to put Xinh out of his mind until her arrival so that he could concentrate more on his work, but it was difficult when he saw her face in that of every passing Vietnamese woman . . . when so many things on the street reminded him of her: vendors selling coconut juice and cubes of steaming sugarcane as young women clad in form-hugging *ao dai* gowns made offerings of fruit and *joss* sticks at curbside shrines mounted in front of their struggling shops.

He saw something of Xinh in the darting eyes of every Saigon girl. Not the proud cheekbones, or the way they glanced with suspicion out of the corners of their eyes when a stranger approached—more that gleam in those eyes, that orderly, inner control despite the disorganized shuffle of events all around them . . . that swirl of danger-laced adventure and electricity common to all women of the Orient.

Abel had been trying to put Xinh out of his mind. The mental plan right now was to completely forget about her until the morning of her scheduled arrival. *Then* he could flip out with glee. *Then* he could act the nineteen-year-old, amazing her with five poker sessions a night. And we weren't talking cards.

None of the mind games worked, of course. It seemed he saw Xinh's face reflected in every mirror and store window by day, every dark room and drifting wall of mist by night.

Abel and Thornton found themselves stopped at a red light on the Bolsa Strip. Several cars ahead of them, a Rolls Royce was bouncing about on customized air shocks as its occupants argued loudly with several Vietnamese youths in a black Nissan Maxima.

"Don't tell me that's Stitch Baxter's car," Abel groaned.

"Okay, I won't tell you." Thornton shook his head from side to side slowly as he checked to make sure a live round was seated in the chamber of his service weapon.

"Hit the siren," Abel advised his partner after they had caught up with and pulled behind the Rolls Royce.

Baxter instructed his driver to pull over even before Abel had his red Kojak light up on the Malibu's roof.

"And to what do we owe this displeasure, Lieutenant?" Baxter hopped out of the car as Luke and his partner dismounted from their unit and started up toward the Rolls. Abel believed that Baxter wore the expression of one of his split personalities.

"Christ, I *told* you we were making a mistake with this punk." Bomber jacket pulled back and gun hand resting on the exposed gun butt of his holstered Parabellum, a disheartened Thornton stepped behind the Rolls's right rear fender as his partner slowly approached the driver's-side door.

Abel stared down at Queenie. "I thought you and your troupe was headed back up into the San Fernando Valley, Baxter."

"We is, *suh*! We truly is!" A hostile gleam twinkled slightly in the ex-con's eyes as Abel scanned his girlfriend's hemline. All evidence of their earlier agreement seemed to have fizzled.

"Via Bolsa?" Thornton sounded highly skeptical.

"We wanna take the scenic route north." Queenie batted her long eyelashes at Thornton.

"I wouldn't exactly call I-Five the scenic route," he replied.

"Well, that's the nice thing about this lovely country of ours, isn't it?" Baxter sneered at a carload of elderly Vietnamese slowly passing by. "We're all entitled to our opinions—*despite* the yellow horde invasion."

"Cut the crap, Baxter." Abel moved within fighting

distance of the gang leader. Baxter rose up straight and tall, until the two were both the same height. In his peripheral vision, Luke noticed the black Nissan Maxima coasting slowly past his Malibu. "I've already read Lui and his Steel Dragons the riot act, so now I'm tellin' you. Again."

Stitch feigned total boredom while directing an obscene gesture at the four men inside the passing Nissan.

Abel grabbed the front of Baxter's shirt and pulled him closer, nose to nose—so there would be absolutely no misunderstanding. "I'm not going to tell you a third time." He spoke slowly and firmly.

"Hey!" Queenie objected quickly. "Ain't that POlice brutality?"

"Yeah!" the four skinheads seated behind her chimed in right on cue, but Abel ignored them.

"You get back in your Roycemobile and Rolls on out of here, *ya hear*?"

"Or we's gonna *slice* your fuckin' *ears* off and wear 'em on our dog-tag chains." Thornton glided up next to his partner until his lips were nearly rubbing one of Stitch Baxter's earlobes. "You *savvy*?" his whisper was a harsh rasp.

"Now, you listen, pig." Baxter lost the Tinsel Town smile. "You boys better be sharp Night One of the Gook Tet Party."

"Yeah?"

"Gonna be some serious patriotic action by some real tough dudes to show the slopes who's gonna win this war. You get my drift?"

Abel grabbed Baxter, threw him down and, pinned him on the hot pavement with his foot. "Listen, sonny boy. You tell your 'tough patriots' to keep their fucked-up politics out of this town or they'll have more heat then they can handle. You got that!" Abel let him up.

"*Di-di-mau* or die," Thornton muttered under his breath.

Baxter just smiled and picked himself off the street. Without a word, he got back into the Rolls and signaled the driver to start the engine.

"Screw him," Abel told Glenn as the Rolls drove off. "He ain't worth the paper work, brother. . . ."

Lui had directed his driver to pull over, and Abel began walking over toward the parked Maxima when it suddenly swerved out into traffic and accelerated. "Aw, shit," Thornton muttered, as it quickly caught up to the Rolls.

"Talk about felony stupid. They can't even wait until we're out of sight."

"Let's go!" Glenn yelled as the Maxima pulled up beside the Rolls and verbal insults, then empty beer bottles were exchanged.

In a few seconds, he had pulled up alongside Lui's gang and cut them off.

His pistol extended out the Malibu's passenger-side window, Thornton was casually waving the Maxima over to the side of the road.

As soon as both vehicles stopped, the Maxima's left rear door flew open, and Le Van Lui jumped out. His fists were raised. "Come on, Abel!" he threatened. "You wanna stay on my case all fucking week, then let's *do it!*"

"Hey, hey!" Glenn Thornton glanced over at his partner as they rushed from the brown Chevrolet. "Let's oblige him, Gus. *Please!*"

Abel's .45 automatic had failed to clear gun leather, however. His two hands were raised, unclenched, palms out. "Mellow out, Lui!" He forced a smile.

"Why you bastards always gotta roust me, Abel?" Lui turned slightly, motioning the rest of his group to remain inside the four-door sedan. "Why you always gotta be . . . so . . . *bad*?"

"Because bad becomes me, Louie-Louie. But, like before, I'm gonna cut you some slack. I happen to know Baxter there"—he pointed to the Rolls Royce disappearing down a side road in the distance—"provoked your boys. Probably even threw the first beer bottle . . . Ol' Stitch was just tryin' to get my goat, that's all . . . just playin' the usual game of mindfuck."

"Then why didn't you *arrest* his ass!?" Lui demanded, losing all composure. "I'll sign the goddamned complaint *personally*!"

Remaining calm, Abel wanted to see if he could out-psyche the gang leader. He wanted to see Le Van Lui jump up and down on the side of the road, kick a dent in the shiny new Nissan. "Because I wanted to talk to you, Lui." Abel wrapped an arm around the young career hoodlum's shoulder.

Lui was unnerved as the bigger American guided him back over toward the Malibu. He kept glancing back over a shoulder to see if his boys had observed the unprecedented physical contact. "Knock it off, Abel!" He tried unsuccessfully to break free. "Just what the *fuck* are you up to? You're signin' my fuckin' *death* warrant with this buddy-buddy bullshit, man!"

"Look, Lui"—the fingers of Abel's fist clamped onto Lui's sparse collection of chest hairs as the gang leader was lifted up onto his tiptoes—"I'm gonna level with you. No more games. Me and my men have enough problems just tryin' to bust your punks for extortion, robbery, and prostitution. I've got more pressing problems. This white-on-Asian rumble. Nothing I can say or do will keep you bastards apart. Nothing but brute force. So if that's what it takes, *be advised*"—he lifted the gangster up even higher, until they were nose to nose—"violence will be met with violence. So, back off. You and your Steel Dragon clan lay low. Until after Tet. I don't want civilians getting killed in the crossfire. Do we understand each other?"

"I don't control the Blue Bamboo boys," Lui said simply.

"Have a talk with them. Tell them that a Tet truce is in their best interests."

"You sound like Henry Kissinger in 1973—before he sold my country down the Saigon River. Go fuck yourself—okay, Abel?"

"So be it. But tell the Blue Bamboo what I just told you."

"They'd just as soon draw a bead on us as the white meat scopin' Bolsa," Lui sneered. "They're *dinky-dau*."

"Then I'll back you up if you need it. Arrange a meet' with Blue Bamboo, and I'll have half the detective division lurking in the shadows to save your ass if things go bad."

"There's no way the police could protect us."

"You talk that way because you're a know-nothing punk." Head lowered in resignation, Abel pushed the Steel Dragon leader away and started around to the Malibu's driver's side.

"You made us what we are, Abel." Lui twisted the knife of guilt.

"What?" Abel froze at the car's rear fender.

"You Americans," he said, waving his arms out to encompass the sea of anonymous Asian faces crowding the Bolsa Strip. "You created this junkyard full of dislocated refugees. We are what America has become . . . and there is no way to get rid of us now. . . ."

"You can't talk me into a guilt trip, Lui." Abel's smile was a sad one. "I've already been there and back. A million times."

"We'll take care of business, Abel. I'm out of here."

Abel raised his arms in a hands-off gesture.

"Just do me one favor, Lieutenant. Hit me, okay?"

Abel did not question Lui's request. The hood wanted to look good in front of his boys—tough and defiant, not like a cooperating wimp. Or worse, a snitch.

"Watch your back," the investigator said, reaching forward to embrace Le Van Lui in a bear hug. " 'Cause this scene is a show of weakness. Every punk in your car is gonna start questioning your authority. They're gonna test you, Lui. I just wish I'm there when it happens."

Lui pushed himself away from the American violently and spat at Abel's feet. "You'll regret this, Abel. You and Little Saigon."

≡ CHAPTER 15

BY THE TIME he had dropped Thornton back at the substation and picked up an extra six-pack and reached his apartment, Abel's watch read 0400. The first time in weeks he had actually finished his shift on time. He entered the dark living room catlike, prowling out of habit, yet hoping not to rouse the three birds. He could see the parrots' beedy little black eyes, watching his every move from their cage in the corner. But they remained silent as well—except for a few feathers ruffling in muted panic. Abel was thankful parrots saw only blurred images in the dark.

When he reached the bedroom and turned on the light, the telephone began ringing, and Dirty Harry called out after him, "Fuck it."

"Yeah, no shit," Abel muttered as he fought the urge to simply draw his .45 and riddle the irritating contraption with hollowpoints. Finally, he reached for the phone and began pacing. "Abel here."

He froze in his tracks at the sound of the voice.

"Lucas? It's me . . . Xinh."

"My God!" Abel whirled around, her countless wall photos closing in on him now. "Xinh!" He was instantly soaked in sweat, heart thumping, toes and fingers tingling, vision blurred.

"Gus, I miss you so bad . . . I'm still here. I'm still in Thailand. . . ."

"Oh, Jesus!" Abel dropped his head back in disbelief. Xinh! It was really her. A terrible groan set free the great weight that had been pressing down on him all these years. His eyes darted from picture to picture hanging on the walls all around.

"Talk!" He listened to static reclaim the phone line. "Talk to me, baby!"

". . . The police . . . the Thai police say I have only three minutes to speak, Lucas. I want you to know I am coming to U.S.A. very soon—to be with you again. Do you still want me? Do you even remember me, *Dau-che-tao*?"

Dau-che-tao. Pain maker. Her nickname for him. Her little joke: He always caused her heart so much pain. "Xinh, this is Luke you're talking to! *Luke!* I've never forgotten about you. I got your telegram, but there was no way I could call back . . . no address to—"

"Yes, I know . . . I know—the Thai authorities . . . they are so strict. They hate us, you know—we Vietnamese refugees."

"I miss you so bad, honey—it's so good to hear your voice again. Are you *all right*?"

When Xinh did not immediately reply, an icy swirl cleaned out Abel's gut. "Xinh?"

"I know soon we will be together again. Same before. Same Saigon. Please wait for me, Lucas. Last night, I dreamed you had American wife and six children. But I know that is silly." Her voice was taking on an almost desperate tone. "Tonight, I will write you letter. Tell you everything. Tomorrow Thai police say they will give me address so you can write back. Maybe phone number, too. But it will be too late. Okay, I will get you the flight information—yes, that's what I'll do. . . ."

He could hear her sobs now. "Yes, honey. You do that. Find out all the details for me. Get word to me somehow. I'll be waiting, Xinh. I'll be waiting for you at the airport. I love you, babe!"

There was a slight commotion in the background—a

weird chimelike ringing on the overseas line. Xinh
speaking to someone in pidgin-Thai, then her lips brushing against the mouthpiece again. "They tell me I have
to go now, Lucas. They pay for me to use phone, but
only three minutes. I almost forget my English, but
somehow I remember. Good-bye, Lucas. I have to go
now. Don't forget about Xinh. She coming to see you
soon. . . ."

Abel listened to Xinh hanging up the phone receiver,
ten thousand miles away.

Fourteen years, and she forgot to tell him she loved him.
But Xinh had always been that way. Abel nodded at the
rush of memories as he sat down on the edge of the bed
and stared up at the largest portrait of her—a collage of
bright oils on felt: Xinh in her black-and-purple *ao dai*,
standing before the Xa Loi Pagoda in Saigon.

"Xinh's alive!" he raced through the apartment, waking the neighbors, waking the pets. Dogs howled in a
courtyard below his balcony window. He opened the bird
cage, and the three parrots soared through the living
room, flapping about in excited circles, sensing his joy
and happiness.

Le Van Lui stared long and hard down at Ricky Pham
as they sat in the Steel Dragon's safe house after the other
gang members had left. There was something odd about
the kid. The boy was slow, reaction-wise, at times—and
recklessly swift at others. Lui knew about the youth's
father being an ex-Saigon cop. It didn't matter. He was
easily influenced and molded—the perfect gang initiate.

Tonight, Ricky wore cut-off jeans, tennis shoes, and a
black windbreaker. His dark hair was combed forward,
the strands on top an inch or two long—the sides shaved
close. His nose was flat and wide. He wore wire-rim
glasses and a much-practiced sneer.

"It is time for you to move one rung up the Steel
Dragon ladder of seniority, Ricky. Yesterday, you were
clinging to the bottom. Today, you ascend one level. To
shooter."

"I am ready." The youth nodded.

"This is a .45-caliber pistol." Lui jerked the weapon's slide back, chambering a round. He flipped the safety into place, and brought its operation to Ricky's attention. "When you want to fire it, flip this lever here on the left side, straight down. Got that?"

Ricky nodded. "What do you want me to shoot up?"

"Not what, but *who*." Le Van Lui grinned. He produced a newspaper clipping that contained a grainy photograph of police Lt. Luke Abel. "Do you know this man?"

Ricky swallowed hard. "I've seen him around Little Saigon. He is a cop." He suddenly remembered all the back-alley meetings he'd had with the M.A.G. detective in secret—all the information he'd passed to Abel about the gang's movements and activities, though it had never really been anything vital. Small-time extortions, vandalisms to cars owned by the Blue Bamboo boys. Abel hardly had time for it. But that was not what troubled Ricky now—he was remembering everything as if for the first time. And he wondered what he was doing here, nodding his head as Le Van Lui gave him instructions to terminate the only American who had ever taken an interest in his welfare.

"Lucas Abel reports for work Thursdays thru Monday, seven P.M to three A.M. at the substation where Bolsa meets Brookhurst."

"I know the building." Ricky nodded. "Second floor. Above the Chinese market."

"That's it." Lui smiled again. He would not have to lead this kid around by the hand. "You're to go there tonight, wait for Abel under the stairwell, and when he appears, jump out and shoot him in the back of the head before he can react."

"In the back? The back of the head?" Ricky's eyes grew large. His jaw went slack.

"Yes. Then you are to return the gun to me. But not directly. The pigs might bring in dogs, and they would track you here or to one of the other safe houses. You proceed directly to Brookhurst and Hazard streets. There will be a bicycle there, chained to a light pole. Here is the key. Behind the rear tire will be a glass filled with pepper. Sprinkle it all around the bike—it will confuse any dogs the K-Nine cops bring in—then proceed west, all the way to Magnolia, then south, down to our clubhouse on Head Street, where I will be waiting for you—is that understood, or do you need me to go over it all again?''

"It's understood."

"Good. Now go. You're one of us now, Ricky. Don't let me down."

"What if Abel is with his partner?"

"Then you shoot both of them, stupid."

"Of course. I knew that."

Ricky Pham was drenched in sweat. He lay hidden in shadow, crouched beneath the stairwell that led up to the M.A.G. task force's second-floor offices. He checked his watch: 7:15 P.M. and still Luke Abel's brown Malibu had not arrived.

Then, he heard footsteps—one set of them—approaching from the rear parking lot. Soft footsteps—barely perceptible: rubber beneath a big man against unyielding blacktop. And he spotted the M.A.G. lieutenant, carrying a large stack of file folders. He must have parked behind the complex.

Ricky held his breath as he squatted there, his shirt off, draped over the sweat-slick .45 he clutched in trembling hands, and Abel passed by without noticing him.

After the police detective had proceeded up a couple of stairs, Ricky jumped out into the open and froze in a defensive stance he'd seen in more than a few TV shows: knees bent, arms extended.

At the first alien sound, Abel dropped the stack of file folders, grabbed the railing, and vaulted over, out into space, back to the ground.

He landed on his feet, automatic pistol extended in a two-fisted combat crouch. The front sight came down in front of Ricky Pham's chest. Abel's eyes locked on the black windbreaker draped across the boy's forearms.

"Ricky!" He immediately lifted his service weapon

skyward and secured the safety. "You scared the crap out of me, son! What's goin' down, little brother?"

"I . . . I . . ." Ricky Pham stood there frozen, his hands holding the concealed .45, his finger pressing the trigger harder and harder without any result as he struggled with his emotions: the *good* rules his father was forever trying to instill in him, the *right* thing to do in life, versus Le Van Lui's law of kill or be killed. "I . . . I . . ."

As he locked eyes with Abel, Ricky completely forgot about the safety mechanism Lui had showed him. His hands began to tremble as he watched Abel holster his own Colt and began wondering why the .45 under the windbreaker refused to fire.

"You . . . you *what*?" Abel mimicked him.

"There's something I want to tell you."

"I'm listening," Abel's smile was warm, trusting—unsuspecting.

"Uh, n-nothing. You're busy. It can wait."

"I'm never too busy to shoot the shit with you, Ricky. What's troubling you, son?"

"It's cold tonight." Ricky seemed to regain a calm composure almost instantly. "You are always working out on the street with nothing warm on." He slowly lowered his arms without letting the windbreaker fall away. "I wanted you to have this jacket."

"Save it, pal." Abel laughed. "I've got my M.A.G. bomber jacket back in the car. But I appreciate the offer. Wanna come up for some of Luyen's ice coffee? She's working at the substation tonight, and I know how you *love* that Vietnamese-French brew she whips together."

Ricky's tense smile faded. "Some other time," he said slowly. "I gotta go."

"Okay, well . . . watch you ass, kid. The streets are gettin' *bookoo* mean lately. Be sure to let me know if—"

But Ricky Pham had already backed off into the shadows and disappeared. Abel listened to his footsteps fading in the distance.

In the M.A.G. office upstairs, Abel poured himself a

cup of coffee, then asked Luyen, "Did Ricky Pham speak with you just a while ago—before I arrived?"

"Ricky who?" Luyen glanced up from her computer console.

"The little kid I been trying to steer away from Lui's gang. The one who always follows me and Glenn around Bolsa."

"I guess I just never paid any attention, Luke." She resumed working on a rape statistics report. "Sorry."

Abel scratched at the stubble on his chin in reflection. "The oddest thing happened downstairs tonight."

"Huh?" Luyen did not look up this time.

"Oh, nothing. Forget it. Probably just my imagina—"

One of the three hot-line phones hanging from the west wall interrupted him.

"Abel here."

"Shelley, Lou. Just gettin' ready to send some units down to the barrow ditch, south side o' Bolsa, couple blocks west of Euclid on the east edge of Little Saigon. Possible homicide victim. Female Vietnamese. Lying facedown and butt naked behind a McDonald's restaurant."

"A gang girl?" Abel wondered why the thought crossed his mind.

"Looks that way."

"Luyen and I are enroute. Glenn's over at Santa Ana P.D., briefing the guys there about security precautions at the Tet Festival. Raise him on the pager and have him meet us at the scene."

Abel slammed the phone down and told Luyen, "Let's haul ass, honey. It's started."

She was in her early twenties, and had been an attractive woman before they cut off her nose and ears. Abel knew she'd once been pretty—he'd seen her hanging out on Bolsa with some of Lui's boys. Thuy was her name. So many girls in Little Saigon named Thuy, but he remembered this one as he stared down at her pale buttocks, glistening in the moonlight, streaked with blood and jagged, discolored tears from shoulder blades to haunches.

She had thrown a brick at their Malibu one night. Thrown the brick, then just stood there, defiant, daring them to arrest her. And they had—dragged her kicking and screaming to the substation, where Zamora whacked her a couple of times and still didn't get anywhere. Thuy had been a pure hate machine. Lui was her god. He supplied her with free crack cocaine, and she'd take on cops, crooks—anyone for him.

Luyen recognized her, too. Lai's older sister—the girl who had brought her female bullies to the Cultural Center.

This was not the work of a sadistic Asian, though. A Rebel flag was stuffed down into Thuy's mouth. It appeared she had been gang raped, as well.

"Any witnesses?" Abel asked the district car, which had beaten them to the scene by a few minutes.

"Negative, Lieutenant. The call came in anonymously. Some old guy, said he was walking his dog—didn't wanna get involved."

"Did he call on Nine-one-one?"

"Nope—too smart for that. Dialed direct, in through one of the non-emergency lines. But I think it's pretty obvious who your prime suspects are." The officer's flashlight beam fell across the tip of the Rebel flag protruding from the edge of Thuy's lifeless snarl.

"It's never that cut-and-dried, bud." Abel broke out the crime-scene gear. "Not in Little Saigon."

≡ CHAPTER 16

"CHECK *THOSE* WHITE boys out." Thornton pointed at a pink Mercedes that had appeared down the street just as the two M.A.G. agents were about to pull into the substation lot. Luyen had taken Glenn's car back to the morgue to do the follow up, while he and Abel headed back.

The Mercedes was cruising slowly through one of the many commercial districts of the Bolsa Strip. Its occupants appeared to be casing the closed shops and dark storefronts.

Abel pulled in between two parked cars and doused his headlights, just as the Mercedes executed a U-turn and coasted into the Man Wah complex. Thornton already had his folding binoculars out and trained on the expensive auto.

"Skinheads," he announced.

"Aw, fuck . . ." Abel clearly wasn't in the mood for another confrontation with punkers.

"They're getting out," he whispered, though the Malibu was parked far out of earshot. "Six of the suckers."

"Mercs," Abel muttered.

"They're walking up to the Golden Buffy Gift Shop. Two of 'em are picking up a trash can, Gus . . ." His voice grew tense.

Abel pulled back out into traffic and floored the gas pedal. "Shouldn't we wait until they smash the front window in?" Thornton said. "Then we'd have a prosecutable crime!"

"It's fucking oh-two-hundred," Abel answered irritably. "Do *you* wanna do the paper work this late?"

"You're right." Thornton folded his binoculars back up and rolled a heavy Kel-light from beneath the seat. "Want me to call it in?" He noticed a black van parked across the street. Vic the Vet. The interior was dark. The one-legged hero was sleeping it off.

"I think we can handle it. There's only six of 'em, for crissakes!"

"Yeah, right . . ." Thornton swallowed hard. "The area watch commander'll have a cow, though, if we FI six skinheads by ourselves—" But Abel already had the Malibu skidding up beside the Mercedes.

Thornton trained their spotlight on the six youths standing frozen in front of the shop's huge plate-glass window, as Abel approached the Mercs, pistol in hand. "Police officers," he announced, barrel pointed casually at the ground. "Sit the fucking trash can down or I'm going to plant you in it."

"And you can shove your badge up your ass, man!" one of the skinheads replied. Nevertheless, they set the trash can down, *then* started walking toward Abel, with a menacing gait.

"Grab some pavement, assholes!" Thornton appeared in front of the Malibu's headlights. A shotgun had replaced his steel flashlight at the last moment, and the spotlight's beam silhouetted its gleaming, no-nonsense barrel.

Slowly, the six complied, dropping first to their knees, then completely prone across the cool blacktop. They knew the routine.

"And just what the hell were you expecting to do with that goddamn trash can?" Abel asked. He moved from figure to figure, patting them down for weapons as Thornton kept the shotgun trained on the group.

"Ain't doin' jackshit, man. . . ."

As he spoke, two Garden Grove units pulled up to the scene, headlights off. They parked a good fifty feet behind the Malibu, drivers' sides together, and watched the roust in silence—available if needed, but preferring not to interfere in an undercover investigation unless requested. Neither patrolman bothered to get out of his unit.

"I don't think you scrotebags were planning to rip off this shop." Abel flashed his partner a sign indicating the six were unarmed. "You sure don't need some Saigon trinkets or Vietnamese desktop flag sets—which is about all the Golden Buffy stocks anymore. I think you were about to smash-and-trash it instead."

Thornton waved one of the Garden Grove units up. Lowering his shotgun, he asked the officer inside, "Can you spare me some FI cards, bud? I'm all out."

"You M.A.G. dicks been busy today." The patrolman spoke civilly despite what some on the force might consider territorial infringement.

"*Too* busy." Thornton thanked him, then walked up next to Abel.

"Get up," Abel ordered the six punks. "And anybody tries to be macho-man, I'm gonna blow his kneecaps off."

"I don't suppose any o' you maggots stopped by the McDonald's Drive-In tonight," Abel muttered.

"No chance, Chief," one of them said.

Making a show of brushing dust from their trousers, the teenagers stood up slowly. There was now a vulnerable uncertainty in all their movements, except for one. Five stared at their jungle boots. The sixth one locked eyes defiantly with first Thornton, then Abel—the youth who had done all the talking up to this point . . . the threatening . . . the stare-downs. Abel singled him out for further questioning. "You girls all look like curfew-violations-in-the-making to me," he said.

"We're all legal." The obvious leader snickered. "Everyone's old enough to vote, or they don't ride on my wheels."

"Then you're old enough to fight," Thornton said. "Why aren't you in Marine boot camp, hero?"

"There's a bigger war being waged right here at home," the top skinhead replied.

"I think all six of you sorry-assed punks would wash out of boot camp the first week," Abel challenged, motioning toward their combat boots.

"You don't *deserve* to wear that army surplus!" Thornton said.

"Break out some ID," Abel directed.

One of the youths darted into the shadows of the nearby storefront and, before Abel or Thornton could give chase, two gunshots rang out from above.

Everyone—Mercs and M.A.G. agents—dropped prone across the blacktop. "Don't shoot us!" the nearest teenager lying spread-eagled beside Abel yelled. He obviously feared a shoot-out and swift police retribution. "Whoever the fuck's up there, he's not one of *mine*!"

As much was obvious to Luke Abel as he and his partner rolled out of the streetlights' glow and against the wooden edge of the storefront's raised walkway: Two of the boy's companions had not dived to the ground, but dropped—mortally wounded. The night came alive with the squeal of tires spinning as the police Plymouths roared up into the kill zone.

"The roof!" Abel was directing the police spotlights skyward. "Get on the horn and request Air One if he's available!"

"You got it, Lieutenant!" Two uniformed patrolmen were kneeling beside their unit's engine block as the surviving gang members finally rolled into the shadows beside Sergeant Thornton.

"None of you clowns make any more moves!" Abel told the wide-eyed gang members.

"No problem!" their spokesman said. "We ain't goin' anywhere!"

"It's the zipperheads, man!" another Merc was saying. "It's gotta be them Steel Dragon assholes who smoked Ed and Larry!"

Abel glanced over at the two youths lying on their

backs in the center of the parking lot. Already, pools of blood were forming around their shaved heads. "I'm going after the rabbit!" he told Thornton.

"Right!" Glenn waved him on. "I'll keep an eye on these scrotes!"

No additional gunshots from the roof of the Golden Buffy had followed the first two. Abel sprinted down along the storefront until he came to a narrow corridor running between two shops—the same avenue of escape the fleeing skinhead had opted for.

Pistol out defensively in front of him, Abel started down the dark alley. He heard a few footfalls overhead, on the roof, but they stopped as soon as he froze. Back against the wall and eyes shielded from the bright moonbeams, Abel gazed up at the roof. A few seconds later, Air One swooped in above the Golden Buffy. The police helicopter's dual floodlights swept back and forth over the buildings.

In the distance, a screaming alley cat and rolling trash can marked the escaping gang member's path. Abel resumed the chase, running faster again—his prey's position all but pinpointed by the racket up ahead.

Abel wanted to yell out at the youth—try to talk him into surrendering. But instead, he found himself prowling the changing, ever-shifting shadows in silence, following the boy through the gloom, yet geared up for even bigger game—the two shooters racing across rooftops overhead. Sooner or later they would have to return to the ground—probably before the police got organized and saturated the area with canine units. It would not take the dogs long to flush out any intruders. With Air One hovering over the whole operation, the VC didn't stand a chance.

VC. Abel shook his head.

He could feel them rushing along through the dark up there, even now. Just like Saigon. Abel often suspected much of the Asian criminal element operating in Little Saigon today were ex-Viet Cong. There were always rumors about vast tunnels crisscrossing like catacombs beneath the refugee community—installed *after* American involvement in their faraway war ended. And he had been through enough sniper attacks after seven years in the Nam to know how their rooftop riflemen operated: Pick a building with full-circle visibility and easy access to a maze of back alleys as well as lower-level, connecting roofs. Fire no more than a half-magazine of semi-auto down at the American military policemen, then flee into the night before they can surround the suspected gunman's lair or call in gunship support. It worked almost every time. Out of dozens of such one-sided shoot-outs in downtown Saigon, he had managed to track down and eliminate only two VC snipers.

Tonight, in the heart of Little Saigon, he found himself walking slowly and pantherlike, just like in the Nam—eyes unblinking, focused on the grainy outlines in the dark ahead, rather than on what might have appeared to be actual objects. It was the only way to remain one step ahead of Charlie. His ears were in tune with the night, as well. Now and then, he could hear the pitter-patter of little feet high above—on the second and third stories. He knew they could not possibly be following him—that they were only making their way farther and farther from the bustle of activity back at the storefronts. But it was an eerie, haunting feeling nonetheless.

Abel detected the youth's heavy breathing. The white boy was leaning against a doorway, trying to catch his breath, oblivious of the M.A.G. detective's presence. Abel took a moment to inspect the young hood's clothing and demeanor. He appeared unarmed. Perhaps still high on drugs, as well. Most probably PCP. That would account for his bolting from the scene back at the Golden Buffy. Above, the gentle slapping of footfalls again.

Abel breathed deeply and closed his eyes tightly, psyching himself up for the takedown. The M.A.G. lieutenant wanted desperately to effect the capture without alerting the Vietnamese on the roof of their presence. Of their presence . . . Frozen with indecision, Abel bit his lower lip: They already knew, he decided. About the running Merc, in any event. That was why their path took them in this same direction. They, too, were after the juvenile Abel hunted.

A train's whistle several miles away seemed to bring every activity and movement, all motion and life, to a startled standstill. That was when Abel glided across the open alleyway and latched onto the Merc's throat. In a split second, the youth was slammed facefirst to the ground. Without words, Abel rammed the handcuffs into place.

"Let's go!" Abel's harsh whisper in the boy's ear propelled him to his feet and back down the alley. Suddenly, the investigator slid to a halt and jerked his prisoner into a doorway. Sensing a presence overhead, he leaned out from under the doorway's sloping arch for a better view— his .45 pistol extended out like a protective face mask.

Two faces stared back down at him. Vietnamese. The flash from an AR-15 muzzle erupted, lighting up the dark corridor, and Abel fired off four rounds at the purple vision outlines in his memory. A head flew back, its face split down the middle, and blood poured down onto them.

"Stay put!" Abel yelled at the Merc hoodlum. He produced a spare set of handcuffs and slipped them through the pair already in place, securing the gang member to the bottom rung of a nearby fire escape. Then he chased after the sound of fading footfalls.

Grabbing onto a protruding pipe, he swung himself up toward the roofline only to have the Vietnamese—blood gushing from a scalp wound—race down the connecting corridor one level below.

Dropping back to the ground, Abel chased after him. "Freeze, ya son of a bitch," he muttered under his breath, too exhausted to yell out as he forced his limbs to run, pleaded with his innards not to explode . . . for his system to survive just one more adrenaline rush tonight.

The shooter darted down a fork in the corridor that headed back around toward Bolsa. Abel kept with him, but the distance was fast separating between them— despite the runner's wound.

"Come on, you son of a bitch." He found himself hoping the punk would whirl, raise the AR-15 so he could blast him in the gut, cancel his ticket—not that it wouldn't already be classified a righteous shooting if he just offed the sucker. Bullets in the back made for bad press, though.

The cluster of connecting corridors seemed to go on forever. Every time Abel sensed he was catching up, the suspect disappeared around another bend. Tenement walls rose up three and four stories on both sides—they were now in a residential housing project, far from the Golden Buffy's shopping plaza yet still running parallel to Bolsa. Abel resisted the urge to turn up his pak-set—he'd kept the portable radio's volume switch off as soon as the foot chase began. Such was routine. And now, when stealth was no longer paramount—the suspect obviously knew he was being stalked—he remained on his own, electing not to air his position.

It had become personal to Luke Abel. It was just him against Victor Charlie.

"Hold it!" Around the next bend, the Vietnamese gang member was only a few feet away. He had tripped and fallen—was now nursing a sprained ankle as well as the deep scalp wound, the AR-15 slung across his back. "I said *hold it!*" Abel repeated as the youth turned away and resumed running despite the painful injuries.

The lieutenant had almost caught up with the limping gunman when he, too, slipped on the same unseen patch of engine oil that the sniper must have slipped on. "Jesus!" His pistol clattered across the concrete, but the Vietnamese made no move for it. Instead, he continued down the corridor, limping wildly as Abel fought to regain his own footing.

He scooped up his service weapon, checked its safety on the run, and continued after the teenager—gaining slowly, but gaining nonetheless. A door suddenly flew open, striking the gang member flush in the face and catapulting him backwards, off his feet.

A dim, yellow porch light flashed on, but Abel ignored the man emerging into the corridor from the ground-floor dwelling. His shadow fell across the M.A.G. detective as he struggled with the stunned hoodlum, finally forcing his arms behind his back and the plastic set of spare flexicuffs around his wrists.

When Abel finally glanced up at the man who had cut short the foot chase, he found himself face-to-face with Sgt. Pham, the old, retired *canh-sat*—a contented smile creasing his sleep-dazed features—staring back down at him, .38-Special in hand.

"A pussy misdemeanor traffic warrant! He ran because of a pussy *traffic* warrant?" Thornton could not believe it. He poked his head into the patrol car's back window again, inspecting the prisoner Abel had handcuffed to a fire escape ladder during the foot chase. The youth now lay facedown on the seat in his own vomit, curled up in the fetal position, leg shackles attached to his handcuffs. He had passed out back at the fire escape ladder, and two patrolmen had had to carry him back to the shooting scene. "Jesus *H*!" Thornton said. "What a fucking moron."

"You can't treat him like an animal!" the largest Merc was protesting.

Using the driver's licenses his partner had collected, Abel matched photos with faces. The loudmouth's name was R. Allen Casselmann. "R. Allen, eh?" he chuckled. "Rich stock, no doubt."

"A breed above the rest." Casselmann lifted his chin slightly. "And my hometown's being invaded by fucking foreigners from Japan, man! They just zapped two o' my brothers! Are you skates gonna track 'em down, or not?"

"We got 'em, kid." Thornton scratched at the stubble on his chin.

"Invaded! *Yeah*!" The youth standing beside twenty-year-old Casselmann stepped a pace closer to Abel. "And we're determined to let them know they're not wanted."

Abel slowly shook his head from side to side. "First of all," he told R. Allen, "they're not from Japan . . . they're from Vietnam." He stared down at the two blanket-covered corpses.

"A gook is a gook, man. And it's open season on all slant-eyed motherfuckers tryin' to take over Orange County."

"So you come down here in the middle of the night to bash in some storefronts, huh?" Thornton lowered his shotgun barrel to Casselmann's groin. "Real brave, boys . . . real brave." He waited for them to slip, boasting about the girl at the McDonald's—or at least start to slip, but recover at the last moment. Even that was too much to ask for. But Abel's M.A.G. team didn't have much time to smoke out the rats infesting Little Saigon.

"These people *know* they're not wanted or liked by certain Orange County residents. They don't need pukes like you to remind them." Abel sighed.

"I can't even read most of the signs," one of the youths complained.

"Then after tonight, I suggest you stay the fuck out of Little Saigon and up in the Sci-Fi Valley, where you belong."

Abel stared down a nearby back alley where Zamora was completing a tow slip on a parked Camaro. He was sure the car had been abandoned by the Viet snipers. He could barely make out the personalized license plate from here: CHA-CHA in the Kel-light. "But for right now, report over to police headquarters. I want witness statements from all you lowlife scrotes." He glared at their polished jump boots and bloused jeans.

A thought struck Abel, and he reached out, grabbing the front of Casselmann's shirt. "This one gets held for forty-eight hours," he told one of the uniformed officers. "For questioning."

"Questioning about fucking *what*?" the Mercs' lieutenant threw his chin out at Abel.

"We had a little gang-rape-slash-homicide down the street a few blocks, which I'm sure none of you boys knows anything about," Abel muttered. "But since some of the evidence at the scene seems to indicate skinheads of the white-power persuasion might have been involved, I'm keeping you behind bars—at least until I get the coroner's report back, and we dust the whole scene for prints, and run a microscopic on the corpse.''

"Yeah? What's the charge, motherfucker? Fucking slant meat ain't the Merc way.'' Casselmann didn't seem intimidated.

"How's protective custody sound?'' Abel grabbed a wrist, twisted his arm behind his back, and forced him to his knees.

"It sounds like wimp shit,'' Casselmann spat back.

"Well, then, I guess it applies, don't it?''

"Thanks for nothing,'' Casselmann hissed as a uniformed officer snapped the cuffs in place behind his back and jerked him to his feet. "I'll take your name off our death list.''

"This is the last time I wanna see your faces down here on Bolsa,'' Abel told all of them. "At least until after the Tet Festival. *Then,* if you get the itch to visit, *phone* me first. For fucking permission.''

"You aren't messin' with some amateurs, mister!'' Casselmann threatened.

"Oh, that's exactly what I'm messing with, kid.'' Abel started back toward the Malibu. "Because if I took you punks half-serious, I'd have blown you away back at that shopping plaza.''

Sergeant Thornton paused to educate the Merc leader even more. "Abel's Law Number Sixty-eight, *Mister* Casselmann: Real cops take no prisoners.''

≡ CHAPTER 17

"MANY THANKS FOR lift, Lieutenant. I enjoy exercise, but only after sunrise. It would have been a long walk."

Abel glanced in his rearview mirror. "It was my pleasure, Sergeant Pham."

The old, retired *canh-sat* laughed. "Oh, I am no longer a policeman, my young friend," he said. "That was long ago. Very many years before. Now I am just old man."

"Once a cop, always a cop." Thornton got out and pulled the seat forward. "The lieutenant here told me about how you came to his rescue, Smith and Wesson in hand. Sounds like you haven't lost the old touch, sir."

"My son, Ricky"—Sgt. Pham's countenance grew serious—"I do not want him working for police. He will only end up in early grave, like his older brothers. We left Vietnam to avoid war and communists. Sometimes I think it is worse here, in U.S. I just don' know anymore, my friends."

"Your son has been working for me almost three months now," Abel said. "He has provided us with valuable information."

"He doesn't know any better. He's retarded."

"I'm not using him—he comes to me," Abel said, taken aback. "Besides, he's not retarded. He's just slow sometimes—that's all. You should be proud of him."

"How can I be proud of a boy headed for the next life?"

"We are expecting trouble at the Tet Festival this year," Thornton told him.

"So I have heard." The old man nodded.

"Your son might be able to help us prevent it."

"The gangs will win, Lieutenant Abel. They are the tentacles of one giant serpent, whose history reaches back thousands of years . . . an elusive creature with many names. Now its influence has spread to U.S.A. I pity your country. It will become like a plague." The retired *canh-sat* pulled a small Vietnamese-into-English dictionary from his trouser pocket, flipped through some pages near the back, and nodded again. "Yes," he said, "plague . . ."

"We only need him until after Tet, Sergeant Pham." Thornton's words were reinforced with respect.

Without looking back, Pham started toward his flickering porch light. His gun hand waved in the air beside his face slightly. "Do what you must," he said. "I am only an old man. How can I argue with you? No one listens to me anymore, anyway."

Abel stared at the pistol butt protruding from the refugee's back pocket as he entered his apartment and switched off the porch light, leaving them in the dark.

"This split-shift business sucks," Rachel Zamora confided in her partner as they cruised Bolsa at high noon. "I miss nights."

"It wasn't Luke's idea," Sgt. Verdugo defended the M.A.G. lieutenant. "It was Sanders's."

"Who awarded him a Ph.D in planning, anyway?" Zamora noticed some activity behind the Vietnamese Cultural Center and executed a perfect U-turn through heavy traffic.

"What the Colonel wants, the Colonel Chicken gets," Verdugo sighed. "And what he wants is M.A.G. on split shifts 'til we crack this case: Abel and Thornton on nights, you and me on days. But I gotta side with you,

Rachel: I fucking hate getting up so early just to come to work. Fishin'—now, that's another matter entirely.''

"Hey, we got a knife fight goin' down back there!" Zamora reached for the radio mike as she pulled into the Cultural Center's rear lot and hit the siren.

A large group of women had surrounded two bruised and battered female combatants—both of whom brandished knives. There was little left of their skirts and blouses except torn cloth and shredded silk. Exposed breasts swayed from side to side wildly as the women danced about, jabbing at each other with the blades. Vietnamese girls formed one semicircle, white girls the other. Likewise, the fighters represented Rebs and Steel Dragon.

"Knock it off!" Zamora jumped from the car pumping a round into her shotgun after she brought the Plymouth into a sideways skid directly up to the arguing women. She instantly recognized the white one: Stitch Baxter's girl, Queenie. She was wired on something, probably PCP.

"She *saiiiid*: Knock it off!" Verdugo appeared in a low crouch behind the unit's engine block, revolver leveled across the hood. "Everyone on the ground! *Now!* Spread-eagle, and don't be modest about it!"

"These bitches came flying' in here outta nowhere!" one of the Vietnamese girls complained. "Like they *own* the place!"

"Look at that sign!" another Viet gang girl pointed to a colorful banner hanging from a nearby wall. "It says *Vietnamese* Cultural Center—not *honky-tonk*! Get yo' lily-white asses out of here!"

Screaming incoherently now, Queenie dropped her knife, only to throw a punch at the Asian woman. It connected across the lower jaw, knocking her off her feet and flat on her back.

"I wanna hear cold steel bouncing off the floor!" Zamora directed. "*Everyone's* cold steel." That included guns, for a half dozen revolvers clattered to the ground. A reassuring sound reached Zamora's ears, then: sirens. Nearly a dozen of them.

Within five minutes, they had the entire bunch searched and subdued. Zamora called an ambulance for the girl suspected of ingesting drugs, and F.I.'d everyone present—expecting Lui or Stitch to show up at any moment, but neither one did.

She placed the knife wielders under arrest, and ran the rest of them off. As the ambulance was pulling away, Queenie, strapped down inside, screamed at the top of her lungs: "The Rebs are gonna burn your small dick gook guys in their own fucking houses, bitch!"

"What a pleasant personality." Verdugo shook his head.

"It's why I love this job so much," Zamora said sarcastically. "You get to patrol the Bolsa Twilight Zone, meet unusual personalities . . . And kill them before they get a chance to reproduce."

"You should have seen her," Verdugo told Abel and Thornton. " 'I wanna hear cold steel bouncing off the floor—*everyone's* cold steel!' And they fucking complied. It was great!"

"Yeah, we all know Rachel knows how to kick gang ass, Vinnie," Abel said, not looking up from his ballistics microscope. He was examining spent shells from recent shootouts, trying to find a match he could trace. "But why're you wasting your off-duty time telling us when you got some hot ying-yang waiting?"

"Guess I'm just sweet on Old Glenn here."

"Hey, listen up, beaver breath!" Thornton rattled his newspaper in preparation for reading something to his partner. "I've finally found it.

"What—a new brain?"

"Up yours, greaseball. It's the perfect plan. A way we could both retire rich, and in a short amount of time."

"Jesus," Abel muttered, switching bullet trays.

"We can corner the Japanese chopstick market, Gus!"

"We can *what*?" Abel refused to look up from his microscope this time.

"I'm readin' this story here, and it turns on enough light bulbs inside my head to light up the town. . . ."

"Little Saigon would suffice."

"Did you realize the Japanese throw away two hundred million chopsticks a day—even though they have a shortage of wood?"

"I know what you're thinking"—Abel chuckled—"but it's already been done. . . ."

"Huh?"

"*What's* already been done?" A female voice drew their eyes to the substation's entryway. Rachel Zamora sauntered in, wearing tight-fitting jean shorts and a bulging halter top. She walked over to Abel's desk and plopped down on it. Behind her, Luyen—still dressed in her C.S.O. uniform—was closing the door.

"In Minnesota," Abel told Thornton, "where all these laid-off people in this one town used to be steel workers and auto union diehards. Now they have the biggest chopsticks plant in the world."

"Oh . . ."

"Speaking of chopsticks"—Abel moved a pyramid of leaning reports off two chairs so the women could sit down—"I could use a little pre-shift food."

"That's why we stopped by—to see if you wanted us to pick you two up any take-out. We're headed for Pho-75."

"How 'bout some of those spring rolls?" Glenn exchanged winks with Luyen.

"*Goi cuon* can hardly satisfy the nutritional requirements of a growing boy," she teased the detective.

"Boy?" he stood up, and Luyen retreated playfully toward the door.

"Here"—Abel pulled his keys from a pocket—"take the Malibu."

"I don't like that bomb," Zamora said, crossing her legs again. "It's *tacky*."

"*My* Malibu is tacky?" Abel leaned back in his chair and clutched the ignition key tightly against an expanding chest. "Surely you jest, *Patrolwoman* Zamora."

"I mean, it's . . . Christ, Lou, it's fourteen fucking years old. Why don't you requisition a new package from the motor pool?"

"Sentimental value," the lieutenant replied quickly.

"We used Malibus in Thailand," Thornton expounded.

"That, too." Abel nodded, a reminiscent smile in place.

"I'm still not drivin' that death trap," Zamora said.

"Here." Thornton tossed her the keys to his '88 Plymouth.

"Now *that's* more like it." Rachel headed for the door.

"Just do me a favor and don't turn the air-filter cover upside down, okay?" Abel asked.

"You got it, Lou!"

"But do *me* a favor by gassin' the sucker up on your way to the restaurant, dear." Thornton clasped the fingers of both hands behind his head and leaned back in his chair. "And bring me back some ice coffee and a baggy of steamed sugarcane cubes!" he added as an afterthought.

"And don't call me dear or I'll flexi-cuff you to the queer cage, *Sergeant*!"

One of the three phones on his desk began ringing the same moment the door slammed shut behind the two women.

"Are we here?" Abel asked Thornton.

"Fuck it." Glenn shrugged. "Might as well pick it up. Maybe you won the California lottery."

"Abel here." He frowned into the mouthpiece.

"Dispatch here, sir." A girlish giggle on the other end started his temples to throbbing. "Patching a call through to you." He recognized the redhead's voice.

"Who is it?"

"The party wouldn't identify himself, Lieutenant. But he asked for you personally . . . by name. Sounds Viet."

"Is he on a recorded line?"

"No, sir. He called in on the non-emergency number. Do you want me to put him through now?"

"Wait a second!" Abel jumped up. "Put a recorder on this line!" he told Thornton.

In his haste to comply, the M.A.G. sergeant knocked his cup of coffee off the desk, but had a portable monitor hooked up in less than a minute. "Okay," Abel told the dispatcher.

"Lucas Abel?" The voice sounded out of breath and young, but confident. There was no hesitancy, no fear in the tone.

"Speaking."

"You've meddled in our affairs one too many times, Abel," the voice said coldly. "A . . . device, planted nearby and placing some of your people in peril will go off before you can call the sheriff for help in defusing it. *If* you even find it in time."

"You know my name. Why don't you tell me *yours*, asshole."

"Because that's not the way to play the game, my friend." The caller chuckled lightly. His breathing had calmed considerably. "A bomb will explode within the next five minutes."

"Where?" Abel pulled out his pen. "On Bolsa?"

"No, no, my friend." The caller's laugh grew more hearty. "We planted it much . . . much closer to home. . . ."

For some reason, he thought of his apartment, and the girl living on the ground floor who played Vietnamese music all night. "You'll have to give me more to go on than that."

"Little wheels, spin and spin . . ." The caller's tone turned ugly, and Abel knew from experience he was dealing with a psycho.

"What are your demands?" he asked slowly.

"Little wheels, spin and spin . . ." the man repeated. There was a click in Abel's earpiece, and the line went dead.

" 'Little wheels, spin and spin'?" he asked his partner. "Does that mean anything to *you*?"

Thornton started to shake his head from side to side when a deafening explosion outside shattered the office's second-floor windows. Dual firebombs rose from the parking lot, and the building shook as if an earthquake had struck.

"The Malibu!" Abel raced toward the window, but a

dense blanket of black smoke concealed everything below. Two wheels, torn from a car chassis by the thunderous explosion, bounced forth from the billowing columns of smoke and rolled off down the street on their own.

Little wheels, spin and spin . . . The words tumbled through his head, over and over.

Thornton was already on the phone again, dialing the fire department.

"Jesus!" Abel yelled. A breeze had already swept some of the smoke aside, and he could see that the Malibu had escaped the blast unscathed. Thornton's unmarked Plymouth was a pile of molten metal, however. Flames danced along what had once been the roof and trunk. "Rachel and Luyen!" he cried, darting for the door.

Thornton was busy yelling into the mouthpiece as Abel bolted out of the office. "Yes!" he told the fire dispatcher. "Right behind the substation, Bolsa and Brookhurst! Thanks!"

He slammed the phone down and rushed after his partner.

☰ CHAPTER 18

"OH, CHRIST!" ABEL gasped as they reached the bottom of the stairs to find the unmarked police car totally engulfed in flames. A nearby shop owner had rushed up with fire extinguisher in hand, but his efforts were useless. The canister was empty in thirty seconds, and the flames grew stronger.

"Poor Rachel," Thornton whispered.

"And what about me?" Luyen's singsong voice chirped behind them.

The two men turned to see Zamora and Luyen walking through the swinging front doors of the Chinese supermarket that occupied the ground floor of the building housing M.A.G.'s offices. Their faces were blackened with soot, but both appeared uninjured. Zamora was holding an empty sugar cone—the ice cream had been melted by the blast's heat wave.

"We stopped to get some orange sherbert on the way," Luyen explained, a mixture of guilt and relief creasing her features.

Abandoning his usually emotionless bearing, Luke Abel hugged both Rachel and Luyen with all his might.

"Hey, what about *me*?" Glenn opened his arms wide.

"Touch me and you're *history,* pal!" Zamora's laughter was laced with a series of shudders as she watched the Plymouth burn.

"This is getting more and more like Old Saigon every day," Luyen complained as she kept her face pressed against Abel's chest.

"When do we start getting combat pay?" Zamora asked.

"And you thought the *Malibu* was a bomb!" Thornton told her.

"Look at this shit in the *Gold Coast*!" Thornton tossed the early edition of the local newspaper at his partner. They were parked outside Mah's Donut Shack.

The headlines cried about escalating attacks on elderly Vietnamese in Little Saigon by white skinhead gangs. One Viet youth was quoted as saying, "If the police won't make any arrests in these cases, then we'll take matters into our own hands."

"Funny, but the guy they're quoting in this article is our old buddy Louie-Louie."

"The one and only." Thornton nodded.

Abel scanned the headlines again. " 'Police Mystified by Baseball Bat Assaults.' And 'Little Saigon Simmers with Racial Unrest. Where Are Our Police When We Need Them?' I bet Hanoi bankrolls these bastards."

"Station Eighteen to M.A.G.-One-Three," the static crackled across the car radio. "Switch to the Diamond channel."

Abel switched to the scrambled frequency. "Send it, Dispatch."

"Shelley here, Lieutenant. Where the hell you guys at?"

"Mah's."

"Just got a delivery from the G.G.P.D. Detective Division I thought you guys would like to see: composites from that baseball bat murder down on Bolsa. I think you might recognize what the dicks at City came up with."

Abel and his partner made it to the Commo bunker in record time.

"Look like anyone we know?" Shelley cracked an ear-to-ear grin as he handed the composites to the M.A.G. lieutenant.

Abel stared down at the spitting image of R. Allen Casselmann.

Lt. Luke Abel refused to back down in the face of overwhelming objections to his suggestion. "We have to cancel the Tet Festival," he repeated.

"Impossible." Franklin Sanders was seated between Chief Daniels and a female councilwoman—one of the city's political activists known for her anti-police attitude. And her successful fund-raising. They were all angry that Abel had requested this early morning emergency meeting. "There's just too much money tied up in this year's festivities, Abel!"

"If it were last year, then I'd agree," the councilwoman said. "But 1988 was a fizzle, anyway, because of that gang-related shooting. This year, we've blitzed not only the Asian community with advertising promotions, but L.A. TV and radio, as well. For the first time, we've got some reputable Gold Coast investors involved. This could really turn into something big, Lieutenant."

"Why do you think the cities got together to build all those new band shells and bleacher stands?" Sanders asked. "We're expecting some big-name entertainment, as well as investor potential."

"Tell me more about the bombing this morning," Chief Daniels said.

"We were lucky. One of our undercover units was targeted, but no one was inside when it blew."

"Though Detective Zamora and C.S.O. Vo Luyen narrowly escaped death," Daniels told him.

"The bomb squad"—Abel nodded toward the councilwoman—"says the detonator wasn't hooked up to the ignition. Or Luyen and Zamora would be mincemeat right now."

"Whoever planted it lit a fucking fuse?" Daniels asked.

"Yes, sir. It wasn't all that sophisticated. Not even a

timer. Typical asshole VC sapper strategy, if you'll excuse my French, ma'am,'' he glanced over at the councilwoman again. "It was probably that same sonofabitch who phoned in the bomb threat a few days back." Abel locked eyes with Sanders briefly. "He was breathing hard—probably from doing wind sprints from the substation parking lot to whatever pay phone he used."

"You didn't recognize the voice?" Chief Daniels asked.

"Never heard it before in my life. This afternoon, someone else—an entirely different group of individuals from those who planted the bomb in Sergeant Thornton's car—phoned to say the Tet opening ceremonies will be disrupted by a device ten times as powerful."

"What?" the councilwoman rose from her seat.

"We believe they are members of one of two skinhead gangs from up north in the San Fernando Valley but don't have the proof we need yet to obtain arrest warrants," Abel explained. "Therefore, I once again respectfully suggest the Tet Festival be canceled. Otherwise, M.A.G. can't be responsible for—"

"It could be gang related, then?" Chief Daniels asked.

Before Abel could respond, Sanders cut in. "Let's not blow this mad bomber business all out of proportion," he said. "If Steel Dragon was behind destroying Sgt. Thornton's Plymouth, I would think Le Van Lui's just flexing his muscles—trying to show his degree of power to the civil authorities. I don't think we can really tie any of this to the upcoming Tet festivities."

"My office had received complaints about some 'white' gangs causing trouble in the area recently," the councilwoman revealed. "I must confess I didn't take any of it seriously. I mean, *white* gangs? Come on! Don't these kids have anything better to do with their time up there in—"

"You can count on the skinheads attempting to disrupt the activities," Abel said. "We've already had a couple of confrontations between both white gangs, the Mercs and the Rebs, with Lui's gang as well as local citizens."

"There're always going to be arguments between

blacks and whites, Mexicans and whites, Asians and whites," Sanders maintained. "In the old days, they threw switchblades at each other, and once in a while someone got stuck: pin the tail on the punk. No big deal. Not big enough to cancel the festival, anyway."

"These days they're carrying AK-47s and Uzis," Abel reminded him.

"What about communist agents?" Chief of Police Gordon Daniels removed his wire-rim glasses. "Spies from Hanoi, sent to disrupt social events in the Vietnamese community perhaps . . ."

Abel was relieved the man had chosen to sit in on this briefing with Sanders and the councilwoman. At fifty-nine, Daniels was much respected not only in the Vietnamese community, but also by the men under his command—which was even more important. He used to be all over Abel regarding M.A.G. tactics and priorities. But during the last few months, Thornton and Zamora had been treating the chief to drinks at the Can Tho Cabaret while his wife, a Naval medical officer, was away on active duty off the coast of Iran. And Daniels was beginning to like the undercover detectives. He appreciated the obstacles confronting them down in Little Saigon a bit more, it seemed.

"There're not that many flaming commies running around Garden Grove anymore these days—not since we caught that group responsible for fire-bombing the newspaper editor . . . and *that* was just a two-man show, not some huge underground conspiracy."

"Well, we'll just have to increase our foot patrols along Bolsa." Sanders locked eyes with Daniels. "Right, Chief? Saturate the area with marked cars and uniforms, even if it does put somewhat of a damper on the activities."

"A heavy police presence might make the citizenry feel safer," the councilwoman countered. "Let's not forget this is a three-day event. If the first twenty-four hours transpire without incident, the public will probably flock to Bolsa in droves. I can guarantee you the news media will be there in force. Waiting for something . . . *any-thing* to happen.''

"Unfortunately, I believe you're right.'' Abel nodded. "This is going to be a true media event. The press will be praying for disaster—you know how they are.'' He ignored Sanders's burning glare.

"Bearing all that in mind, Lieutenant,'' Sanders said, ''and the fact that this festival is crucially important to the welfare of the merchants and city offices involved . . .''

"Especially ours,'' said the councilwoman. ''We were facing some financial difficulty recently. Now it looks as if the Vietnamese business leaders are bringing a wealth of new investors into the city from Taiwan and Hong Kong. They're already talking about building a high-rise apartment complex and luxury hotel somewhere near the New Saigon Mall. Our portfolio has never looked better. And as far as solvency—''

"Then it's settled.'' Daniels cast an apologetic frown in Abel's direction. ''The festival goes on. And M.A.G. patrols the grounds in alternating, back-to-back, twelve-hour shifts—in plainclothes—twenty-four hours a day, until it's over.

"The Tet Festival is scheduled to kick off with a bang in less than seventy-two hours—no pun intended.'' Leaning back in his chair, Daniels cleared his throat. ''Am I going to be able to tell them we expect to proceed with the festivities without incident?''

"Right now, I don't see any problem, Chief.''

"What about all these assaults on Vietnamese locals?''

"The baseball bat murder was basically unrelated to the festival.'' Abel stretched the truth a bit on that one.

"It's just coincidence that that white punker gang picked their target right down the street from the festival grounds?'' Sanders charged.

"Coincidence,'' Abel muttered, glancing out the window of the fourth-floor office at several all-white G.G.P.D. cruisers parked in the Civic Center's backlot. Uniformed officers were inspecting their units prior to beginning the eleven-A.M.-to-eight-P.M. cover shift—instituted specifically for the week of Tet.

"What are our chances of taking those assholes into custody before tomorrow morning?" Daniels asked him. "The ones who are going around with a baseball bat?"

"We've got a plate." Abel was rubbing at his temples now. "And a possible ID, complete with composite and DMV file photo. Dispatch put out a metro-wide BOLO. It's only a matter of time."

"And what the flying fuck is a *BOLO*, Lieutenant?" Sanders leaned forward against his edge of the table.

Chest deflating, Abel emitted a long, dejected sigh. "It stands for Be on the Lookout, *sir*."

"That's what I thought." Sanders turned toward Chief Daniels and thrust his chin out. "He's using that goddamn military police crap again, Gordon! Christ, he's got all the dispatchers using it, too. It's not regulation and it's driving me insane!"

"What's the big deal?" Daniels removed his glasses and rubbed at his eyelids with massive knuckles. "So long as the message gets across, right, *Commander*?"

"This is Los Angeles . . . I mean *Orange County*!" Sanders hissed, turning to Abel again. "We use 'APB,' Lieutenant! *All Points Bulletin*! Not *BOLO*! You got that?"

"Yes, Sir." Abel shrugged. "I've *got* that."

"And another thing"—the Korean Fried Chicken pulled out his own pocket notebook—"I was informed by Communications that you already *had* the Mercedes punks *in custody* last night! How the *FUCK* did you let them get away?"

"That's the problem with living in a free society, Captain." Abel fought to keep the contemptuous smile suppressed and his features as grim as freeway gridlock. "Not enough probable cause. At the time."

"Now why don't we call this meeting a rap, and head for Bolsa," Daniels said. "Would you like to join us, Luke?"

Abel stood first. "I've got about a thousand leads to follow up on and—"

"Just keep your back to the wall and that partner of yours nearby."

"You can bank on it, sir."

"Okay, then it's settled: The Tet Festival goes on as scheduled. I'm putting my faith in your M.A.G. teams, Lieutenant." Daniels spoke to Abel, but he was staring at Sanders. "Now let's get the hell out of here."

"Can we handle that, Lieutenant?" Sanders smiled at his subordinate.

"No problem." The undercover detective rose to leave. "On with the show. I just hope it doesn't get too much like the real Saigon around here."

Ricky Pham stared down at his severed pinky finger lying curled up on the butcher's chopping block. Tears streamed down his face, but the fourteen-year-old fought the urge to cry out loud. If his father ever found out what was happening right now, the old man would chop off his *head*. Then go after Lui and his boys. One at a time. He would hunt them down. It did not matter that this was America, and no longer Vietnam. His father would make these bastards pay. But he would no doubt be ruthless with young, mutilated Ricky Pham, too.

"How does it feel, Ricky?" Le Van Lui slammed the meat cleaver down onto the severed finger, slicing it down the middle. A gut-flopping fear tore through Ricky as he watched what was left of his pinky finger spurt blood and peel away from the tiny, exposed bone. "Huh?" Lui struck the finger over and over again, filling the small, dark room with the sound of bones crunching. "How does it make you *feel*?"

Lui grabbed Ricky Pham's chin, pulled his face up close, until they were nose to nose. Eyes tightly closed, the boy finally said, "It makes me feel like . . . shit!"

"And do you know what will happen to you if you fuck up again, kid?" Lui slapped Ricky viciously, hurling him across the barren room of the ramshackle third-floor apartment. "You blow your last chance at getting into Steel Dragon."

"I know!" Ricky started toward the open door leading into the kitchen hallway, but Lui latched on to him again.

"We gave you the gun. We gave you the photo of Luke Abel. All you had to do was walk up, aim between his eyes, and pull the trigger. But you fucked up, Ricky. You fucked up royally."

"I'm sorry, Lui. But he was nice to me. I tried, but I couldn't do it."

"Well, you're so fucking lucky today, Ricky." Lui walked over to a closet, dragging the boy behind him. He opened the door and lifted a small shoe box off the floor—the only item inside. The gang leader opened up the top, revealing a block of plastic explosives attached to a timer. "Today, you get a chance to make amends."

"I can do it, Lui. I know I can kill the cop this time!"

Lui twisted the timer and connected a wire to the base plate. "Well, now is your chance to prove the other men wrong, Ricky. The other men say you're a pussy. They say you don't have any balls."

"I do, Lui! I *do* have balls. And I'll prove it too—"

"That's exactly what you're going to have to do, Ricky." Lui handed him the box. "Prove yourself. Show me you're worthy of membership in Steel Dragon." He guided the boy over to the window overlooking the Can Tho Cabaret parking lot. "You see that brown Chevy parked down there?"

"I see it." Ricky's eyes seemed to glow slightly.

"Take this bomb and attach it to the Chevy's undercarriage. It's set to go off in thirty minutes. Abel and his partner are on duty—they only just pulled up to the cabaret five minutes ago, and will stay less than a half hour. Then, they'll cruise Bolsa for another hour before heading back to their office. During that hour of limbo, they will be blown back to Bien Hoa."

"I can do it." Ricky took the box.

"Good," Le Van Lui took hold of Ricky's ear. "Because if you fail again, my friend," he held the meat cleaver in front of the boy's face, "I'll fucking lop off your head and stuff it down the toilet in Veterans' Park.

Now how would you like to go through eternity with shit stuffed up your nose?''

''I wouldn't like that, Lui. . . .''. the boy swallowed hard.

''Then get the hell out of here.''

≡ CHAPTER 19

RICKY PHAM STOOD in the shadows, staring at Lt. Abel's brown Malibu, for nearly ten minutes.

He didn't want to kill Luke Abel—not at all—but Lui and his Steel Dragon boys were the only boys he knew who would talk to him and overlook his slowness. They were like the big brothers he'd never had—the best friend his father refused to be. "I have to do it," he muttered under his breath, starting for the car, the shoe box held out in front of his body like a hornet's nest.

"You have to do *what*?" a hand clamped onto his arm, whirled him around.

Ricky found himself staring face-to-face with the ogre all his classmates claimed was a crazy man. The crazy man's eyes bulged as he whirled Ricky around, lifting him up off his feet, snatching the shoe box away. "What the hell you up to, ya little prick?"

Ricky stared up, wild eyed, at the unshaven, unkempt madman that was Victor the Vet. "Let me go!" he screamed. "I wasn't doing nothing!"

"*Choi-oi!*" Victor flipped the box's top off, revealing the C-4 plastique. "What are you, a little fucking apprentice VC or something?"

Two armed security guards standing in front of the Can Tho Cabaret's swinging front doors started over to-

ward the vast parking lot's dark edge. They recognized
Victor immediately and slowed down. "Everything okay,
Vic?" one of them called out.

"Yeah," he yelled back. "Just caught some punk
thinkin' about stealin' hubcaps!"

"Want us to notify the cops?"

"Naw! Forget it! He's history!" Victor hurled Ricky
against a big truck's unyielding quarter panel and watched
the boy scamper off down a nearby alleyway.

Cradling the shoe box under one arm, Vic the Vet then
limped off toward the black van parked a few feet away,
his crutches scraping against the blacktop.

Franklin Sanders pounded his desktop four times. He
was obviously pissed that he had to meet with Abel after
hours.

"What's the real lowdown on this Rebs versus Steel
Dragon shit, Abel? And I don't want none of the horse-
shit sweet talk you gave Daniels and that councilwoman
cunt yesterday. After that coroner's report on the dead
girl, I want the real lowdown."

"Nothing has changed since I gave my last report. If
it did, you'd be the first to know."

"You're square with me on that?" Sanders narrowed
his eyes at the veteran investigator.

"Square, sir. If there's any new developments, I'll
surely—"

An intercom box began squawking on Sanders's desk,
and he slammed a palm down on its red Transmit button.
"M.A.G.-One!" he answered the call.

A secretary's high-pitched voice crackled from the receiver. "Phone call for Lieutenant Abel, sir," she said.
"It sounds urgent—from Sergeant Shelley in Dispatch."

"Put him through." To Abel, he said, "That middle
phone there." And he rose from his seat and walked over
to a massive plate-glass window that overlooked the police parking lot below.

Abel listened to the air wheezing forth from Sanders's
chair again as it inflated and, as he reached for the receiver, one of the incoming lines began blinking.

"Just press the button that's lit up," Sanders told him. "You needn't pick up the receiver."

Abel was feeling defiant. Defiant and in need of privacy. Ignoring Sanders's instructions, he picked up the receiver, but Shelley's voice erupted over the intercom anyway. "Abel here."

"We're just about to air it, Lieutenant," Sergeant Shelley advised him. "At Bien Hoa Billiards. A gang fight brewing."

Sanders whirled around. "Let's get on down there and round 'em up for questioning!" he told Abel. "Every last one of the little squirt gang bangers. Bring them in! And *now*!"

Abel's grin had returned. He pocketed the pen and notebook and shrugged on his bomber jacket. Once the shoulder holster was concealed again, he headed for the door. "I'll keep you posted."

"You won't have to." The M.A.G. commander grabbed his jacket as well. "I'm coming with you."

Frowning, Abel shot out of the office without bothering to hold the door open. "Suit yourself," he muttered.

"Oh, and Lieutenant!" Sanders called after him. "About your request for two weeks of vacation time, starting tomorrow. The one that's been sitting on my desk for a while now . . ."

"For about a *month*!" Abel paused in the hallway outside, sensing the coming blow. He'd all but forgotten about the paperwork, considering such written requests routine—they had never necessitated a reply in the past. He rarely requested vacation or comp' time, but when he did, it was routinely granted. And without a reply in writing. This latest request had been perfect timing, however—it would coincide almost exactly with Xinh's arrival from the refugee camp.

"Well, I'm afraid I'm going to have to disapprove it for right now." Sanders's eyes seemed to gleam.

"What?" Abel demanded.

"At least until after this Tet Festival is over and done with. Chief Daniels and the City Council want me to expedite some positive results, and you're the best man

for the job!'' As he rushed up to join him on the stairs,
Sanders slapped Abel on the back in a rare show of confidence—a display Abel immediately knew was as phony
as a buck with South Vietnamese President Nguyen Van
Thieu's face on it. ''The faster we get on it, the faster
you can go AWOL for a week or two with your *tealock*.''

''That's mighty generous of you, sir. . . .'' Abel's enthusiasm had drained like blood from a decapitated
corpse. *Tealock* was Thai for shack-up girlfriend. Abel
resented the use of the word by anyone who hadn't actually served in Thailand or Nam.

''Sorry about your wife or your girlfriend or whatever
she is!'' Sanders was taking the steps two and three at a
time alongside Abel. ''I just can't spare you right now.
Anyway, it'll be good experience for your . . . woman.
What's her name?''

''Xinh.'' Abel's sigh was a long, heavy one. It was
also involuntary. He didn't want Sanders to know he had
won this round in their continuing battle of wits.

''Well, maybe she'll get to see you in action. They
love to watch the TV, you know—these foreign women.
Do they still have TV on the other side?''

''Not anymore.'' Abel wasn't sure, nor did he care.

''Well, you'll see: She'll be so glad to be stateside she
won't even *want* to travel outside the country so soon.''

''You might be right,'' Abel muttered. Then, under
his breath, ''But I kinda fucking doubt it. . . .''

''Hell, you'll probably even *thank* me when this is all
over.''

They burst through a set of double doors, into the
bright sunlight outside, and jogged toward the Malibu.

The car's engine was off, but music from Glenn's personal, jury-rigged cassette player drifted out to them in
a drum-thumping crescendo. Abel recognized the pursuit
music. Hugo Montenegro and another Clint Eastwood
soundtrack. The M.A.G. lieutenant's smile returned. His
foot came down on the two-door sedan's rear bumper, in
an attempt at startling Thornton which never worked.

''Yo, *bwana-san*!'' The stocky sergeant jumped from

the undercover unit and issued a snappy salute when he saw Sanders.

"I *hate* this fucking car," Sanders grumbled, ignoring Thornton's disrespectful antics.

Abel headed for the passenger-side door. "You drive!" he told his partner with a winking wave. The body language informed the heavy-footed investigator to leave no curb unstruck.

"Aw, gimme a break." Sanders hesitated climbing into the backseat when it became evident who would be in control of his immediate destiny. He despised Thornton's driving skills far more than the Malibu's looks.

It was the only way Abel could think of to retaliate on such short notice.

As they got into the Malibu, the triple-toned scrambler was clearing the police radio net of nonemergency traffic. "All units, vicinity Brookhurst and Hazard," the dispatcher announced, "in front of Bien Hoa Billiards . . . several reports coming in of gang fight in progress . . . that location . . . approximately fifty subjects . . . armed with chains and knives. . . ."

"Let's *di-di-mau* and *now*!" Abel slammed his door shut and clamped the flashing Kojak light to the Malibu's roof.

Without further encouragement, Thornton floored the gas pedal, switched the siren toggle to Yelp, and roared into the traffic crowding Bolsa Avenue. The Malibu's rear tires were smoking like a chimney fire.

Police cars were skidding up into the Bien Hoa Billiards parking lot from all directions. Nightsticks were flying. Officers wearing riot helmets rushed about, trying to keep from hitting one another as they chased down drug-crazed gang bangers in all the wild confusion. The brick walls rising up all around were aglow with flashing red and blue lights. More units raced in from the surrounding agencies, and dozens of wailing sirens drowned out the night as Dispatch called for a status and nobody took the time to radio back the situation.

"Man, the little fuckers are comin' out of the wood-

"I count about two dozen Rebs and twice as many Vietnamese," Abel said.

Thornton pointed to a group of arrestees being led over to the Garden Grove paddy wagon. "There's a bunch over there!"

"Wouldn't it be great if they'd all just waste one another?" Sanders finally joined the melee when it looked safe enough.

"It'll never happen," Abel said. "This is just the start of an all-out race war."

Luke Abel glanced up at the clock. Twenty-three-hundred hours. Sixty minutes before midnight. The so-called witching hour. In Little Saigon, it was simply three hours before the bars closed—three hours left to drink, dance, line up a lay, and reminisce about Old Saigon, twelve thousand miles and as many broken hearts away, where eleven P.M.—or twenty-three-hundred hours—meant martial law curfew, and a bullet in the brain if you were caught out on the street.

Lui, leader of the Steel Dragon gang, was lying low. Neither Abel nor Thornton had seen him on the street since their last confrontation.

Five officers were hurt at the gang fight that night—three from Santa Ana, when a machete-wielding Reb on crack went berserk; and two Westminster officers who were run down when a carload of Steel Dragon gang bangers tried to escape in their Volvo. The Volvo sustained two hundred and thirty two bulletholes from alert officers nearby. Two twenty-year-olds with felony narcotics warrants were killed.

Forty-four other Steel Dragon gang bangers were in the jail ward of County General Hospital, suffering everything from mild concussions to broken jaws. One had a backbone fractured in seven places. Another had both arms broken in bloody compound fractures.

Stitch Baxter didn't show up at the fight—just lesser members from his gang, it seemed. Ten hard-core Rebs and twenty-two initiates were taken into custody.

During questioning later, Thornton managed to talk

one of the Rebs into phoning Baxter so Abel could attempt to arrange a Tet truce between the gangs, but there was no answer. He also agreed to call Casselmann's girlfriends' house, but she told the M.A.G. detectives she hadn't seen the "two-timing bum" in over a week.

Abel stared up at the wall clock again. Twenty-three-oh-one hours. He sighed heavily as his eyes roamed across Thornton's substation movie poster from *The New Centurions*—only its highlights were visible in the darkened room.

Glenn was leaning back in the swivel chair on the opposite side of the cramped office, shoes up on his desk, head back, suspended in darkness—out of the lamp's glow.

Four hours until they could officially call it a night. He didn't dare sneak home early—even with Xinh due into Los Angeles International Airport in less than twelve hours. Sanders was on the warpath.

He turned down the lamp on his desk and laid his head on a stack of crime reports, trying to imitate his partner, but the computer hum from three consoles made sleep impossible.

☰ CHAPTER 20

FOLLOWING THE GANG fight at Bien Hoa Billiards, the paperwork alone kept his team at M.A.G.'s Little Saigon substation until sunrise, and Xinh's plane was due in at Los Angeles International Airport around eight o'clock that morning.

His loyal partner, Sgt. Glenn Thornton, accompanied Abel on the forty-minute ride north to LAX. They took the souped-up Malibu, and Thornton drove. He did a lot of talking, too: Lucas appeared scared to death.

He definitely needed the moral support. Today was the day. He and Xinh were finally going to be reunited. But what would he find at LAX? Whom would he greet at the arrivals gate? Surely she could not be the same Xinh of old. Not after what she had been through during the last sixteen years.

As they approached the exit ramp to Century Blvd., Abel's weary eyes locked onto a Singapore Airlines jumbo jet passing low over the freeway less than a mile up ahead, and he worried that Xinh's plane might have arrived early.

It hadn't, of course. Thornton had radioed Shelley twice already, since leaving Orange County, and the desk sergeant had checked with the airport police: Xinh's flight was still forty-five minutes out over the Pacific. They had plenty of time.

"You checked the spare tire?" Abel swallowed as they roared through a construction zone and passed several disabled motorists changing flats.

"I checked." Glenn smiled, shaking his head slowly. "Mellow out, brother. I'll get you there."

"Sorry." Abel sighed, checking his watch. Sixteen years since he'd last actually *seen* Xinh . . . fourteen since the fall of Saigon . . . forty-eight hours since he'd gotten any sleep.

They passed a man walking along the shoulder of the road carrying a gas can, and Abel leaned to the left, eyeballing the fuel gauge, but he didn't say anything.

There was the usual traffic jam at LAX, but Thornton placed the flashing Kojak light on top of the roof, and then began swerving in and out of trucks, buses, and other commuters until the Malibu was coasting up to the busy International terminal.

Xinh's plane was early. A woman was announcing its arrival over a loudspeaker even as they were pole vaulting through the metal detectors, badges in hand.

A huge 747 jumbo jet was coasting along the endless plate-glass windows on their right, and Abel asked, "Is that the one?"

"Over there!" Thornton had been listening to the woman on the loudspeaker. He pointed in the opposite direction.

Another 747 was already sitting at the gate, but none of the passengers had as yet disembarked. "*That* one!" Thornton nodded confidently, as doors leading to the gate corridor swung open and two flight attendants appeared, loaded down with a computerized flight manifest and looking exhausted after the eighteen-hour trip.

Several American and Filipino businessmen strode off first, and then a thirty-member Japanese tour group dressed in identical blue-and-white blazers and sun hats followed.

Welcome to the U.S.A. Abel gritted his teeth as they took what seemed to be an agonizingly long time getting

out of the way. Two globe-hopping families from Australia were next, and when one of their teenage children got
a strap from his backpack tangled on the security railing,
the long line of travelers ground to an unceremonious
halt.

"Aw, Christ . . ." Abel groaned.

"Hang in there." Thornton patted him on the back.
The detective sergeant was no longer smiling, however.

A commotion in the distance caught both their attention, and Abel tensed when he observed doors at the next
gate over flying open. Dozens of Asians—both men and
women—began streaming out. "Are they from *Xinh*'s
flight?" He grabbed Glenn's wrist. "Comin' out doors
on the other side of the plane?" Abel demanded.

"No way." Thornton started in that direction, though.

Suddenly, Abel heard a woman's nervous laughter.
Xinh's laughter.

She was standing alone in the arrival gate's doorway,
behind the throngs of departing Japanese tourists. All the
other passengers had come and gone. Xinh was just as
he had remembered her—more beautiful, in fact, than
ever before. She had done something to her hair—pulled
it back in some combination of Asian braids and feathered temples that still left the jet-black bangs cascading
down her forehead. She wore no lipstick or makeup, yet
Xinh was as attractive as any of the younger, twenty-
year-old stewardesses he'd seen since arriving at the airport—her cheekbones high and proud, her lips full and
rose-petal red, her nose narrow and finely chiseled, not
flat.

He had thought she would be wearing one of her *ao
dai* gowns, but today Xinh was clad in a modest purple
skirt and blouse. The same clothes she had worn when
he had taken her to see Barbra Streisand and Ryan O'Neal
in *What's Up, Doc?* Their last date before he left Saigon.

Somewhat uncertainly at first, Luke Abel started toward her. She stood tall for a Vietnamese—nearly five-
seven—but she would still have to look up into his eyes.
As always.

Xinh's resolve crumbled as Luke drew closer, however, and she seemed to slip toward the ground, nearly fainting, only to recover as the tears burst forth and she darted out from the doorway, arms open.

"Xinh!" Abel cried as they embraced, and he lifted her off her feet. He thought he might black out, but not caring . . . squeezing her back . . . kissing her again, drinking in the sweet, musky scent of her.

"I missed you, Lucas," she said, drawing her head back to gauge his expression. "I missed you so much I wanted to die! I died a little bit every day, I missed you so much!"

"Never again, Xinh . . ." He held her tightly, so tightly he was afraid he might break her, but try as he might, Luke Abel could not let go.

"What?" Xinh's laughter made him hug her even harder until he felt a seam along one side of the dress split a couple of threads. And he forced himself to control these strange, alien emotions—this love gushing up from a heart grown black after all those years. But Xinh was back. She would breathe new life into him. Like before, after the gun battles. "What?" she repeated, running her fingertips across his eyelids the way a blind girl might.

"I'll never again leave you like that," he promised, tears streaming down his face now. "Never ever again, Xinh."

She was still crying, too, but there was an amused, unsettling look on her face. Abel still held her in his arms, but Xinh placed the palms of her hands flat against his chest and pushed away in mock rebuke. "Do you know me, Lucas?" she asked, the tears still flowing freely.

"What?" Abel felt himself being strangled with emotion. "Yes, of course I do, Xinh. You're the woman I love. The woman I've been waiting for . . ."

"Are you sure?" She seemed to be taunting him. Xinh—the same old Xinh. She had been practicing. He could tell.

"Am I sure? Of course!" He tried to hug her again, but Xinh's elbows were locked.

"I dreamed that you married," she said, eyes narrowing with accusation. "I dreamed it many times." Xinh scanned the airport terminal the way a cop on stakeout would. Abel winced at the sight of so many pretty, tanned Southern California blondes strolling about. "I dreamed you married American woman."

There was no anger in her voice, only regret . . . sorrow. "No, Xinh." Abel stared into her eyes. "I'm here, aren't I? I waited for you, *manoi*. . . ." And he brought his wrists together behind the small of her back, forcing her elbows to bend.

There was no further resistance. Xinh wrapped her arms around her man and hugged him long and hard.

"Welcome to your new home," Abel told her. "Welcome to America. I love you, Xinh. I love you forever."

"I love you, too, Lucas." she finally allowed him to pry her arms apart so they could move. "Forever . . ."

But Xinh's forefinger wrapped around Abel's, refusing to let go. It was a sign of commitment from the old days—a funny little practice, but one nearly every Vietnamese woman he had met before Xinh liked to teach their boyfriends as well.

Abel had all but forgotten.

Xinh seemed to notice the stocky man standing behind her for the first time. She glanced up at Luke questioningly.

Abel chuckled. "This is Sergeant Glenn Thornton. My partner."

"I am honored to meet you, Sergeant," she said, extending her hand. Thornton hugged her instead. Abel feigned a burst of jealousy in separating them. "I'll get your bags." Glenn took her boarding pass and luggage tickets.

Later, as he escorted the two reunited lovers back to the Malibu, Xinh took notice of the many young, tanned, and shapely blondes crowding the airport terminal. "California girls." She seemed awed, not upset. "Just like the Beach Boys song." Her eyes drifted up to Luke's and narrowed suspiciously. "I know you butterflied on me, Lucas, but it is okay—how could you resist?"

"Jesus, Xinh," Thornton said, producing the most serious expression Abel had ever seen on his partner's face. "Luke here ain't mentioned another woman except you ever since I've worked with him—and we've been partners coming up on four tours of duty now!" He set Xinh's luggage down beside the Malibu and unlocked the trunk.

Xinh started to speak, but hesitated, seeming to consider Glenn's words. "You lie, you die," she warned him.

"Really, Xinh," Abel spoke in his own defense now as her eyes narrowed at his partner but the slightest hint of a smile appeared. "He wouldn't lie to a Saigon city girl! Nor would I! You'd find us out in a minute—just like back in Nam."

"*Viet* Nam," she corrected him.

"Viet Nam. You always knew when I was up to something—or you *thought* I was up to something. I never butterflied on you, though. Never."

Xinh seemed to notice the freshly washed and waxed Malibu for the first time. "Such a big car!" She sought to change the subject. "Is it really yours, Lucas?"

"It's *ours*," Thornton smiled proudly, as Xinh started to get into the backseat.

She froze, though, and ran her fingers along the rippled contours of the right rear quarter panel. "Are those . . ." Her fingertips probed a line of jagged punctures. "Are they *bulletholes*?" One eyebrow rose. But it was obvious she already knew the answer.

"We're assigned to Little Saigon," Thornton was trying to respond with a joke, but it backfired.

"There are many beautiful *Vietnamese* girls wandering around Little Saigon in search of an American husband, no?" Xinh grilled the man holding her hand.

"Where to?" Thornton turned over the engine, and Xinh tensed as the monstrous 440 rumbled to life, sending a vibration through the two-door sedan's floorboards.

"My goodness . . ." she whispered, clutching Abel's arm with both of her hands in a manner that said she expected the car to ascend into the skies at any moment. Aside from smoking Saigon buses and the small blue-

and-gold Renault taxis, the only "private" vehicle Xinh had ever ridden in was Abel's MP jeep.

"Drop us off at my pad," Abel responded. "Where else?"

"Roger your last." Thornton nodded. He was still smiling at the fact that there were no parking tickets clinging to the windshield wiper. "ETA: forty-five minutes, *bwana-san*."

"We *should* have gotten into the backseat." Abel laughed as his hand automatically fell to Xinh's thigh and she covered it with both of her own. "I'm not so sure I can wait."

He expected a mild reprimand from Xinh, but instead, she said, "I cannot wait either, Lucas. . . ." One of her hands began sliding toward his crotch.

"Don't mind me." Glenn Thornton stared straight ahead, tight grin intact. "Hear no evil, see no evil . . ."

"Dispatch to M.A.G.-Thirteen . . ." The radio hanging from the dashboard between Xinh's knees crackled to life, and the Saigon city girl nearly jumped into Abel's lap.

"Nobody's home," he told Thornton.

"I guess we better answer it," Thornton muttered. "Shelley knew why we were coming up here. He wouldn't bother you 'less it was urgent."

"Aw, fuck . . ." Abel sighed, grabbing the mike. "M.A.G.-Thirteen."

"Got a one-eighty-seven for you down in Little Saigon, Lou," Shelley advised them of a homicide.

"I think you are a very important man." Xinh held on to his arm again. "Like before. In Saigon. When you were an MP sergeant. All the time, people want you to come to places full of trouble and straighten everything out. Like that time I rode with you—the time your captain got so pissed off and threatened to send me to Chi Hoa jail and you to Germany."

"Hang in there, baby." Abel leaned over and kissed her cheek. "I'll get us out of this one, too."

"I thought life in America would be so peaceful." She saw that Thornton already had the Kojak light out from under the seat, and that its red lens was flashing with muted urgency. "I thought there would be no more . . . trouble. No more . . . headaches . . ."

"Saigon was a vacation compared to cop work in Southern California, Xinh," Abel told her, before thinking.

"Behind the McDonald's, Bolsa at Euclid, Lou," Shelley continued. "In the alley. A Caucasian female in the dumpster."

"A white chick?" Thornton locked eyes with him. "In Little Saigon?"

"Christ." Abel shook his head. "So it begins: retaliation. They're goin' after the women now," he told Thornton.

"Sergeant Verdugo's on-scene," Shelley advised further. "He's already ID'd her on a visual, and insisted I notify you ASAP."

"Send it." Abel swallowed hard as a dozen guesses teased him.

"Stitch Baxter's woman."

The extra effort was unnecessary. "Hit the siren," Abel told his partner.

≡ CHAPTER 21

XINH HAD SEEN death many times before—on the riverbanks of the *Song Saigon,* in alleyways near her home, even on the balcony of her own apartment the night Abel shot a *cao boi* sneaking along the rooftops at midnight—but the grisly sight of a young woman naked and mutilated, her head cut off and placed with the face ''licking'' the crotch, was almost more than she could handle.

Abel had insisted she remain in the car, of course, but moments after he and Thornton were down on one knee, checking for evidence, Xinh appeared standing over them—jaw set firm, hands on hips—her old days as an interpretor for the 18th MP Brigade fresh in her mind again. Abel thought he recognized the look: Xinh had noticed the many policewomen milling about, he decided; she was simply establishing territorial boundaries, announcing her arrival: Lucas Abel was taken, she was the taker, and that damn well better be understood. Abel doubted she had counted on finding such culture shock, decapitated, in the blood-soaked dumpster.

''Gimme the tweezers,'' he told Thornton. The lieutenant frowned when he noticed Xinh standing over him, but did not advise her to leave. Murder and mayhem were nothing new to her. The annoyed expression told him she just did not expect to find it so blatantly displayed in America.

"Can I ask questions?" she said.

"Go ahead." His expression stated he might not have any answers, however.

"Why do you wear plastic gloves?" She was thinking back to all the mornings he had dragged himself home from night watch, covered with caked blood. It hadn't seemed to bother him back then—Abel rather enjoyed the horror of it, she thought . . . wearing the crimson smear like a badge of honor. Perhaps he had finally tired of the stench of it.

Abel's chuckle was an irritated one, but he was not mad at Xinh. "The world has changed a lot in the last fourteen years, honey," he said simply. "I'll explain later."

"Okay." Xinh's eyes scanned the grim faces of the dozen or so officers securing the crime scene with yellow barrier tape. "Do you know who did this to her?"

"We have a few people in mind," he gently lifted the dead woman's head out from between her tangled legs and examined the hacksaw marks along her throat. Blood gushed from the empty eye sockets, and Xinh gasped.

Abel located a metal filing—possibly from the tool used in the street surgery—and cautiously removed it from the ugly flaps of flesh. He placed it in a large plastic vial, snapped the container shut, dated the evidence seal, and affixed his initials. "We'll have to let the boys in Forensics give it the once-over. You got a case number yet?"

Sergeant Verdugo gave it to him, and Xinh watched Abel scribble a six-digit number across the chain-of-evidence label. "I want photographs from every conceivable angle," he told Vinnie. "Black-and-white *and* color. Two different detectives to take them, too. Got that? I want *all* irregularities noted, and it'll take two dicks to do that."

The M.A.G. sergeant nodded. He appeared tired and bored. "Is this the Mrs. ?" Verdugo smiled at the woman standing quietly in Abel's shadow.

Abel nodded back. "Meet Xinh, Sergeant Vinnie Verdugo."

"Welcome to the strip," Vinnie's hands were covered with dried blood flakes, and he extended neither one.

"Thank you." Xinh lowered her eyes slightly. "I think."

"Good answer." Thornton grinned with approval. *I'm gonna get to like this lady,* he thought to himself.

The ceiling fan he had had installed nearly a year ago, in anticipation of this day, twirled lazily overhead, splitting the hot, muggy air inside the bedroom, cooling the two of them as they lay tangled together on the blue satin sheets—Xinh finally on top of him again, having just shed her skimpy black nightgown several minutes ago . . . breathing heavily as she moaned with delight, crotch grinding against his, the tips of her breasts barely brushing against his lips each time she slid back and forth.

Her long black hair cascaded down into his eyes—the scent reminding him of the magic, tropical nights they'd lain together in the heart of a city at war, thunder and lightning clashing about overhead, raindrops tapdancing on the roof.

She was moving her hips in rhythm to the drumbeat of Huynh Anh's *Men ruou ly boi* now, as she had back then, so many lifetimes ago. Singer Thanh Thuy's melancholy voice lingered in the background, drifting up from the tape player's speakers. But this was not Saigon. There were no flares floating on the edge of the city . . . no danger of rockets crashing down on them, interrupting the pounding of flesh against flesh with the ear-splitting roar of exploding metal ripping limbs away or splashing brain matter across the shrapnel-riddled walls.

Vietnam is in the past, he told himself as Xinh threw her head back—fingernails digging into his chest muscles as her arms locked tightly at the elbows, and her back arched, catlike. Nipples rigid, and the skin along her throat taut, Xinh's lips drew back away from her teeth, and a soft whimper left her mouth. A shudder swirled from her groin, up through her belly and chest, finally

affecting her limbs and fingers. He felt her toes curl, and
then she collapsed across his chest, with a long, pain-
purging sigh. The bottoms of their feet rubbed together—
Abel's soft, Xinh's coarse as sandpaper from so many
barefoot years toiling sunup to sundown in dried-up, un-
productive rice paddies.

After a few moments of silence, she whispered, "Your
turn, Lucas."

He could feel her heart thumping wildly against his,
and the stream of tears dripping from her face onto his
chest. "I already did." He kissed the top of her head,
eyes glued to the black, silky negligee sliding off the
edge of the bed.

"What?" She did not move as he stroked her long
hair. "You came the same time?"

"Um-hmmm . . ." Luke sighed. Xinh hugged him
tightly.

Later, after they had bathed together and were standing naked before the parrots' cage in Abel's living room,
feeding Sherlock and Bronson and Dirty Harry, Xinh
asked, "Who was the dead girl, Lucas? You seemed hurt
by her death."

Abel stared at the parrots who, in turn, stared silently
at Xinh, ignoring their birdseed. He was grateful they
had yet to utter an obscene word in this beautiful stranger's presence. He wondered how their manners would
change once they became used to seeing her. "I take it
hard anytime a young lady is murdered on my beat," he
tried to explain. "That's my job, Xinh. To protect people
who can't protect themselves."

A tense smile remained on Xinh's face. She didn't
enjoy delivering the continuous barrage of questions, but
it was simply not in her nature to ignore subtle signs of
fate and destiny when Buddha saw fit to reveal them to
her. In Saigon, she and Lucas had argued all the time.
But they never went to sleep without first making up—
by making love. Today, her eyes were never still. They
roamed the third-floor apartment continuously, ever
amazed at the seeming opulence Luke Abel indulged
himself in. After postwar Vietnam, Garden Grove was a

rose garden. Xinh forgot that, when Abel had paid the rent in Saigon, their apartment had been equipped with nearly as many appliances.

"You must love this woman very much." Xinh pointed to one of the poster-size enlargements of herself. They decorated every wall in the apartment. Dozens of them. "She will be jealous, I think, if she comes home and finds me here. . . ."

"Very jealous." Abel's smile returned the taunt. "She might very well cut off my dick and pickle it for *nuoc-mam* sauce."

"So many pictures." Her eyes grew sad as she went from photo to photo, examining a much younger Xinh. "You must be . . . obsessed with this woman. Is that the right word?"

"I was. I still am," Abel quickly corrected himself. He rushed over and embraced her, ran his tongue along the nape of her neck, tried to drag her back to the bed. Xinh resisted with a playful giggle—but only slightly—and they tumbled back onto the sofa again, instead . . . Luke filling his lips with the sweet taste of her breasts, and Xing simply savoring the touch of their bodies molding together so naturally.

The honeymoon-like bliss lasted only a minute or so, however, for Xinh could not confine herself to simple matters or a childlike innocence. There was just too much on her mind. She needed to give Luke Abel a piece or two of it.

"Tell me about the murders, Lucas," she rejoined him on the couch after spending several minutes at the balcony railing, gazing down on Bolsa. "Tell me why the Vietnamese are killing each other in your Hometown U.S.A. when there are no VC behind any of it." Her words stabbed at him like a dagger twisting in the small of his back, yet she was practically sitting on his lap now, hanging on to his arm, the side of her face against his chest.

"It's been going on since 1975," he told her. "Since the war ended. Since the refugees began congregating here in Orange County. But lately, it's been getting worse.

The white people—some of them—are causing trouble.
They are harassing the Viet gang members, and some
of the innocent citizens, as well. It is a bad mess. The
Tet Festival is coming up soon, and I think it's going to
be 1968 all over again.''

"Will the white gangsters come after me, Lucas?"
She clung to his arm.

"Not if *I* have anything to say about it." He kissed
the bangs concealing her forehead.

"I think you are so important a man here in Little
Saigon"—a shudder went through Xinh, so hard Abel
felt it—"that this gang called Steel Dragon will try to
kill you. Where would Xinh be then? Alone again? Defenseless. I would rather die beside you." She was trac-
ing hearts between his chest scars.

"I don't think it will come to that." Abel touched her
lips with his fingertips until her eyes rose to meet his.
Then he lifted her chin, and they kissed.

It was around noon. It rained a little bit, bringing the
sea breeze to Bolsa and, for a moment, it felt and smelled
and tasted like the Orient again.

Xinh was holding his gun hand in both of hers, and
she brought the scarred and calloused knuckles up to her
lips. "I think you do not get paid enough to do this job,
Lucas. Not enough at all."

"I think you are most enlightened on the subject and
one hundred percent right." He nodded solemnly. "But
it's what I do. It's the only work I know. The cops, the
street . . ."

"Come here." Xinh had laid back against the sofa's
edge. Arms held out to him, her knees fell slowly apart.
Abel watched the thighs spread wide like the wings of a
golden butterfly. "I know something else you do well,"
she said.

A squawk drifted over to them from the bird cage.
Dirty Harry bobbed his blue-and-white head up and down
with apparent anticipation.

"Shut up, you feathered fuckup!" Abel pointed a
forefinger at the bird in warning, and Dirty Harry flapped

his wings defiantly as the other two birds erupted into chirping laughter.

"You know me." Xinh's fingers fluttered, motioning him closer. To her, the birds were no more deserving of her attention than cockroaches falling from the apartment walls in Saigon. "I don't take no for answer. . . ."

Abel's grin returned. "I'm no longer nineteen." His tone was only slightly apologetic. "I'm not sure I can do it four times a night like in the good old days. . . ."

"Give it your best try, Magic Man." Xinh thrust her chin out at him in a teasing gesture.

That was when the phone rang.

"Aw, fuck . . ." he groaned, hesitating . . . deciding if his job was more important than Xinh right now. "Abel here." He finally picked up the receiver. Shelley's voice. "What can I refuse to do for you, Sarge?" Abel sighed as Xinh started to roll off him, then decided against it. She snuggled up across his chest, long legs squeezed together and between his own now.

"Sorry to be callin', but we just got a bomb threat down on Bolsa. The caller was a Vietnamese male. Said this time they weren't fucking around—those were his exact words. Said they weren't going after pig Plymouths this time—that they were going to blow up one of the new band shells before Tet. Then another bomb—twice as big as the one they're planning to set off tonight—will go off on Day One of the Tet Festival."

"Shit. Did the caller make any demands?" Abel glanced at his wristwatch, but his eyes refused to focus.

"Negative. He just said for me to make sure 'Lieutenant Abel and his partner were notified.' Sounds like he's targeting you personally, sir. Maybe you better watch your ass out there. Sergeant Thornton has notified me he is en route."

"I'm sure he can handle a simple nine-ninety-six." Abel yawned, and Xinh began licking the nipple over his racing heart.

"Sanders is on the warpath, claims he's en route to the scene with Chief Daniels, half the City Council, and every friggin' insta-cam TV crew in the metro area."

"What?" Abel's loud groan sent the three birds fluttering about in their cage.

"I don't know if the colonel has blown a gasket or his hemorrhoids flared up, or what, but he wants you down there to brief him on M.A.G.'s progress in the on-going gang investigations, and he wants you down there yesterday."

"Holy Christ." Abel bit into his lower lip, glanced at Xinh, then back at their reflections in the dresser mirror. "It's going to take me awhile to get us untangled." Abel's tone was a self-pitying one, but Shelley didn't sound apologetic.

"Yeah, that's what I figured. Why don't you let the Malibu have a day off. I'll have little Miss Vo Thi Luyen come by and pick you up in one of the Plymouths."

Abel swallowed hard. Sensing that something was wrong, Xinh's head rose up off his chest, and she stared into his eyes. *'No!* Have Glenn come pick me up," he told the desk sergeant, wondering if she had heard Shelley's scratchy, metallic words. And Luyen's name.

"Okay." He sighed. "You spoilsport—hope your whanger's been rubbed raw. But what ever happened to your spirit of adventure?"

"It's still there," Abel assured him. "I just don't want to wake up with my pecker liberated and hangin' out of my mouth. If you . . . catch . . . my . . . meaning."

"No need to spell it out," Shelley replied. "Catch you later. *Xin Loi,* GI."

Abel hung up the phone without wasting the mental energy on a reply.

"Fuck it," came a squawk from the other room. Abel glanced over Xinh's shoulder, at Dirty Harry perched innocently in the birdcage. The profane farewell had been the bird's, not Luke's. Obviously feeling more comfortable in Xinh's presence, *The Good, the Bad, and the Ugly* were starting up again. He hated to leave her alone with them but had no choice.

"Trouble?" Xinh asked, that knowing gleam in her eye.

"I have to go out in the field." He kissed her long but

softly on the lips. "I love you, baby. I'll be back later tonight. Before sunrise. I promise."

"I suppose so. Xinh has no choice in the matter: she's too lazy to go with you, and you would probably not allow her to tag along anyway. . . ." She watched him dress and holster his service weapon.

"You're probably right." Abel smiled.

≡ CHAPTER 22

GLENN THORNTON WAS sitting atop a fire truck when Abel pulled his Malibu up to the central band shell. "Always wanted to ride one of these suckers," he called down at his partner.

"Finally got your chance, huh?" Abel responded, noticing a black van parked across the street. "What else is shaking?"

"We got a deadline."

"What deadline?"

"Thirty-six hours or so before the Tet Festival is ready to kick off, and we've got to figure out why some anonymous puke out there wants to go ruin everything by plantin' bombs instead o' brotherly love."

"They actually found something this time?" Abel's eyes had finally opened all the way.

His partner pointed to three sheriff's deputies wearing full-cover body armor, kneeling in the dust below the wooden stage of a band shell. "The bomb squad's trying to figure out right now whether to blow it in place or transport."

"What have they got?"

"An old fragmentation grenade taped to some aging C-4. One of the guys told me it was partially disassembled when they rolled up, though. Oddest thing."

"Plastic explosives?"

"Yep. Vintage Nam stuff. Vic the Vet over there called it in. I guess he's not such a weirdo after all. Said he didn't see no one. Just woke up when he heard tires squealing, and the bad guys leaving. Said it might've been a Maxima, but he wasn't sure."

"Where's Sanders?"

"Oh, him and Daniels cruised by, but didn't stop when they saw none of the news media maggots showed up."

"What about this 'half the City Council' I was warned about?"

"Yeah, I heard the same shit. Why do you think I shaved? Another Sanders bluff to keep us on our toes and lookin' pretty."

"Well, I'm gonna pretty well fuck him up next time he pulls this shit. They don't need two detectives to investigate a bomb that hasn't even gone off."

Abel started walking over toward the bomb squad, when two of the sheriff's deputies rose to their feet, lifting a sandbagged platform between them.

The two M.A.G. detectives gave them ample room as they moved slowly toward the bomb-disposal truck. Several additional deputies standing around a thick steel barrel mounted on the bed of the truck helped lift the platform up. They, too, were wearing head-to-toe protective gear.

Abel watched them cautiously lower the explosive device down into the tank, climb into the black-and-white cab, then drive west—toward the beach—a two-car, light-and-siren escort in front. He motioned after the bomb-disposal truck's fading taillights. "You better go with them," Abel said, rubbing at his temples, "to preserve the chain of evidence, if nothing else. I'll meet you back at the substation when you get in."

"Why don't we both go, *partner*?"

"Because rank has its privileges."

"Roger that." Thornton patted him on the back and disappeared through the maze of police units.

* * *

"Station Eighteen to M.A.G.-One-Three."

Abel frowned as he reached for the microphone. "Some dispatchers just can't bring themselves to say the number thirteen," he told Thornton on the next night's shift. The mike to his lips, he said, "M.A.G.-*Thirteen*, Bolsa and Brookhurst."

"Ten-four, Lieutenant . . . be advised Car Three-twenty-two is responding to the festival grounds on a nine-ninety-six. He wanted me to notify you."

"We're en route."

"At twenty-three-oh-five hours."

"Another bomb threat?" Thornton appeared irritated.

"I'm going to hope for the worst and expect things to turn out twice as bad." Abel was already placing the flashing red light on top of the Malibu's roof.

Two canine teams were already on-scene when the M.A.G. detectives arrived. The five acres of vacant lot running along the southside of the Bolsa Strip between Brookhurst and Bushard streets that had been set aside for the festival had been transformed dramatically since Abel last saw them. Row upon row of carnival-like booths were erected, and three large circus tents rose up through the night haze between brightly decorated band shells. Vendors were already setting up their stalls—it appeared some might spend the night camped out in vehicles parked alongside their rented spaces. A giant ferris wheel and several smaller amusement rides were slowly going up in the midst of it all, and a hundred hammers raced against time to put the finishing touches on four shooting arcades and twice as many booths. "Jesus, they've even got a haunted house back there," Thornton observed.

"Check out the truck." Abel pointed to a tractor-trailer rig parked on the side of the road. It was loaded down with new luxury automobiles. "They're not just selling ethnic food and 'Freedom For Vietnam' bumper stickers this year."

"I heard there will be a total of twelve raffles held," Thornton said. "One for each animal represented in the Chinese lunar calendar. Those cars go to the winners. Can you believe how far these people have come?"

"Yep. It's certainly big time this year. That's where the six TV insta-cams are going to go." He pointed at a small, man-made hill rising above all the commotion and drifting sawdust.

A vicious dog was suddenly bouncing off the glass of Abel's driver's-side window. "Jesus H. Christ!" the M.A.G. detective flew halfway into his partner's lap.

"Kill, King Cong! *Kill* those two faggots in the brown Malibu!" a husky voice commanded.

Boisterous laughter from several leather-clad officers standing outside reached Abel's ears above the nonstop barking of the German Shepherd.

"If you don't call that half-breed mutt off, I'm gonna ram this .45 down its throat!" Abel threatened. Climbing back over behind the steering wheel, he rolled his window down a couple of inches.

"Kill! *Kill!*" the K-9 officer was still screaming. "Off with their heads! Death to the limp-wristed queers!"

Abel actually drew his service weapon, and the dog handler rushed to control his animal. "Hey-*hey*! Lieutenant!" he said. "We were just *kidding*, sir."

"Find anything?" Thornton asked while Abel kept his eyes on King Cong, and the huge police dog strained against his leash in the M.A.G. detective's direction.

"Nothing whatsoever, Sergeant. Nothing *job related*, anyway." He glanced over at a shapely young woman setting up a vendor's booth.

"We'll be on our way then," Abel said.

"Carry on, sirs," the handler's insolent partner muttered, and the two K-9 officers walked off through the mist, dragging their police dogs behind them.

Le Van Lui stared out through a crack in the blinds. At this predawn hour, the streets were still deserted. No patrol cars had even cruised past. From the Steel Dragon safe house on Head Street, he could see the lights along the Bolsa Strip, glowing faintly, beckoning him.

"It is time we move our operations, Lui." The voice behind him sounded distant.

"Steel Dragon stays here, Chung. In Orange County.

I will not be frightened off by a two-bit flatfoot the likes of Luke Abel.''

"Don't sell him short, Lui. He's intelligent. And he's been to Nam. He spent many years there. He knows our ways, and the ways of those who came before us. That worries me. I still find it a blessing from Buddha that his M.A.G. team has not stumbled onto this place.''

Lui stared at his Second in Command and the half dozen lieutenants seated in a semicircle behind him on the large Oriental rug. Lui's riflemen were positioned beside every window, at every door—two to a station, all heavily armed with automatic weapons. "I thought you showed some grit when you cut off the head of that white whore, but now you sound like a woman," Lui told the twenty-five-year-old. "If you want to run away, then do it. *We* will stay and defend our territory.''

The older man laughed. "It is not your turf," he said. "It belongs to the Americans.''

"That means nothing to me. This land came to them through accidents of birth. Now it belongs to Steel Dragon.'' Grudgingly, he added, "And Blue Bamboo.''

There came a series of rapid knocks at the door. Everyone in the room tensed as the entry guards scanned their peepholes. Finally, a runner was allowed in.

Lui accepted a rolled-up newspaper. It was a copy of *Saigon Coi Bao*.

"Breaking legs over protection money and robbing residents of their hidden gold stashes was one thing, Lui.'' Chung leaned over Lui's shoulder, scanning headlines. "But now you've gone and iced two white trash punks, and The Man don't take kindly to that—when you gonna learn?''

Lui tensed. His eyes shifted across the dark room to his driver, Brass Balls—seated against the far wall, drinking a beer. Brass Balls was Chung's best friend. Lui never trusted one, unless he could see the other. Lui's lawyers had just pulled every string in the book to get Brass Balls released from the monkeyhouse on bail.

"Times have changed since we were kids, haven't they, Lui?'' Chung taunted. His men were silently laughing at him now: The headlines were declaring the Tet Festival would go on as scheduled, despite rumors of an impending gang war and actual threats from some of the local gang leaders. The paper did not mention Steel Dragon by name, and that also irritated Lui.

"Then that seals it." He returned to his window. "Today Steel Dragon makes a stand, whether you're with us or not."

"What's the scam, my man?" Chung tilted his head skeptically.

"Today we become Viet Cong." Lui's sly grin sent a chill down the older gangster's spine. "Like guerrillas, we place one final bomb at the festival, to go off during the opening procession. Make it look like Stitch Baxter's Rebs did it. Abel will be there, and the blast will be big enough to take out his entire unit and as many fools who crowd the Tet parade route, ignoring our warnings. My own trusted blood brother shall plant the device." He locked eyes with Brass Balls, seated on the other side of the dimly lit room.

"And also like guerrillas, we ambush the Rebs," Lui continued. "They will surely arrive to monitor the opening ceremonies. Maybe they'll plant a bomb or two of their own—just to make things more interesting. Regardless, we hit them with everything we've got. From the rooftops, the sewers—everywhere. We can out-gun the police. They are fools. I have already checked their security precautions. The patrol commanders have ignored Abel's warnings as well, and are treating this like any other event. Crowd control and some dog handlers to check for hidden explosives along the parade route—that's all. They think we sleep from four A.M. until noon. *Ha!*"

"Then we must act fast." Brass Balls, appearing suddenly sober, rose from his chair. "On the way over here, I spotted the Rebs at an all-night café on Beach Boulevard. Many of them. They definitely mean business, Lui. They're out to avenge that white bitch's death."

The phone rang, causing several of the gang members on both sides to jump. Brass Balls calmly reached over and answered it.

"It has begun." He gently replaced the receiver. "One of the new girls—Lai is her name—reports they're headed down Bolsa. Stitch Baxter and his Rebs."

"Ten-four, thanks," Thornton called in to Sgt. Shelley over his pak-set. Turning to Abel, he said, "Lab just got a laser match on those prints the murderer left on Queenie's breasts. Belongs to some punk named Diem Chung. He's Le Van Lui's number-two man. Lab boys lifted a righteous latent off that Rebel patch stuffed into the dead Viet gang girl's mouth, too. Came right off Stitch Baxter's fucking pinky—can you believe that? I told Shelley to air an APB on both the bastards."

The M.A.G. lieutenant put away his tray of shells and looked up as the phone rang. "Legendary Luke Abel here."

"Now it begins, Lieutenant." The line went dead and at the same moment static burst forth from Thornton's pak-set again. Abel caught the codes.

"Turn that sucker up!" He reached over to grab the portable radio's volume switch as a three-toned scrambler cleared every police channel in south Orange County.

"*Nine-ninety-seven!* Bolsa and Head Street—on the south side! *NOW!*"

"All units . . . One-fifty-four is requesting assistance, Bolsa and Head Streets, southside . . . units to respond, identify!"

"Let's *di-di-mau* and *now*!" Thornton grabbed the pak-set sitting on the desk and started down the stairs to the street below. Abel chased after his partner.

≡ CHAPTER 23

"DISPATCH TO FIFTY-FOUR, what's your status?"

"Gang fight! Forty-plus subjects, with chains, knives, and firearms! Would you guys hurry up and get over here?" Shots could be heard ringing out in the background as the officer calling for help kept his microphone keyed an extra second or two. His car's emergency equipment blasted the airwaves with Yelps and a long, drawn-out Wail.

"Gang fight?" Thornton exchanged bewildered glances with Abel as they piled into the Malibu and he fired up its 440. "At six in the morning?"

"Perfect timing." Abel checked his watch. "The Tet Festival's opening procession starts in exactly two hours. What better way to disrupt the damn thing? Head Street's a T-intersection—right across the street from the festival grounds."

M.A.G.-13 pulled up two minutes later to find nearly a dozen Vietnamese youths beating a pink Mercedes with baseball bats.

"M.A.G.-Thirteen on-scene!" Abel yelled into the mike as they skidded up behind several units.

"Hold it!" Abel got out of his car and fired a shot up into the air. But it had no effect whatsoever. The fighting continued. He holstered the .45, grabbed a nightstick from under the Malibu's front seat, and started toward the battered Mercedes.

"Station eighteen to any unit in the area, another nine-ninety-six at the band shell," the dispatcher aired a bomb threat call, droning on without emotion despite all the excitement on the street.

"King-Niner, responding from Headquarters . . ."

"King-Niner, we need you over at Bolsa and Head Streets, south side!" Abel yelled into his pak-set.

"Roger!"

Abel noticed that the rumble was going down right in front of the Steel Dragons' clubhouse on Head Street, a stone's throw south of the Bolsa Strip. Lui didn't think M.A.G. knew about the place, but Sanders had had people watching it off and on for several months now. The white gangs had certainly picked a poor place to start trouble—or else they underestimated the strength of the Steel Dragons.

R. Allen Casselmann lay across the front floorboards of his Mercedes, skull crushed and lower jaw nearly severed. "Jesus!" Abel reached out and held on to the two nearest Vietnamese gang members. He handcuffed them both to the shattered windshield frame, then turned to find three more approaching with baseball bats swinging wildly over their heads.

"Hold it right there!" He drew his pistol again and began waving it back and forth, side to side.

The trio continued to advance toward him, and Abel shot the closest youth in the midsection. The teenager folded over, screaming loudly and clutching his belly. Bright red blood spurted from between his fingers with each frantic heartbeat as the other two hoods fled—abandoning him to the police.

"This is fast turning into a major clusterfuck!" Thornton was back to back with his partner now as two more carloads of Rebs roared up the street. They were all hanging out windows, brandishing rifles and shotguns.

Abel didn't hesitate. He pulled the pak-set from his belt again and yelled for interagency help: "*NINE-*

NINETY-EIGHT! Head Street just south of Bolsa! Get
the Sheriff's Department in here! NOW!''

"Roger, M.A.G.-Thirteen!" Sergeant Shelley had
taken over the primary Police Communications console
and recognized his voice. "We've already got Santa Ana
and Westminster rolling! Hang in there! Help is on the
way!''

"You boys better think twice!" Thornton yelled at the
dozen or so white youths jumping down from two con-
vertibles. The cars were fancy, but the Rebs looked like
tattooed rejects from a survival camp. "You're talkin'
felony time if you don't call a fucking retreat, and now!''

"We want the gooks responsible for icing Queenie!''

"Stop and go back to your car!" he said, ignoring the
demand.

"Screw the pig!" One of the Rebs was getting anxious, and Glenn drew his pistol. "Yeah, off the porker!''
another one cheered. "We'll take care of the chinks
later!''

A Rolls-Royce roared up through the wave of rampag-
ing hoodlums, and Abel recognized Stitch Baxter behind
the wheel. The Reb leader skidded the expensive automobile up between the M.A.G. detectives and the gang
advancing on them, and climbed up onto his car's front
hood, waving an M-16 automatic assault rifle. "Back off,
Goddamnit!" he demanded of the other skinheads.

"Hey!" one of the Mercs began yelling hysterically.
He was standing on the Mercedes's running board, and
staring down into the front seat. "It's R. Allen! And he's
DEAD!''

With that shocking revelation, the others started backing away. And not a moment too soon. A Sheriff's Department helicopter swooped down into a noisy hover
directly overhead, and Abel and Thornton dashed for
cover as it began dropping tear-gas cannisters down onto
the combatants.

Sirens converged on the gang fight from both sides of
Head Street, and the area was quickly sealed off, pre-
venting anyone from escaping. "Holy shit!" Thornton's
eyes slowly rose above the Malibu's dashboard. "Kinda

remind you of the Nam, Luke?'' he pointed to where the wall of gunsmoke was rapidly parting as tons of brute iron mass roared up toward the rumble.

Turning off of the Bolsa Strip, a V-100 Assault tank—the Sheriff's Department's official battering ram—began lumbering down toward the action on man-high, bullet-proof tractor tires. The armored vehicle's battering ram consisted of a cement-filled barrel mounted on the end of a fifteen-foot-long steel beam that protruded from its armor-plated turret. The .50-caliber machine gun swinging slowly back and forth over the top crewmen's hatch created quite a menacing appearance—even though it wasn't firing. Yet.

A squealing of tires nearby caused heads to turn as a black Nissan Maxima catapulted up out of an underground parking garage beneath the Steel Dragon safe house. Despite the car's tinted glass, Abel recognized Lui behind the wheel. But before he could respond, another car was skidding up into the intersection: Zamora and Luyen inside one of the P.D.-blue Plymouth Furies, siren screaming. The two cars nearly slammed into each other head-on—Zamora swerving to the left, and Lui turning his steering wheel hard in the opposite direction.

Zamora brought her unit into a broadside skid that blocked the roadway. A wall of dust and gravel was thrown up against the Maxima's windshield, but Lui merely swerved onto the wrong side of the boulevard and attempted to make the sharp turn back down onto Head Street—missing the sliding Plymouth by inches.

Rachel's unit fishtailed out of control, but she held on to the steering wheel and hit the brakes as the sheriff's monstrous battering ram suddenly loomed into view.

Lui's Nissan was not so lucky, and the two police women watched helplessly as the Maxima's driver, unable to stop in time, crashed into the tank. The battering ram slammed down through his front hood and windshield, squashing the foreign import like an accordion and pinning Le Van Lui in the wreckage.

''Let's go!'' Abel started cautiously toward the smoldering Japanese four-door. Thornton sprinted past him service weapon already out, safety off. Guns drawn as well, Zamora and a dozen other officers rushed up to the Steel Dragon leader.

"You have the right to remain silent, lowlife." A grinning Glenn Thornton began reciting the Miranda warning to Lui as the sound and odor of leaking gasoline reached them both.

"Please . . . get me outta here before this piece o' shit blows up!" The gang leader's plea was suddenly meek, his vicious defiance gone. He appeared miraculously unscathed in comparison to his totaled-out car but unable to move from the shoulders down due to a warped steering wheel jammed against his chest.

"Now listen up: you have the right to an attorney. . . ." Thornton said matter-of-factly.

"Come on, you guys. Gimme a fucking break! I can smell *gas*!" Lui's bulging eyes darted about frantically.

"We've already radioed for the fire department rescue squad, scumbag. Now, if you cannot afford an attorney—but we all know you can, seein' as how you control half the gambling and prostitution rackets in Little Saigon—one will be appointed to represent you. . . ."

The K-9 unit pulled up—King Cong barking wildly in the backseat as the German Shepherd struggled unsuccessfully to get through a half-open window and sink his teeth into a nearby skinhead. Abel sent the Canine car down toward the bandshells and reviewing stand to investigate the pending bomb threat call.

Several wailing Vietnamese women—Lui's gals—gathered around the crushed and twisted Maxima. Zamora tried to grab Lai's wrist, but she twisted free and ran off into the sunrise.

Thornton produced a Zippo cigarette lighter and flipped the top open. "Who offed Queenie, Lui?" His thumb began rubbing at the flintwheel.

"Chung!" Lui did not hold back long, verifying the lab teams' suspicions. "Diem Chung wasted the honky bitch!"

"Aw . . ." Thornton nodded, his mini-pocket recorder silently turning. "And the two Rebs back at the Golden Buffy Gift Shop?"

"You *know* Tuc was behind that—Abel *busted* him there!" He began struggling to squirm out from behind the damaged steering wheel and the horn started blaring.

"Tuc?" Abel sought clarification.

"You fuckers know him as Brass Balls!" Lui yelled.

"But *you* ordered him to shoot the white boys, right, Lui?"

"No way, man! He was acting on his own! He's ambitious! He was trying to impress Chung. You find Tuc, and you'll have a righteous Murder One arrest to boast about, Thornton!"

"What about the so-called bomb supposed to go off on Bolsa this morning—at the parade," Abel asked. "Where's it at, Lui?"

"I don't know nothin' 'bout no motherfuckin' bomb, goddamnit!" He squirmed and twisted violently now as gasoline soaked his legs and lower torso. "Talk to Stitch Fucking Baxter about *that*!"

"Fire is one hell of a way to die, Lui," Thornton rubbed at the Zippo again. "But I guess we might have to burn Steel Dragon to the ground in order to save Little Saigon."

Abel glanced up toward the Bolsa Strip—already, the ceremonial parade was passing them by. The opening, sunrise procession was headed for the Tet Festival grounds two blocks to the west—its participants oblivious of the goings-on only a half mile down the hill.

"You'll never . . . find . . . it," Lui groaned, a spark of defiance back in his eyes. And then he fainted, overcome by the fumes.

"Well, shit," Thornton muttered, obviously disappointed.

Abel picked up his pak-set. "M.A.G.-Thirteen to King-Niner."

"Send it, Lou."

"Anything?"

"Negative. I've got a sheriff's dog squad on-scene. They've been over the parade route and the bandshells and everything in between with a fine-toothed comb. No devices whatsoever. King Cong is bored silly.''

"Ten-four.'' Abel bit into his lower lip. There was nothing else to do now but wait and hope Louie-Louie was a liar.

As Zamora busied herself at the scene of the gang fight, dividing up the paper work among her fellow officers, Luyen was approached by a young teenager clad entirely in black. His hand was tightly wrapped with bandages where a finger had been "liberated" by Le Van Lui. She did not recognize him immediately, but the lieutenant's earlier remark came back to her: *Ricky Pham—the retired Saigon cop's kid . . . the oddest thing happened downstairs tonight. . . .*

Glancing around frantically to see if any of the gang members were watching, Ricky took hold of her wrist and led her away from all the commotion.

"The bomb,'' he whispered as soon as they were alone. "I saw him plant it. Tuc. Lieutenant Luke calls him Brass Balls. He hid it. Him and Chung. I had to help him. They were testing me—Lui and the others. I know it. They are going to ice me because I failed to shoot Luke. They made me go along this morning—just a game: fuck with the doomed boy. I helped plant it— the bomb. I didn't want to. They made me.''

"It's okay, it's okay!'' Luyen spotted Abel in the shifting sea of P.D. blue and waved him over. "Tell me where they hid it.''

"It's going to go off in the middle of the procession!'' Ricky Pham was talking nonstop now. "As soon as the parade begins . . . the opening ceremonies!''

"Where . . . is . . . it . . . hidden?'' Luyen demanded slowly, in a firm voice. Sirens passing by failed to drown out her words.

"The shrine . . . in the Buddha shrine . . .''

Luyen's mind raced. She could not think of any temples close enough to Bolsa where disruptions there might interfere with the procession or festivities. "The shrine? *Which* shrine?'' she demanded loudly—her voice difficult to hear now as a dance troupe of five-year-olds, clad in traditional costumes, made their appearance and the nearby crowd erupted into an approving roar of applause.

"What is it?" Abel trotted up to them, out of breath. But his expression changed when he saw the terrified look on Ricky Pham's face.

"The bomb . . ." Luyen began, when a single shot rang out.

Blood splattered across Abel's face as the rifle slug exploded out of Ricky Pham's back.

Screaming, Luyen watched helplessly as the boy's lifeless body crumpled to the ground. Her hands, also smeared in crimson, covered her face in shock. The nearby crowd was still going wild with applause and loud murmurs of approval over the tiny dancers.

"Are you okay?" Abel grabbed her shoulders and shook as they both dropped to their knees beside a giant tree trunk. He ignored the dead youth.

"I'm . . . I'm all right."

"Here!" He handed her the small .380 automatic from his backup ankle holster and pointed into the rising crimson sun. "You stay here with the kid. The shot came from that rooftop overlooking the Bolsa Strip. I'm gonna go check it out."

As Abel and Thornton raced toward the fire escape ladder across the street, Luyen rushed to check out the procession, hoping to spot something—anything suspicious that might lead her to the bomb.

Several high school girls clad in thin, form-hugging *ao-dais* passed by first. They were carrying streamers proclaiming FREEDOM FOR VIETNAM! and reminded her of the countless banners that once hung suspended over Tu Do and Le Loi streets. Back in Saigon. But all she could see, over and over again, was the look on Ricky's face when the bullet struck him.

Young boys from the Cultural Center skipped up and down the parade route, blowing horns and lighting long strings of firecrackers. A lengthy assemblage of golden-robed bonzes followed the girls. They carried a heavy, ornamental arch, chanting and humming as their leader struck a gigantic suspended gong with each footfall. They passed a black van parked on the side of the road.

Behind the monks were several dozen ex-ARVN soldiers, many carrying the red-and-gold flag of South Vietnam. In their ranks were scattered American 'Nam vets. They, too, carried flags—Old Glory and the black-and-white Prisoner of War/Missing in Action symbol. Luyen searched for Vic the Vet's face, out of habit, but was unable to spot him, and quickly forgot about the man. None of the ex-GIs seemed to have noticed the distant high-powered rifle discharge over the ear-splitting din and crackle of black cat and M-80 firecrackers.

A procession of smiling Vietnamese nuns followed the grim-faced warriors. Down the block, the floats began. But something being carried behind the nuns caught the Community Service Officer's attention.

A shudder went through Vo Thi Luyen when the sacred Buddhist shrine passed by her. The altar was a miniature replica of the ancient temple at Hue, South Vietnam's Imperial City, and was carried upon the shoulders of four monks, clad in bright orange robes. Luyen was not sure if it was a cop's gut instinct going to work, or woman's intuition, but she suddenly knew that the small shrine was where the bomb was hidden.

That was all it took.

Luyen stepped out in front of the bonzes, Abel's pistol a lightning rod in her extended hands, pointing skyward. "Stop!" she directed, her small feet braced apart in a no-nonsense, businesslike stance.

Though shocked by her outrageous actions, the sight of the snubnosed gun barrel nonetheless brought the procession to an immediate halt. "Lower the altar," she said in a firm voice.

Again, the monks complied, and she motioned for them to move back. As two motorcycle officers rushed up to the disturbance, Luyen pulled open the tiny shrine's gold-layered doors, revealing the fist-sized vial of nitroglycerin dangling from a timer and det' cord inside.

A scream went up through many of the spectators lining the parade route as Vietnamese chatter announced that a bomb had been found. Word spread like wildfire through the throngs of war-weary refugees. They scattered like gazelles being stalked by a Bengal, many trampling over Ricky Pham's blood-soaked body without even seeing it.

"Motor-Seven to Dispatch." One of the 'cycle officers was already off his machine, calling for assistance. "Get the bomb squad back over here, ASAP! *Right now!*" He seemed to recognize Luyen, motioning his partner for restraint as the other cop started to draw down on her.

"According to the timer," the second officer said, following a cursory examination, "we've got about half an hour to get it disarmed."

"The bomb squad is en route, Motor-Seven." Sergeant Shelley's voice rose from the Kawasaki 1000's radio. "Their ETA is zero-five. They ask that you stand by for crowd control, over. . . ."

Tears of relief filled Luyen's eyes as she stared at the tiny Buddha statue cloaked protectively within the shrine's gold-leaf walls. Bringing clasped hands to her forehead, she dropped to her knees in thanks as shots rang out on a nearby rooftop.

People continued to rush about all around her, but Luyen remained on her knees. Her eyes eventually followed the two motorcycle officers' gaze: Lieutenant Abel and Sergeant Thornton were standing over someone's body on the roof line's edge, three stories up. Le Van Lui's number-two man: Diem Chung. They also had a second gangster in custody, bandoliers of ammunition clips crisscrossing his blood-smeared chest.

Brass Balls.

Imitating a Wild West gunfighter, Thornton blew imaginary smoke rings from the barrel of his pistol as he waved down at the applauding crowd on the street below.

Abel was busy handcuffing the dead man's hands behind his back, and wondering how he would break the news to Sergeant Pham about Ricky.

* * *

After the bomb squad had carefully transferred the explosive device to a metal-and-sand container and transported it a safe distance from the festival, the Tet parade resumed. Luyen watched the brightly colored floats for a short time, then headed back to assist in the gang fight cleanup still in progress.

When she arrived back at the fight scene, she met Abel and Thornton leading a handcuffed Brass Balls Tuc to their Malibu.

"Well," Thornton said, "if it ain't our own Wonder Woman." He was holding two confiscated hunting rifles in a long, clear plastic evidence bag.

"Cool it, Glenn," Abel told his partner, then turned toward Luyen who stared over at a team of paramedics working feverishly to coax life back into Ricky Pham. "That was great detective work, Officer," he said.

Community Service Officer Vo Thi Luyen looked down at the ground, then back at Abel. "Thanks. But it was that young kid who saved the festival. And he's dead." Her eyes shifted back to the ambulance crew again, but they had given up, and were peeling the pads and wires off the unmoving boy's chest.

"And this is the scum who killed him," Thornton said, shoving Brass Balls toward the Malibu. "We got him on the roof overlooking the parade just after the bomb squad pulled up. Him and one of Lui's other Steel Dragon assholes."

"Brass Balls here ain't so tough, after all." Abel motioned toward a tarp-covered corpse being wheeled on a gurney over toward the coroner's van. "That scrote in the bodybag there—Chung—actually wasted Ricky. Brass Balls didn't get off a single lousy shot."

"He rabbited as soon as he saw us coming." Thornton grinned.

"But I guarantee you he's looking at thirty years hard labor in Chino or San Quentin, all the same." Abel stared through the gang hit man. "If I can prove special circumstances here today, I'll wager we can grant you a visit with the executioner, too."

"You're dreamin,' Luke," Thornton sneered. "This is California, man."

"He's right!" Brass Balls erupted with hideous laughter, throwing his head back. "I'll be out in three or four years, with good behavior. We'll *all* be out. This is *America*, man! I'll be out—and I'll be *back*!"

"And we'll be waiting for you," Abel said calmly, his gaze still fixed on the Vietnamese thug.

"Ricky Fucking Pham was a traitor!" Brass Balls snapped back defiantly before glancing away. "He deserved to die. Like this bitch," his eyes rose again to lock with Luyen's.

"Shut the fuck up, asshole." Abel belted the hoodlum across the face, bringing him to his knees.

Blood trickling from the corner of his mouth, Brass Balls slowly looked up at Abel, his narrowed eyes burning with hatred and revenge. "You stupid white pigs think it's over, right? That this is the end of it? After a couple of lousy, rumble busts? No fucking way, Abel! There's too many of us. We're growing stronger every day. I've already been replaced, motherfucker."

Thornton yanked the gang banger back up to his feet and threw him through the open car door, into the backseat. "We don't get paid enough to listen to this shit."

Luyen shrugged her shoulders, eyes moist with a growing sadness now. "Trouble is, he's right. Half these kids will be back out on the streets in a few days. You know it, and I know it."

"And we'll be ready for them," Abel ejected the spent clip from his .45 automatic, slammed home a fresh magazine of hollowpoints, then slipped the blood-smeared weapon back into its shoulder holster. "Right now, we got a hot date with Book-in."

The two M.A.G. agents climbed into their beat-up Malibu and left, maneuvering slowly through the maze of squad cars, ambulances, and proned gang bangers, still spread-eagled on the concrete.

Luyen turned to start back toward Zamora's unit, but found her path blocked by a tall American clad in a brown poplin shirt, black tie, and dark green suit—Army green.

Four rows of combat ribbons adorned the formal uniform. A bright green-and-gold combat patch—symbol of the 18th MP Brigade, Vietnam—was displayed proudly on the right shoulder. The man was holding a small baggy of iced coconut juice out to her and smiling. "You did good, young lady." Victor the Vet nodded.

"I only did my job." Luyen stared long and hard at the Vietnam veteran without smiling back. It was the first time she had ever seen him clean-shaven, and with a fresh haircut. The army trousers and jungle boots were gone, as well. With the aid of a prosthesis, that which was actually a stump became whole again. Victor had brought out his Class-A uniform and government-issue "leg" especially for the Tet Festival.

He still gave her an uneasy, creepy feeling though— still sent a shiver down her spine. She could see the souls of a hundred dead soldiers fighting for control of his bloodshot eyes.

"Lost this back in your country. Doing that sort of work," Victor's smile did not fade as he tapped the artificial leg and glanced over at the bomb-disposal truck. Luyen listened to the hollow, metallic sound verify his claim. "Only I wasn't as good at my job as you were at yours this morning."

Luyen swallowed hard. "I'm sorry." She reddened at the sound of her voice cracking. "I'm sorry for *all* you vets."

"I used to think it was all just a big waste." Victor's eyes scanned the multitude of happy, amber faces in the crowd and came to rest on the revolving carousel— joyous Vietnamese songs of celebration blaring from its loudspeakers now as the Bolsa Strip began returning to normal. "This"—he patted the false limb again— "Vietnam . . . the black gash in Washington, D.C. . . . the whole damn thing . . . All nothing but a sad, pitiful waste. But now, after witnessing this morning's events, I realize I've been wrong all these years. Now, maybe I can finally leave Little Saigon."

"I wish you wouldn't. . . ." Trembling, Luyen stepped forward and accepted the coconut juice.

"I would have helped you." Victor indicated an old army medical bag slung over one shoulder and riding his hip. But instead of bandages and medicine, it contained delicate instruments necessary for defusing explosives. "It's filled with all my old . . . 'tools of the trade,' you might say. I was watching from the crowd. I knew about the bomb. I know about everything that goes down in Little Saigon."

"Then why didn't you—"

"Because then *I* would have been the hero here today," he cut her off, smile fading as a throng of reporters rushed toward them, pencils and notebooks out, TV cameras turning. "And that just wouldn't have been right."

Taking his hand in hers, Luyen ignored the barrage of reporters' questions and guided Victor toward the carousel.

Watch for

LITTLE SAIGON: DEATH FOR SALE

*next in the Little Saigon series
coming soon from Lynx!*

M.A.G. Lieutenant Luke Abel and his task force fight
to stop a gang-sponsored plot to smuggle illegal weapons
through U.S. Customs in the next action-packed police
adventure.

NICHOLAS CAIN resides in Little Saigon North (in California's San Gabriel Valley) with his Saigon-born wife, Angie, and works in Little Saigon South (Orange County) where he is active in the Vietnamese community.

As a military policeman, he was awarded the Bronze Star Medal in Vietnam, where his unit, the 716th MP Battalion, was awarded the Vietnamese Cross of Gallantry and Presidential Unit Citation. After a stint as Southeast Asian foreign correspondent for *Soldier of Fortune* magazine along the Thai-Lao border (1979) and later the *Denver Post* (1981), he went on to pen the popular and long-running *Saigon Beat* series in *Gung Ho* magazine. He has authored twenty-five other Vietnam-related adventure novels under various pseudonyms, including Jonathan Cain, Nik-Uhernik, Jack Hawkins, Roger Stone and Dick Stivers.

work!'' Thornton appeared eager to engage the ''enemy'' as he rushed to pull on his sap gloves.

''I take it you want to mix it up.'' Abel appeared too tired to risk soiling his clothing. ''Howabout we just let the line cops kick ass and take names, then we'll mop up and card catalog this fiasco afterwards.''

''No way, Lou!''

''Then let's get it over with.'' Abel started to open his door, but it was immediately slammed shut again by an airborne gang member whom two Orange County Sheriff's deputies saw fit to throw in the direction of a cage car.

''Sorry 'bout that!'' One of the county officers pressed his face flat against the glass before disappearing back into the melee. ''We were aiming for the black-and-white over there!'

Abel forced his door open, stepped outside, and promptly removed two hidden handguns from the young Vietnamese hoodlum. He rolled him over onto his stomach and handcuffed the youth's hands behind his back while he was still dazed.

''Help me throw this jerk into the backseat,'' he told Thornton, but Thornton was already gone.

One Garden Grove officer had tackled a white punker, only to be set upon by three other Valley Rebs, and Thornton was grabbing handfuls of hair and slamming one potential prisoner after another into the nearest brick wall until they sank to their knees, disoriented and bleeding.

''Thanks, man!'' the Garden Grove officer said as Thornton's handshake also pulled him back to his feet. They both took off after other combatants as a squad of deputies charged through the parking lot, gathering up all the fallen fighters.

''Over here, Gus!'' Thornton called to him, and Abel was soon by his side as they went from cluster to cluster, examining bruised and battered faces with the powerful beam from Glenn's Kel-light. ''Us partners got to stick together, dude!''